MW01611157

FLIGHT RISK

AN INGRID SKYBERG THRILLER

EVA HUDSON

VENATRIX

First published 2021 by Venatrix.

978-1-9160195-8-4

FLIGHT RISK

1

The man in the Miami Dolphins cap was going to be a problem. He had been shouting on his cell at the champagne and oyster bar in the departure lounge, and he was still on his phone at the gate. He was still shouting. Alcohol and anger had reddened his face to the point of sunburn. Ingrid wondered if the staff would actually let him board.

Her fellow passengers gripped finely wrapped Christmas presents too precious for the hold. Duty-free bags bulging with festive tipples nestled between their feet. Ingrid clutched her only piece of luggage; a small backpack containing her phone, wallet, passport, FBI badge and embassy ID, plus some lip balm and a copy of The Motorcycle Diaries she'd hastily bought in the airport bookstore. She'd been more attracted to the word "motorcycle" than the prospect of reading Che Guevara's life story, but she was on a search for meaning and in the mood for adventure. The book promised both. She had failed to find a gift for her mother—she guessed she'd end up going home for the holidays—but it didn't really matter because whatever she bought her mom would either end up in a bottom drawer or the goodwill. Unless it was cigarettes or vodka.

Realistically, Ingrid was not going to read on the plane. She had far too much on her mind to concentrate on a book. She had a resignation letter to draft, an explanation to come up with for her unexpected arrival in the States, and an entire future to figure out. The only thing she knew for sure was it was time to leave London. She now had seven hours in the air to decide whether to ask for a transfer to another field office or walk away from the FBI altogether. Unless leaving London without authorization had already taken the choice out of her hands. She could well be fired before the end of the day.

"We would like to invite Premium Economy and passengers with children or special needs to come forward for boarding."

The man in the cap grunted. He gave the impression of someone used to flying business, and traveling with the horde insulted his status. The man was either a Grade-A jerk or the one person on the flight whose life was a bigger mess than her own. Ingrid knew the rates of suicide among middle-aged men spiked around Christmas, and she sensed his rage—though currently outwardly directed—was really for himself. She'd overheard enough of his conversations to know his children were spending their first Christmas with his ex-wife and her new partner. A classic trigger for both homicidal and suicidal behavior.

The gate staff called for the first rows of economy passengers to board, and almost everyone got to their feet. Ingrid had an aisle seat. She would wait till the end to get up. The people who leaped to their feet weren't going to cross the Atlantic any quicker than she was. When the final call for "all remaining passengers" was made, Ingrid approached the desk and offered the clerk her passport and boarding pass.

The woman scanned the documents then scanned them again. Her features puckered before she raised her gaze to Ingrid. "Hmm." She grabbed a roll of blue paper towels from under the counter and wiped the scanner before holding the documents over the laser again.

"Is there a problem?" Ingrid asked.

"Um." The woman, early twenties and heavily made up for the time of day, made Ingrid excruciatingly aware she hadn't bathed and was looking decidedly crumpled. "I just need to get my colleague. Benita?"

Benita—older, even more elegant—joined from the other desk, looked at something on the screen, then scrutinized Ingrid. She scanned the passport herself.

"What's the problem?" Ingrid asked, her heartbeat now fractionally elevated. A gaggle of last-minute travelers lined up behind her and murmured their impatience.

Benita pursed her lips and stood a little straighter. "It's probably nothing, but I need to call airport security. It won't take long. Please take a seat, madam."

Ingrid was not about to sit down. She stepped to one side for the other passengers to board while Benita radioed for backup.

"What've you done, love?" one of the travelers asked. "You on the FBI's most-wanted list or something?"

When the passengers had gone through the doors, the younger woman closed them.

"What are you doing?" Ingrid asked. Anxiety constricted her throat. Had purchasing a ticket without Bureau approval triggered something in a database? Did they know she was planning to walk away from her job and throw her life off a cliff?

"They were the last passengers." The attendant gripped the door handle.

"*I* am the last passenger."

The woman looked sheepish. "Oh, um. Right, okay." She turned to Benita for reassurance, but Benita was still on the radio, nodding as her eyes bored into Ingrid.

A necklace of heat encircled Ingrid's throat. She felt like she was standing outside the principal's office, unfairly accused of cheating on a test.

Benita looked up and over Ingrid's shoulder. "Yup, I can see you now. She is still here."

Ingrid turned to see two uniformed police officers running toward the gate. Both held MK5s across their chests. They were male, one older and white and the other younger and south Asian. Ingrid held out her FBI badge as they approached. "Special Agent Ingrid Skyberg."

"Oh." The older cop looked surprised.

"Are her bags off the plane?" the other one asked.

The younger woman picked up her radio.

Ingrid wasn't about to tell her she didn't have a bag in the hold and speed up the process. "Can you tell me what's going on?" Ingrid asked.

The older cop took a step toward her, his palm extended at waist height. "If you could step this way." He ushered her away from the gate and took her ID. "I take it this is genuine?"

"I take it that was an attempt at humor?"

He sucked his teeth. "Fair point. Listen, take a seat. I'm sure I can sort this out."

Ingrid remained standing as he and his colleague looked at the same error code that had triggered the gate crew's concern. His face adopted a similar expression. He then examined her passport and conferred with Benita who shook her head. His colleague also looked at the screen, then at Ingrid's passport. He grimaced. The younger woman locked the gate door, making Ingrid's stomach twist.

The older cop strode over to her. His sideburns were graying, and the skin around his sea-blue eyes was weathered and lined. "Ingrid Skyberg?"

"You know that's my name."

"I have to inform you that there is a warrant out for your arrest—"

"What? You're kidding me." Ingrid blinked hard.

"You will not be boarding your flight. You will not be leaving the United Kingdom. You need to come with us."

"This is a joke, right?" But somehow Ingrid knew it wasn't. "What the hell are you arresting me for?" Her pitch wavered.

"Ingrid Skyberg, I am arresting you on suspicion of causing death by dangerous driving. You do not have to say anything. But, it may harm your defense if you do not mention when questioned something you later rely on in court. Anything you do say may be given in evidence."

Ingrid was momentarily speechless. The departure gate slowly revolved at the edges of her vision, and the floor rolled beneath her feet. This wasn't happening. This was a joke. A prank. Had to be. The past few days had been chaotic, traumatic even, but she was damn sure she hadn't killed anyone.

The cop bit the inside of his lip. "You need to come with us."

2

Ingrid stood up when the detective from Thames Valley Police stepped into the interview room.

"Miss Skyberg."

"Special Agent Skyberg. FBI."

"Yeah, the Heathrow team mentioned as much." She dropped a folder onto the table. "Detective Sergeant Hayes. And this"—she turned to introduce a skinny colleague bundling through the door with a broad grin—"is Detective Constable Berryman."

"Hi," Berryman said. She was so strikingly beautiful Ingrid wondered if she was an actress researching a role. "Are you really FBI?"

Before Ingrid could answer, her duty solicitor grunted. He didn't get up.

"Hello, Norman," Hayes said. "Always a pleasure."

"Likewise." Norman Middleton shuffled in his seat, a roll of belly fat pressing his diamond-patterned sweater outward. He was one roast dinner away from a heart attack.

Hayes scraped back a plastic chair and sat down. She was broad-shouldered and thick-necked and looked like she played rugby for Samoa or New Zealand. It was unusual to see someone with South Pacific features in the UK. "I take it Norman here has told you why you've been arrested."

"We've both read the warrant." Ingrid's anxiety at the departure gate had morphed into righteous anger in the ninety minutes she'd been waiting. Her plane was somewhere over Ireland, yet she was stuck in a windowless room in Heathrow's Terminal 3.

"Okay then." Hayes leaned over and switched on the recording. "Detective Sergeant Hayes and Detective Constable Berryman commence the interview with Ingrid Anna Skyberg at eleven oh-two. Duty solicitor Norman Middleton also present." Hayes stared at Ingrid. "So, Ingrid Skyberg, you have been arrested on suspicion of causing death by dangerous driving—"

"This much I already know."

"On November nineteenth," Hayes continued, "at around eight in the morning, Matthew Harding was out for his daily jog on Greenacre Lane on the outskirts of the village of Burnt Oak in Buckinghamshire."

Ingrid resisted the urge to interrupt. She had never heard of Matthew Harding or Burnt Oak.

"His injuries suggest he was hit by a motorcycle. An eyewitness reported seeing a bike riding erratically nearby at the time of the incident, and forensics from the scene recovered flakes of paint thought to have been deposited when the bike that hit Harding skidded fifty yards along the road surface." Hayes paused and looked up. Ingrid detected a glint of delight in her eyes. "Analysis shows this particular shade of petrol blue is a custom paint that has only been used on a few hundred vehicles in the UK, one of which is a Triumph Thunderbird registered in your name."

A tiny wingbeat of doubt flapped at the edge of Ingrid's mind.

"We have ANPR data—that's our number plate recognition system—"

"I work in law enforcement. I know what ANPR is." Ingrid realized a fraction too late the cop was baiting her.

Hayes pressed her lips together before continuing. "The ANPR logs show your motorcycle being ridden on the M40 motorway on the night of November the eighteenth, leaving at junction five, which is the turnoff for Burnt Oak." Hayes leaned back in her seat and smirked. "Where were you at eight a.m. on November nineteenth?"

Ingrid looked at her solicitor who shrugged. He was about as much help as a steak in a vegan restaurant. "Off the top of my head, no idea. It was nearly a month ago."

Berryman smiled at her. She was trying a little too hard to be the good cop. Hayes, whose low center of gravity and confrontational demeanor suggested a second career as a pro wrestler, was more than happy to be the bad cop.

"I'd have to look at my diary," Ingrid said.

"Do you have your diary on your phone?" Hayes asked.

Ingrid answered cautiously. "I do."

"You want to get it out?"

"The officers who arrested me took it away." Ingrid raised an eyebrow for emphasis.

In return Hayes wrinkled her nose; a gesture that said 'yes of course they did, I knew that'. "Tess, you want to grab it?" she asked Berryman.

The red-haired rookie blinked rapidly. "Yes. Sure."

When she came back into the room, Berryman offered the phone to her boss who inspected it. A beaten-up iPhone 6 with a cracked screen and a dent in one corner. The solicitor cleared his throat. They would need either his client's permission or the court's permission to unlock it. Hayes passed it over to Ingrid without comment.

Ingrid unlocked it and opened the iCal app. "Eighteenth of November, right?"

"You need to put the phone on the table," Hayes said. "We need to see what you're seeing."

Ingrid placed it face up on the melamine surface and scrolled. Then scrolled the other way. Her chest dropped, her posture slumped. There was absolutely nothing in her diary for the Eighteenth. Or the nineteenth. This was going to take longer than she'd hoped.

"Well?" Hayes asked.

"This is my personal phone," Ingrid said, her voice already a little unsteady. "You see, until recently I was undercover, so I had a second phone for my alias. That's why this one is so blank."

Hayes flared her nostrils. Berryman's eyebrows arched.

"And where is your UC phone?" Hayes asked.

"At the embassy. Where I work." It was a guess. Ingrid wasn't sure what had happened to the possessions belonging to her alias.

Hayes looked up from her notes. "So, you don't know where you were on November eighteenth?"

"No. But my assistant will be able to tell you. You just need to call her. Her name's Jen. Jennifer Rocharde."

Berryman wrote down the name.

Hayes wasn't going to be told how to conduct an investigation. She squared her paperwork. "Can you confirm you are the owner of a Triumph Thunderbird 1600 with a blue petrol tank, registration number AG03 PFA?"

Ingrid's eyebrows lowered. "I am," she said carefully. "Do you ride?"

"No."

Berryman almost giggled before shaking her head.

"Trust me," Ingrid said. "You hit a pot hole at forty miles an hour and you end up on the deck. If I had hit someone hard enough to kill them, I think I would have noticed." Saying it out loud made her realize how preposterous their allegations were. The dark wing fluttering on the periphery of her thoughts could damn well fly off. There was just no way this had anything to do with her.

Hayes pushed up the sleeves of her taupe jacket. "I'm not saying you didn't notice. I'm saying you didn't stop." She pressed her palms into the table. "Why were in you in Burnt Oak in Buckinghamshire last month, Miss Skyberg?"

Ingrid stopped herself from insisting they call her 'agent'. "I wasn't."

The solicitor coughed into his fist, and Ingrid turned hopefully. He indicated they should continue. He didn't have a point to make, he just needed to clear his throat.

"At approximately eight twenty a.m. on November nineteen,

a witness saw a bike matching your description riding erratically through the main street of Burnt Oak." Hayes paused. "At nine a.m., the wife of Matthew Harding started to worry her husband hadn't returned from his morning jog and used the Find My Phone app to locate him. She drove to a location on the B3562, known locally as Greenacre Lane, where she found her husband dead in a ditch at the side of the road. When the paramedics arrived, they estimated he had been dead for over an hour."

Ingrid had sat on the other side of the table enough times to know that the surest way to bring this to a close, and to get on the next flight to DC, was to remain calm, answer their questions and hold on to her temper. *Deep breath, kiddo*.

"I'm very sorry to hear that, but I don't even know where Burnt Oak is."

Hayes sniffed. "Just because you don't know where it is, it doesn't mean you haven't been there."

There was a knock at the door and one of the uniformed officers who'd arrested her popped his head into the room. "Got those documents you were after," he said.

Hayes accounted for the interruption on the recording while Berryman took the folder from him. The uniformed cop didn't make eye contact with Ingrid in breach of the code. Normally, when one cop arrests another, the code says you treat them like a distant family member. You put the kettle on. You go out of your way to make sure their stay is as pleasant as possible. No one apart from Berryman was playing by the rules.

Suck it up. This will be over soon.

Berryman placed the recently delivered notes in front of Hayes and pointed to a particular paragraph. Hayes nodded. "When was the last time you were at Heathrow Airport, Miss Skyberg?"

Something inside Ingrid deflated. She came close to letting out a groan because she knew her answers to the next few questions were not going to paint her in a good light. "Three days ago."

"That was a short visit," Hayes said, pointedly. "And what was the purpose of your flight three days ago?"

Ingrid inhaled deeply. "I was returning home."

"You live in London?"

"I have lived in London for the past five years."

"And what was the purpose of your flight today?"

Ingrid tapped her index finger as she considered fabricating a family emergency. But the risk of her mother contradicting anything she said was too high. The truth wasn't convenient, but a lie could make things worse. "I was also returning home. This weekend I decided to move back to the States."

Hayes and Berryman both looked surprised. "Just like that?" Berryman asked, sounding almost impressed. "You must have had a really rubbish three days."

"Actually, the past three days haven't been too bad." Ingrid ran a hand through her unwashed hair. "But the weeks beforehand were, as you say, rubbish. Life has been a little... difficult lately. It felt like it was time to move on."

Hayes jutted out her bottom lip and narrowed her eyes. "Difficult how?"

There was no point in lying. Ingrid knew they thought she was fleeing the country to escape prosecution, so it was important everything she told them checked out. "Number one," she extended her thumb. "My apartment burned down. Two, the undercover work I've been involved in for the past two years got nixed. And three," she uncurled her middle finger, "my ex-fiancé was murdered. Oh, and I saw a colleague killed right in front of me." She eyeballed them. "Like I say. Difficult." She hadn't even mentioned the funerals she'd attended, or the week she'd spent in her childhood home being berated by her formidable mother for not producing any grandchildren.

"I see," Hayes said, though there was no way she could. "So, you returned to London on Friday and first thing on Monday morning you're flying out again?"

Ingrid saw no need to answer.

"And I understand your daypack is your only luggage?"

Ingrid sighed. "I just wanted to leave everything behind. You ever felt like that? Like you want to start over?"

"Can't say I have. Now," Hayes said, "our colleagues visited your flat in Sutherland Avenue on Saturday, and again yesterday. Where have you been since you arrived in the UK, Miss Skyberg?"

Ingrid stiffened. "Is that really relevant, sergeant?"

Hayes's eyes narrowed. "Answer the question, Ingrid."

Why did she keep refusing to call her 'agent'? Ingrid inhaled hard. "I've been staying with a friend."

"And what's her name?"

"Tim."

"Tim what?"

Ingrid closed her eyes. "McConnell. Or maybe McConnahey?"

"You've stayed with a friend for three nights and you don't know his surname?" Hayes jaw hung loose like a bulldog's.

"Correct."

The solicitor coughed.

"What? I'm the only one that's gone home with a date?"

Berryman gave her a half smile.

"Thank you. See, it's not that unusual."

Hayes shifted in her seat. "So, this is what you want us to believe… You come home from America having been away, according to these records, for three weeks and you do not go back to your flat. You pick up a guy in a bar, you stay with him all weekend, and then decide to leave the country." She paused. "What did he say to you?"

Ingrid scratched a forearm. "It wasn't like that. I did go to my apartment, actually. For about three minutes. Then I stayed with Tim. He's a nice guy but not nice enough to hang around for. So, I bought a ticket and… here I am."

Berryman steepled her fingers under her chin, her red hair bouncing around her symmetrical features. "Hmm. See, it seems to me, Agent, there's another way of interpreting these facts. The way I see it, you left the country three weeks ago because you anticipated being arrested for the hit and run. Then, after three weeks, your contacts, or your access to police databases, whichever, reveal you're not on any list, so you figure it's safe to return to London." Berryman chewed her lip before continuing. "Then you get to your flat, speak to your contacts at the Metropolitan Police and realize you're in trouble. There is a warrant out for you after all, so you find a bloke to shack up with—classic cop move, by the way, utterly untraceable—and arrange a hasty flight back to the States before the Border Agency process our All Ports Message."

Weren't you meant to be the good cop?

"It's not looking very good for you, is it?" Hayes said.

Ingrid's solicitor leaned forward. "I'm not a barrister Izzy Hayes, but even I could convince a jury that you've got nothing. A partial plate from a witness several miles away from the crash, a paint flake that may or may not have anything to do with the accident, and ANPR hits from a motorway journey the night before. So long as my client can account for her whereabouts at the time of the accident, you really should be letting her go." He cleared his throat for emphasis. He wasn't as useless as he looked.

Hayes sat up a little straighter. "Yes, but your client hasn't accounted for her location, has she? What she has done is say she has never been to the area when we know, thanks to the ANPR, she has. So, all we can be sure of at this point is she's not particularly acquainted with truth." She smiled wide enough to show her teeth. "Now, Ingrid, why don't you tell us what you did with the bike?"

Ingrid looked from Hayes to Berryman. She was a little surprised they were asking that question.

"Well, where is it?" Hayes said.

"I damn well hope it's where I left it."

"And where is that?" Hayes asked.

Ingrid paused before answering. Now she thought about it, she wasn't actually sure when she had last seen her bike. She hadn't ridden it for at least a week before she left for the funerals in the States. That meant she hadn't set eyes on her ride in well over a month. "In the underground parking lot at the embassy." A speck of doubt modulated her voice.

Berryman and Hayes looked at each other.

"Well, that would explain why we couldn't find it," Berryman said.

Ingrid's head fell into her hands. She wasn't going to be getting on the next flight. She'd spent the past 24-hours in mental anguish. She'd pounded the streets of London for hours and hours as she weighed up the wisdom of walking out on her own life. And having made the choice to step off a cliff without knowing what was at the bottom, Hayes was yanking her back. Ingrid had had one foot over the edge, she had prepared for the freefall, and now Detective Sergeant Isobel Hayes had wrestled control of her destiny away from her.

"Everything all right Ingrid?" Hayes asked.

Ingrid didn't even want to look at her. Ingrid knew her only route out of London, and her path to the future, was going to have to take an unwelcome detour via the embassy and her old life. She blinked back her frustration then propped up her chin, her elbows resting on the table. "I guess we better go to the embassy."

The two cops exchanged looks.

"Let's get this over and done with. You can check my office diary. Inspect the bike. Examine my leathers, because I'm telling you if I had hit someone and skidded across the road as you're suggesting, they'll be shredded. This is such a massive pile of BS and I can prove it."

3

Lexi Traynor from the embassy's legal unit was waiting for them in the parking lot, four levels beneath the US Embassy in Grosvenor Square. Ingrid knew Lexi a little from the embassy gym and was glad to have representation she could trust. Lexi was tall and slender and accessorized her expensive skirt suit with a stylish natural afro and outsize retro glasses. She trained for ultra-marathons and it showed. She made Sergeant Hayes appear less rugby and more sumo.

Lexi opened the door, sucking the stench of gasoline inside the Thames Valley Police squad car. "You're not in handcuffs. That's a good sign," she said with a smile. Rain dripped off the bottom of the door as Ingrid stepped out. The weather on the drive from Heathrow had been end-of-the-world storm clouds. It was just as well they were now below ground.

Hayes introduced herself and Berryman, her voice echoing off the concrete walls. The strip lights flickered overhead.

"If you would wait here for a moment, ladies," Lexi said, "I would like a word with my client." She pulled her belted cashmere jacket a little tighter and maneuvered Ingrid away from the cops. "They do this to you?"

"Do what?" Ingrid asked.

"I've seen you after HIIT sessions in the gym and you never

17

look like…" she waggled a perfectly manicured hand in front of Ingrid. "… this."

Ingrid blew out hard. "I look that bad?"

Lexi tilted her head. "Uh-huh."

"Sadly, this is all my own doing. I left it so late to leave for the airport I didn't have time to shower."

Lexi tutted. "You wanna fill me in on what's going down here?"

"What do you already know?"

"Honey, I just got a message from my secretary saying one of our FBI agents was with the Metropolitan Police, but I see from the police car you're with some out-of-town cops, so assume I know precisely zero."

Lexi made 'uh-huh' noises as Ingrid explained. When she'd finished, Lexi put a reassuring hand on Ingrid's shoulder. "I don't think we got a damn thing to worry about here."

Ingrid liked the use of 'we'.

"Okay," Lexi said, turning to the cops. "Let's take a look at this motorcycle then, shall we?"

Ingrid led them down a level and along an almost empty lot to the designated motorcycle bay. It was hard to see why the embassy needed so much parking space, but Ingrid guessed when the US first took over the building many more employees drove to work. Now half the payroll seemed to cycle or run.

The motorcycle bay was busier than usual. In winter, the fair-weather riders left their Vespa Scooters and Japanese road bikes at the embassy to protect them from the elements.

Ingrid's skin iced over. She couldn't see her bike.

The garage walls pressed in and the scent of gasoline stung her nostrils. She picked up speed. Her breathing deepened. Ingrid raced toward the regiment of bikes, propped up on their stands like wounded soldiers.

She spotted the Triumph and her shoulders slumped with relief. Her pace slowed. It had been parked behind a bike shrouded in a heavy canvas cover.

"That beauty really yours?" Lexi asked when she caught up

with Ingrid. "You are getting paid way too much if that's your ride."

"It was a gift," Ingrid said, her voice still a little panicked.

"Wish I had friends who gave me presents like that."

The cops said nothing as Ingrid patted the gas tank, cold under a thin layer of grime. The Triumph Thunderbird was an icon of motorcycle design that combined the curves of a pin-up with the grit and swagger of a cowboy. And this particular bike was loaded with extras from the custom paint job on the gas tank to the chrome roll bars and calfskin seat. Ingrid inspected her steed: no dents, no scratches. Her bike had definitely not been in an accident.

"Here it is," Ingrid said to the cops. Her hand lingered on the tank. Something about it was different. "You're going to have to get yourselves a new suspect."

Hayes curled her lip. "As you say, it's been a month. You could have easily had it repaired. Place like this probably has a team of mechanics who could do the work for you."

Ingrid tipped her head back. "Really? That's your reaction?"

Hayes couldn't hide a flash of envy from her features. She crouched down and inspected the tires while Berryman stared at the Triumph the way Ingrid looked at the make-up counter in department stores: blankly.

"You got the key?" Hayes asked.

Ingrid checked in with Lexi before answering. "I don't think so."

Hayes' eyebrows knitted together. "How come?"

"Remember I said my apartment burned down?"

Lexi's eyes widened.

"Yep, well, the key was in my apartment. Which got cleared by a removals firm. Which got redecorated by a team of contractors hired by the insurer." Ingrid rested a hand on her hip. "I've got no idea where the goddamn key is."

"We still need to impound it for forensics," Hayes said.

"Listen," Ingrid said, exasperation infusing her voice. "This bike did not kill anyone. I did not kill anyone—"

Lexi outstretched a hand to stop Ingrid digging an even deeper hole. She smiled at the cops. "Officers, please. My client is an FBI agent. She's a very experienced motorcycle rider. She says she isn't involved, and I think you are failing to consider that she might be telling the truth." When they didn't respond, she continued. "Between the decorators and the house clearers and the loss adjusters, any number of people could have gotten their hands on Agent Skyberg's motorcycle key."

Ingrid hadn't considered someone else might have been riding her bike.

"All you've got, detective, is a partial plate, a flake of paint which obviously hasn't come from this pristine motorcycle and a timeframe with more flexibility than Simone Biles. Time to let my client get on with her day, wouldn't you say?"

Hayes crossed her arms. "This place must be covered by cameras," she said. "It is one of the most secure buildings in the country. Why don't we examine the CCTV? Maybe Miss Traynor is right—"

"*Ms.* Traynor."

Ingrid loved that Lexi was so badass.

"Maybe someone else did gain access to your bike. I'd like to see who was riding on the night of the eighteenth."

Ingrid had thought she'd be half way over the Atlantic by now, and she was finding it hard to process that she was back in the embassy. At least the security footage would put an end to the farce and let her get on with the rest of her life. "Sure," she said. "Let's speak to Steve."

"Who's Steve?" Berryman asked.

"The garage manager."

On the next floor up, Ingrid tapped on the open window of the mechanics' kiosk. A man she didn't recognize sat behind a computer monitor. Even mechanics did paperwork these days. "Is Steve around?"

He swung his seat around. "Steve? No."

"Know when he'll be back?" Ingrid asked.

"Try never." He waited for the shock to materialize on Ingrid's face. "He quit. About three weeks ago."

"Oh." Ingrid would have liked to have said goodbye. She'd gotten on well with Steve. He liked to talk about bikes and was always super helpful whenever she needed an embassy car. "That's a pity."

"Not for me." The guy beamed. "I'm the new Steve. Eddie."

Ingrid leaned against the window frame. "You know how to work the CCTV yet, Eddie?"

He shrugged. Eddie hadn't received that training module, so Ingrid reluctantly walked everyone over to the elevator and punched the call button. She stared at the descending numbers above the doors, disbelieving that she was about to return to her office. It was a journey she thought she'd never make again.

The doors opened on the fifth floor and Ingrid took a deep breath before stepping out into the corridor. The closer she got to the Legal Attaché's suite of offices, the heavier her heart felt. She'd not been in the office since she left London to accompany Marshall's coffin back to Charleston, and she knew colleagues would want to talk to her about his funeral. Ingrid kept her eyes on the floor as she led the way through the bullpen where the FBI's administrative staff labored at ancient-looking computers.

Ingrid lingered for a fraction of a second outside the door to the criminal division and the office she shared with her assistant. She felt less prepared to deal with Jen's questions than she did with another inquisition from Hayes.

Jennifer Rocharde spun around the moment Ingrid stepped into the room and beamed at her. Her smile contracted a second later when Hayes followed.

"What's going on?" Jen got to her feet and nervously pushed her long strawberry blond hair behind her ear. Her eyes widened when Berryman and Lexi entered.

"I see you put Christmas decorations up in my absence," Ingrid said in an attempt to make her return seem as casual as possible.

"You know how I like a celebration." Jen was the sunniest, most optimistic woman Ingrid had ever known.

"That I do." Jen stared at the three women behind Ingrid. "What's going on?"

Ingrid gave her the lowdown and asked her to pull up her diary for the eighteenth and nineteenth of November. On her own computer, Ingrid dialed into the security database and searched for the CCTV images from the garage.

Ingrid's desk was tidier than it had ever been. Jen had obviously taken her absence as an excuse to turn ordered chaos into neatly labeled piles. Her stack of correspondence was crowned with an embossed invitation to the Christmas ball at Winfield House, the ambassador's official London residence. When the new administration entered the White House in January, the ambassador would be leaving her post. She was using the ball to thank everyone who had helped her during her tenure, and Ingrid was touched, although more than a little surprised, to have been included on the guest list.

Once Ingrid had logged into the system, it was surprisingly easy to find the right footage. She only needed to key in the date and her license plate and the computer did the rest. Only the image on her screen wasn't the one she expected.

"There must be a mistake," Ingrid said.

She looked over her shoulder at Lexi whose cat-like expression was unreadable. Hayes's face was more straightforward.

"Do you want to zoom in?" Hayes asked.

The four of them stared at Ingrid's monitor that showed a black-and-white image of Ingrid sitting astride her Triumph waiting for the barrier to let her out of the parking lot. The time stamp was 17:12. Ingrid's palms were so sweaty the mouse slipped under her grip.

"I take it that's you?" Hayes said.

Berryman pointed to the Belstaff motorcycle jacket on the coat rack. It was quite obviously the same as the jacket on the screen. Ingrid's pulse pounded in her neck. She said nothing, then nervously typed in her license plate for the following day. When the footage showed her riding back into the embassy at 11:42, her stomach constricted. Her nostrils buzzed as if a nosebleed was imminent. She blinked at the image several times. This was not looking good.

"Ingrid." Something in the way Jen said her name meant it wasn't the first time she'd called her.

"Good. I've got your attention."

Ingrid saw the diary application open on Jen's monitor.

"Okay, so, looking at those dates you wanted…" Jen paused. Her face crumpled in apology. "They're totally blank."

"Because that was when I was undercover, right?"

"Yep."

"What about Natalya's diary?"

Jen's expression darkened. "It's been locked."

"Really?" Ingrid closed her eyes slowly and kept them shut.

"Who is Natalya?" Hayes asked.

Ingrid opened her eyes and looked at the ceiling with its familiar pattern of missing tiles and yellow stains from when people still smoked at their desks. "Natalya was my undercover alias." The image from the parking lot still filled her screen.

"What do you mean, 'locked'?" Hayes asked.

Jen scrunched up her features. "I've never come across it before. Guess when they shut down Ingrid's alias, they, like, sealed all Natalya's files."

Ingrid's scalp tightened. "How do we unlock them?"

Jen shrugged. "Dunno. But I'll totally find out." She picked up her phone and started dialing.

"Listen," Ingrid pushed her chair backwards, rolling over Berryman's feet. She didn't apologize. "You ever worked undercover?"

Jealousy fluttered across Hayes's features. "No, I have not."

"Well, when I was undercover, I worked on sensitive material. It's understandable that the Bureau will have classified it." Ingrid turned back to her assistant. "Jen, can you please show Sergeant Hayes the diary for the previous month? Or any month from the past two years?"

Jen tucked the phone under her chin and scrolled through the diary to reveal intermittent blocks of gray.

"You see?" Anger infused Ingrid's voice. "It's not like it's just those two days I can't account for right now."

Hayes wrinkled her nose. "So, what was this UC gig?"

"You know I can't tell you that." Ingrid's tone was increasingly indignant.

"Then who here can vouch these blanks correspond with your UC work?"

Ingrid and Jen sighed simultaneously. "Marshall," Ingrid said.

"And who is he?"

Ingrid wanted to let out a scream. Was there anything else that wasn't going to go her way today? "He was my boss. He was the one I told you about. He was murdered last month."

Berryman's eyes narrowed. "You said it was your ex-fiancé who was murdered."

Jen piped up. "He was also, like, her ex."

Hayes took a step back. "So, you're saying you weren't involved in the accident, even though this footage shows you were the one who rode your bike out of this building the night before and back a few hours afterward? And you are also saying the only person who can give you an alibi is dead?"

Ingrid's jaw began to tremble and Lexi leaped into the fray. "Detectives," she said, making sure their attention was on her and not Jen's screen before continuing. "I will undertake to get you access to my client's locked diary. I believe you wish to take her motorcycle for forensic analysis, which she consents to."

Ingrid hadn't, but if Lexi was going to make this carousel stop spinning, she'd go along with it.

"I am a lawyer. My client is a Special Agent with the FBI. We have both taken professional oaths. I am employed by the State Department of the United States government. Agent Skyberg is an officer of the Department of Justice." She tilted her head. "You know what ladies. I think you can trust us to act in good faith here because we really don't want no diplomatic incident. I suggest you do what you gotta do. Meantime, we will bend over backwards to get you gals what you need, and my client and I will attend an interview at your station house whenever you like." Lexi tipped her head the other way. "What d'you say about that?"

Ingrid felt the pressure inside her head decrease with every word that came out of her lawyer's mouth.

Hayes jutted out her jaw.

"You ain't really gonna take my girl into custody, are you now?" Lexi's stare was intimidating.

Berryman looked to Hayes for a decision. She gave a very good impression of this being her first day out of uniform.

"You'll have bail conditions," Hayes said.

"Naturally," Lexi said.

"And because you were intercepted at Heathrow, you will be deemed a flight risk. You'll have to surrender your passport."

"No problem."

No problem? A piece of Ingrid still thought she might be getting on a flight later in the day. She couldn't bring herself to look at Hayes. She just wanted her out of her sight. "Fine," she managed. Anything to make the sergeant disappear.

"And you'll have to report weekly to a police station."

Just say what you need to say and get the hell out of my office. Ingrid's patience was hanging by a thread.

"So, we're agreed, then?" Lexi said.

Ingrid grunted her consent like a petulant teenager.

"Okay then, let's get this sorted."

When the paperwork was signed and Ingrid's passport had been seized, Lexi offered to escort Hayes and Berryman from the building, leaving Ingrid and Jen alone.

"Bet you missed me, huh?"

But Jen wasn't feeling playful. Her lip trembled and her eyes threatened tears. "Why were you at Heathrow, Ingrid?" Her voice was suffused with as much vexation as Ingrid had ever heard from Jen. "You were just going to leave?"

A lump rose in Ingrid's throat. It hadn't even occurred to her that leaving might hurt Jen. "I can explain—"

"You weren't even going to say goodbye?" Jen's face was blotchy with anger. "No warning?"

Ingrid's eyes stung with tears. Jen's fury had taken her by surprise. She didn't know how to respond. "Jen, I'm sorry, I would have—"

"You're right. I did miss you. I have also been worried about you." Jen wiped away a tear. "I stupidly thought you might have missed me too." Jen stood up. "One day, Ingrid Skyberg, you are going to realize that there are people in this world who actually care about you."

Jen's shoulders shook as she marched out of the office. Ingrid knew she should run after her, she knew that was what a caring, compassionate, remorseful human being would do, yet all she was capable of was slumping down into her chair. She let out a groan and shut her eyes.

This was not how her day was meant to go. How had she gone from making the decision to walk out on the embassy and the Bureau to this? Now she was trapped. She couldn't leave until she'd cleared her name. Resentful didn't come close. Anger burned in the base of her stomach.

"Oh, Jesus, no. Not that too."

The thought that the Bureau would force her back into therapy—why are you so angry, Ingrid? How do you feel about Marshall now, Ingrid?—made her jaw clench. But those emotions paled against the shame she felt at walking out on Jen. Everything else had been out of her hands, but not saying goodbye to Jen was on her. That had been her choice, and Ingrid knew she was going to have to find a way to make it up to her.

She wiped her eyes.

The CCTV image was still on her screen. Something wasn't right about it. She glanced across at Jen's desk. Either the diary on Jen's screen was wrong, or the CCTV on hers was. The two pieces of information contradicted each other, didn't they? Ingrid scratched her chin.

When she was undercover, as the diary on Jen's monitor showed she was, Ingrid had operated under a very strict protocol that prevented her from riding her own bike. To be absolutely sure her real identity stayed secret, whenever Ingrid left the embassy to become Natalya, she always wore a different set of leathers and rode a rental bike.

If she was undercover, then she simply couldn't have been riding the Triumph.

26

She stared at her monitor. Her mouth suddenly dry. The only explanation was that the footage on her screen had been faked. Not only did someone want to frame her for Matthew Harding's death, they had hacked into the embassy's security servers to do it.

And she had thought her day couldn't get any worse.

4

Ingrid showered in the embassy gym and returned to her office. She'd found enough deodorant and hair product in the bottom of her locker to make herself look respectable. Jen wasn't at her desk, which was probably just as well as Ingrid hadn't yet figured out how to apologize.

"Oh. Hi." Maisie Millane, one of the counterterrorism agents, popped her head through the door. "When did you get back?"

"Friday night."

"And how was it?" Millane wrote a note for Jen on her desk. "Marshall's funeral?"

"Oh, pretty awful," Ingrid said, not wanting to have such an intimate conversation with someone she didn't really trust. "His parents are strict Baptists so... very traditional."

Maisie perched on the edge of Jen's desk. "We were all thinking of you, you know."

Ingrid didn't know how to respond.

"We sent flowers. I don't suppose you noticed if his parents received them?"

Ingrid scrunched up her features and gave a half shrug. "There were a lot of flowers."

"Well, he was a young man. And the way he died..." Millane trailed off as Ingrid's memories returned to the sight of Marshall lying in a pool of blood.

"Sorry," Millane said. Then, deliberately changing the subject, she waved the note she'd just written in the air. "I think I found what Jen's looking for."

Ingrid said nothing

"She's been searching for a pair of earrings for her wedding. They're pink pearls. Apparently the First Lady wore them at the G7, and I think I spotted something similar at a jeweler in Clarges Street yesterday."

This was more than Millane had spoken to Ingrid in the past year, and it was making her feel uncomfortable.

"And didn't you go to another funeral while you were home?"

Ingrid was surprised Millane had paid enough attention to have noticed. "Yep, Agent Rennie. He'd been over here working a case."

Millane looked down at her hands. "Of course, I'm sorry, I forgot. He was killed right in front of you, wasn't he?" She made an awkward face. "I didn't mean to be so insensitive." She used a change in tone to shift the conversation forward. "Have you heard who's getting Marshall's job?"

Ingrid hadn't given it any thought. "No. Have they appointed someone?"

Millane's eyes narrowed. "So, it isn't you then?"

"What?" Ingrid spluttered. "Not a snowball's chance."

"Oh. I kinda figured you'd be a shoo-in."

Ingrid's eyes widened. "Really?"

"Sure, why not?" Millane smiled before softly making her way out into the bullpen, leaving Ingrid to shake her head.

What just happened? One of the CT agents was A) being nice, and B) suggesting she was in line for a promotion? Ingrid blew out hard. The only thing she'd be getting was a pink slip if she was convicted of the hit and run. Ingrid glanced at the open door. She really, really hoped she wasn't getting Millane's sympathy because everyone thought she was still hung up on Marshall.

Ingrid had no undercover work anymore, no boss to assign her cases, and no ongoing investigation. Until someone of a higher rank told her otherwise, her priority was finding out who had killed Matthew Harding. She opened a browser and Googled him.

The top return was his corporate profile at the financial services firm he worked for. It was still written in the present tense. The next entry was a report on the accident on a website called Buckinghamshire Today. Ingrid took a moment, then clicked.

Matthew Harding had been thirty-eight, married with three kids and judging by the photos illustrating the report, was a man with an envious future ahead of him. He was a marathon runner and a tennis club champion. He had been a senior executive on a substantial salary, living in the kind of house most people could only dream of.

Ingrid stared at the images. He was a young, fit, man who she'd expect to survive being struck by a bike, albeit with broken bones and a long recovery. It wasn't like a truck had run him down. He must have hit his head, she reasoned.

Why might someone want him dead? A jealous mistress. A jealous mistress's husband. A debt. A deal gone wrong. A dormant grudge. Nothing in her search revealed why anyone might want to kill such a decent, likeable man. After an hour of scanning Facebook posts and financial records, the most likely explanation was that his death really had been a tragic accident.

So why would someone try to frame her for it?

Ingrid put in requests via the police database for a transcript of the 999 call. Then she asked to see the ANPR logs for herself, both from the night before and the morning after Harding was killed. She also requested the images taken from the ANPR cameras. She knew it would be hard to prove who was behind a full-face helmet in a grainy black-and-white photograph, but there was a chance those photographs would definitively rule her out.

The CCTV image of her leaving the parking lot was still on her screen. The more she looked at it, the more troubling it was. Out in the bullpen, keyboards hammered and printers spewed out reports, but they didn't mask the sound of her own heavy breaths as her brain tried to parse the facts. The image itself was real, but getting footage of her riding in and out on her Triumph wouldn't be hard because she did it most days. However, seamlessly splicing footage and doctoring the security record of the United States embassy should be virtually impossible. Ingrid chewed the inside of her cheek. It was one of the most fortified buildings in the world. The embassy's systems were among the most robust in the world. A chill scurried over her skin. In all likelihood the person who had set her up was on the inside of the firewall. That meant it was someone inside the embassy.

Unnerved, Ingrid got to her feet and paced the office, her sneakers slipping on the worn carpet tiles. The embassy was due to move into a brand-new building, so for several years maintaining the existing premises had been a low priority. The threadbare carpet and missing ceiling tiles lent the place a decidedly neglected feel. The only new thing in the room was the stationery.

Ingrid peered through the slats of the Venetian blind at a small gathering of protestors braving the rain in Grosvenor Square below. Their handmade placards demanded the US stop selling weapons to Saudi Arabia.

She thought about what Lexi had said, that any number of people could have gotten hold of the Triumph's key after the fire in her apartment. She needed to speak to someone who could tell her who had been in the saddle on the eighteenth, and that person was Steve, the former garage manager. He'd always loved her bike and he would have noticed if anyone had touched it, let alone taken it out of the building. She picked up the phone and called HR.

"This is Agent Skyberg with the Legal Attaché Program."

"This is Barnaby Jackson. Are you calling about the new Deputy Special Agent in Charge?"

"Um, no. No, I'm not."

"Only we've had a few calls asking if we've made an appointment."

"And have you?"

"I wouldn't be authorized to tell you one way or another." The HR executive sounded a little too pleased with himself.

"I'm actually looking for the contact details of an employee who recently quit. I need to speak to him urgently. It's Steve. Thompsett is his last name, I think. He worked in the garage downstairs."

"Ah, now that I can't help you with. Data protection, you see."

"This is a criminal investigation. Doesn't that make a difference?"

"Not unless you get a subpoena."

Somehow Ingrid managed to keep the sarcasm from her voice when she thanked Barnaby for his help. She pulled out a drawer. Years beforehand she'd been given a print-out of emergency embassy contacts. It was just possible Steve's cell was on the list.

Jen had tidied Ingrid's drawer as well as her desk. The mélange of paperclips, Post-Its and charging cables had been ordered into a neat grid of easily identifiable objects. There was no dog-eared list of numbers. Ingrid closed the drawer, then immediately opened it again. Something had caught her eye.

Her Russian passport. It had been issued to her undercover alias, and presumably should have been withdrawn, or at least locked away when Natalya was retired. Ingrid didn't know who she should hand it to. It was only when she was keying Steve's name into various police databases it occurred to her it probably should have been surrendered to Thames Valley Police.

She found a contact number for Steve in the Met's system, which Ingrid duly rang. A recorded message announced the number was unavailable. She pulled up Facebook, where finding Steve proved to be a cinch. Their eleven mutual friends—all embassy workers—allowed Ingrid to see enough of his profile to understand why he had left his job so suddenly. He had moved to Portugal. It was the middle of December and there he was on the Algarve, wearing short sleeves and drinking beer in the sunshine at a bar called Monkeys and Peanuts. The comments showed Ingrid wasn't the only one who was envious. She sent him a message and a friend request saying she needed his help.

Even if Steve could testify that someone else had been riding, what she really needed—what all successful prosecutions required—was a witness to the accident itself. She wasn't going to find one of those sitting at her desk. Ingrid checked the clock on the wall. Almost two o'clock. She glanced at the window. There were still a couple hours of daylight left. If she hurried, it would be worth it.

She reached under her desk for her helmet before remembering Thames Valley Police had taken her gear for analysis. She'd have to get a car. Ingrid instinctively dialed the garage, but hung up before anyone could answer. Until she knew who had breached the embassy's security, she couldn't alert anyone in the building to the fact she was investigating the case herself. Taking an embassy car with a tracker on it to the scene of Harding's accident was out of the question.

She rang Hertz, and five minutes later walked out of the office. She stopped at the threshold to the bullpen and turned back. She needed to leave a note. Disappearing again without explanation wouldn't do anything to heal the rift with Jen.

After she had written her own message, Ingrid picked up the note Millane had left. She really didn't like that a member of the counterterrorism unit had a better idea of what Jen wanted for her wedding than she did. Pink pearl earrings? Really? Wasn't that very conventional? Even for Jen? The First Lady's school marmish fashion choices were responsible for her tabloid epithet of 'Principal Brady'. Surely that wasn't the bridal look Jen was going for?

No matter. If anybody was going to get those earrings for Jen, it was damn well going to be her.

5

It was still raining hard, and the windshield wipers left a smear in the middle of her vision with every swipe. The satnav directed Ingrid west out of London, passing several turnoffs for Heathrow. She shook her head at each one. This was not the day she had planned.

The steel gray sky deepened into charcoal as she reached the outskirts of the city, and she scanned the dash of her rental for the light controls. She tried one button after another and inadvertently turned on the radio and caught the evening news. The announcer sounded so sober compared to the bulletins she'd listened to back home. Her ears tuned in at the mention of Heathrow.

"The American Airlines flight 3046 was forced to divert to Shannon Airport in Ireland when a disruptive passenger attempted to open the emergency exit mid-flight…"

Ingrid pictured the man in the Miami Dolphins cap.

"The man, a Florida resident in his forties, was arrested by the Garda. It is not thought to be terrorist related. Passengers have been further inconvenienced by bad weather as Storm Tanya has grounded all flights from Shannon for the time being."

Ingrid managed a smile. Her day wouldn't have gone the way she planned anyway. She switched over to a music station and found herself singing along enthusiastically to an anthem about swinging from a chandelier.

It took an hour and ten minutes to reach Burnt Oak, a village sixty miles west of London. It was big enough to have a high street with two banks and a collection of upmarket boutiques. A cook shop sold premium kitchen wares, a florist offered gifts for gardeners, an old-fashioned menswear store displayed tweed caps and silk handkerchiefs in the window, while several clothing stores served women in the market for floaty garments with elasticized waists. It was the epitome of middle-aged and middle class. There was probably a tennis club and a rugby club and an annual beautiful gardens competition. Even in the pouring rain, Burnt Oak looked pleased with itself.

London was encircled with towns and villages just like it where—even in 2016—ninety percent of travelers on the early morning trains were men in suits commuting to well-paid jobs. Their wives practiced yoga and made batches of soup from home-grown vegetables between the school runs. Ingrid had a name for places like Burnt Oak: Stepford.

She drove straight through the village and out the other side, following the directions to Greenacre Lane, a long road that curved through sodden fields. A small herd of cows sheltered under a large, bare oak, its branches reaching out to the rumbling clouds as if inviting lightning to strike.

A heap of tattered and decaying bouquets of flowers marked the place where Matthew Harding lost his life. It was at a curve in the road, so Ingrid drove on a little way and found a safe spot to pull over. She looked through the rear window at the floral shrine, the rain blurring her view before a sharp swipe of the rear wiper brought it back into focus. Ingrid was one hundred percent certain she had never been there before.

Ingrid switched off the engine and pulled up the hood of her jacket. She stepped out onto a gravel verge and scanned Greenacre Lane, squinting against the rain. Harding had been killed at a long curve in the road. It was a classic spot for an accident on two wheels; just when you think you can straighten up you veer into the gulley. Especially if the weather was this bad.

Ingrid jogged through the puddles to the fallen regiment of bouquets and crouched down. Some of them were a month old, were well on their way to becoming more trash than tribute. Rain and grime slicked the cellophane wrappings, and handwritten notes of condolence were pulpy and smudged. A couple of cards had been laminated, including one from the local tennis club that read, 'You cannot be serious'. The only other legible card simply said 'Semper Fidelis', a Latin inscription equally beloved by college fraternities and tattoo parlors. From what she knew about Matthew Harding, she'd be surprised if he had set foot in either.

The light was fading. Ingrid wiped the rain from her face and hurried back to the car. The windows started to steam the moment she closed the door. She opened Google maps on her phone and waited for the app to pinpoint her location. Apart from a golf course and a farm, her screen was entirely green save the bisecting white line of Greenacre Lane. There was almost nothing there, which explained why no cars had passed since she'd parked.

With no traffic, and the encroaching gloom, Ingrid wasn't going to find what she needed if she hung around. Her priority had to be finding a witness, someone who could give a description of whoever had been riding on the morning of the nineteenth. She turned the car around and headed back toward the village. She slowed when she saw a pub.

The Barley Mow was more down-market than she expected. It was about a mile out of Burnt Oak, nestled between a gas station and a sign-maker's workshop. Six cars were parked outside. That seemed like a brisk trade for an isolated establishment in the middle of the afternoon.

Inside, slot machines blinked and flashed while two large flat screen TVs showed an Italian soccer match. It wasn't a surprise to find she was the only woman in the place. What was a surprise was that the food smelled good.

"Are you still serving lunch?" she asked. She was suddenly famished.

"For you, of course." The bartender was tall, slim and intense, reminding her of Novak Djokovic. He wore track pants and a hoodie with the logo of an Australian surf club. He handed her a laminated menu. "Anything to drink?"

Ingrid peered over the bar at the glass refrigerators behind him. "Is that an orange juice?"

"Orange and mango. Ice?"

"Thanks."

He opened the bottle and poured the viscous orange liquid into a glass. The menu was not inspiring. Burgers, breaded fish and lasagna. A burger seemed safest.

"You want chips with it?"

"Sure." If the burger was inedible, at least she'd have eaten something. They couldn't screw up fries, could they? Chips was the British national dish, wasn't it?

"Where are you from?" Below his right ear he had a word tattooed in such a cursive script Ingrid couldn't read it. Probably his girlfriend's name.

"The States."

"You on holiday then?"

She took a sip. It wasn't too bad. "No. House-hunting." It seemed as good a lie as any.

"Oh, right."

"Anywhere you'd recommend?"

He peered over her shoulder and Ingrid shifted on the bar stool to see a man look up from his newspaper. "Johnnie's yer man. Got his finger's in everyone's pies." He gave her a wink. "Johnnie?"

"Yes, mate?"

"This lady here would like your advice."

Johnnie smiled at her but didn't get up. He was severely over-weight and standing was something only to be attempted if entirely necessary. He gestured to an empty seat at his table and Ingrid sat down opposite him.

"Hi, I'm Ingrid."

They shook hands, and he folded his paper. He'd been looking at the racing pages and marking up his picks. Ingrid pumped him for general information about the area and maintained her cover story by asking about schools, commute times and road safety. Johnnie didn't mention the hit and run. Instead, he pointed to the map on her phone and told her the pros and cons of buying in each fold of the valley.

"You know your stuff," Ingrid said.

He was a local boy whose business, he said, was 'buying and selling'. He owned garages and parcels of amenity land, and when he got planning permission, he sold them on to the highest bidder.

"What about this area here," Ingrid asked, pointing to the point on the map where Harding had been killed.

"All around there," he said, "are estates that I think are owned by the Duke of Westminster, one of them big land owners, anyway. Not a good idea to go wandering about there looking for a plot. They've got guard dogs and electric fences." He took a mouthful of beer and tapped his nose. "Probably men with guns and all."

Ingrid must have looked shocked.

"It's fox hunting territory."

"Ah."

"And if you don't get hit by a bullet, you want to look out for golf balls."

"I do?"

"Swanbury's over that hill." He nodded in the direction of the fireplace.

"Swanbury?"

"They had the Ryder Cup there last year. Second greatest golf course in the world."

"Which is the first?"

"Depends who I'm talking to. Given you're a yank, I'm going to say Augusta."

She thanked him for his time and moved to another table when her burger arrived. It was better than she'd dared to hope. She'd been hungrier that she'd realized. What did the instructors at Quantico used to say? Better to run on calories than adrenaline.

When she got back outside, the rain had relented and the sky was dark even though it was only ten past four. Ingrid pulled back out onto Greenacre Lane and headed for Burnt Oak. She'd driven five hundred yards before a black sedan driving in the other direction caught her attention. It was another hundred yards before she realized why. It had a diplomatic license plate. They were rare outside of London, and she needed to know if there was a connection to the embassy.

Ingrid checked her mirrors, swiftly performed a three-point turn, and accelerated until the sedan came back into view. It pulled off at a junction marked by a sign saying 'Private Property —Trespassers Will Be Prosecuted'.

Ingrid drove on, pulled over, waited two minutes, then drove back to the junction and took the turnoff. After a hundred yards, the road surface turned to gravel and then became a mud track with a central spine of grass between rutted tire tracks.

She couldn't see cameras or patrolling dogs, but was going to assume both were present. She came to a forged iron security gate and slowed. She peered through and made out the sedan's headlights bouncing through the valley beyond. Ingrid carried on a few yards, switched off the engine, opened the window and listened. No dogs barked. No traffic noise. Just crows squawking in their roosts and the wind shifting through the bare winter trees.

Ingrid picked up her phone from the passenger seat. She waited patiently for Google Maps to pinpoint her location until she was a lonely blue dot in a featureless green rectangle. She switched to satellite view, hoping to reveal what lay on the other side of the gate. The image was pixilated at first, but when it loaded, she zoomed in. This time the image stayed pixilated. She zoomed again. Now the pixels were even bigger.

Ingrid exhaled so hard she whistled. The location had been deliberately blurred. Not even Buckingham Palace was blurred out on Google Earth. Or the Pentagon.

What the hell was beyond those gates?

6

By the time Ingrid made it back to the embassy, Jen had gone home for the evening. The building had an end-of-term feel not just because it was almost Christmas, but because many of the diplomatic staff wouldn't be returning after the holidays. When President Brady left office in January, his successor would appoint a new London team. Screensavers on idle computers showed log fires flickering under canopies of tinsel and baubles.

Ingrid wasn't very good with Christmas. She had wonderful memories of one Christmas in the late eighties when her cousins visited, but after her father died when she was ten, the festivities became a standoff between her and her mom. Svetlana Skyberg had grown up in Soviet Leningrad. After defecting to the US in 1976 following a bronze-medal winning performance at the Montreal Olympics, Svetlana tried hard to be the all-American wife, and the all-American mom. She demonstrated this at Christmas with elaborate, if inedible, meals and endless, unwanted, gifts. "In Soviet Union, this was the dream," Ingrid was told. Whether it was Halloween or Thanksgiving or the Fourth of July, Svetlana went all out to display two things: her allegiance to the nation that had accepted her, and that she could do everything on her own.

After Marshall's funeral, Ingrid had visited her mom. Svetlana still took care of the pigs—even in the Minnesota winters—

and still smoked forty unfiltered cigarettes a day. She also kept saying, 'You don't need to visit' when, if Ingrid didn't, she'd only be asked why she never visited. Svetlana had felled her own tree from the woods and dragged it into the house before decorating it with so many baubles and streamers it was hard to see a single pine needle.

Ingrid turned her attention from the miniature Christmas tree on Jen's desk, twinkling to itself, to her own computer. She needed to find out what was beyond those gates on Greenacre Lane. The only aerial imagery she could review immediately was on public access databases, and the location was blurred on those too. She could put in a request to see the unblurred images from the CIA's satellite, but that would take time.

The Ordnance Survey map of Buckinghamshire showed what looked like a farmhouse on the land she was interested in. A Land Registry search revealed the property was called Uppenham Hall and owned by Kingfisher Holdings. Unsurprisingly, the next thing she learned was that Kingfisher Holdings was an offshore trust, a shell company that allowed the true owner to remain anonymous. Ingrid fired off a request for information to the registrar, but didn't expect to hear back.

Uppenham Hall was important enough to have a Wikipedia entry. It had been built in the 1780s by one of the proprietors of the sugar company Tate and Lyle, and the seventy acres of gardens had been designed by Decimus Burton, a landscape gardener famous enough to have his own Wikipedia page. It was one of the largest private residences in the southeast of England, and previous owners included a duke, a lord and a prime minister. For all its wisdom, Wikipedia had nothing to say about who currently owned the land.

"Ingrid. You're back!"

She glanced up from her screen to see Marshall's secretary in the doorway. She was almost sure the woman's name was Penny.

"Hi."

"Jen's already left, then?" Penny was so stylish she looked French.

"Guess so."

"Will you be joining us, or are you chained to your desk?"

Ingrid didn't want to admit she hadn't been invited to whatever the event was. "Still got lots to catch up on."

"You must have. I think Jen's planning several of these parties so she can say goodbye to everyone." So, Jen was having a leaving party and Ingrid wasn't on the guest list. Ouch. "Um. How was it? We were all thinking about you."

"You mean the funeral?"

Penny nodded.

"Fairly tough. Marshall was only thirty-seven you know… Sorry, of course you know." Ingrid had launched into her usual defensive platitude mode when Penny had been as close as anyone to Marshall. "It was really hard on his parents. Obviously." Ingrid tensed with awkwardness. "It must have hit you pretty hard too."

Penny pressed her lips together and blinked back tears. "Yup. I still think he's going to fly out of his office demanding something gets done yesterday."

"Sounds like Marshall."

Penny paused. "Maybe see you later, then?"

"Sure." Ingrid returned to her screen.

"Oh, almost forgot." Penny hovered in the doorway. "I've not really done anything with Marshall's office. I mean, there's no word on his replacement, and, well, what with your history together… Well, I wondered if it would be better if you went through his things rather than me? You know his family and everything."

Ingrid was taken aback. "Sure. Of course."

"Thanks," Penny said. "I don't think there's a rush. No one's said anything about needing the office."

"Leave it with me." Ingrid didn't like that co-workers assumed she'd had a special relationship with Marshall. Sure, they had a shared, if volatile, history, and she did care for his family, particularly his little sister Carolyn, but Penny's implications of intimacy made her uncomfortable. However, if she found something sentimental in his office, it would be a good excuse to give Carolyn a call. She really should check up on her.

"Nice to have you back," Penny said before leaving.

"Enjoy the party."

Ingrid returned to her work. She inputted data about Uppenham Hall and Kingfisher Holdings into the FBI's open-source database that scraped news sites, social media profiles, alumni periodicals, government and public records as well as 4Chan and Reddit feeds. It served up connections and patterns in minutes that had previously taken weeks of research to deliver. Ingrid let it whirr away in the background and checked her emails. She was pleased to see there was one from the Met responding to her request for a transcript of the 999 call Matthew Harding's wife had made.

"Sorry, we don't have the manpower for transcripts at the moment, and I haven't had time to find the exact call you requested, but here's the link to the database and you can find the call you're after. The password below will be active for the next twenty-four hours. Wish I could be more helpful…"

She clicked on a link to hear the recording of a 999 call and was presented with a list. Each entry was a recording of someone calling the emergency services. The first was a report of a trash can on fire. The next call was just screaming. Calls from several counties had all been handled by the same data center, and there was no way without listening to know which call was asking for an ambulance, the police or the fire department. Each call started the same way. "Emergency. Which service do you require?"

Ingrid leaned back in her seat and linked her hands behind her head. It was going to be a long evening. She would need fortification. The clock on the wall told her the basement canteen would still be open.

Fifteen minutes later she was back at her desk with the last portion the canteen had of Thai curry and two bottles of German beer. She opened the first of them on the edge of her desk and set to work. After a forkful of food, Ingrid clicked on the next link. And the next. She knew roughly what time Mrs Harding had made the call, which narrowed down her search, but there was no option to select by location. It was only when she clicked to listen that she could see where the call had been made. If it was from a landline, then the exact address was given; if it was from a cell, the GPS coordinates and cell tower information was listed.

The next entry had been logged at 0808 hours. on November nineteen.

"Emergency, which service do you require?"

No answer.

"Emergency, can you hear me?"

"Yes."

"Which service do you require?"

After a long pause, the caller said, "Ambulance."

"Where are you calling from?"

There was some background noise before the call went dead. No location was given, only the cell tower number, as it hadn't lasted long enough to be triangulated.

"Emergency, which service do you require?"

"Fire brigade. Quickly."

"What's the problem, madam?"

"I'm burning with desire."

"I need to inform you that it is a criminal offense to make non-emergency calls to this number."

"But I need a man with a giant hose."

Ingrid didn't need to hear anymore. This was not a good use of her time. It was the sort of task she would normally ask Jen to do, but Ingrid knew getting Jen to do something so tedious was no way to make amends. She kept clicking on the links, hoping someone might have called 999 to report dangerous driving or a motorcycle out of control. The chances were slim—people just honked their horns or made hand gestures—but she kept listening until she heard the call made by Harding's distraught wife, Amita. It was logged at 0904 hours

"Emergency, which service do you require?"

"I don't know."

"Ma'am, which service?"

"I don't know. He's dead."

"What's your name?"

"Amita."

"Okay, Anita, can you tell me what you know."

"My husband is dead."

"I'm so sorry to hear that. I am going to dispatch an ambulance. I just need to check your location. Then I can talk you through some first aid. Is that okay, Anita." The call handler kept mispronouncing his wife's name.

"It's too late for first aid." She sounded incredibly calm.

The call lasted seven minutes and, in that time, Ingrid did not hear a single car pass. There was no sound of rain or wind. Nothing to indicate bad weather was involved in the accident. She pictured Amita kneeling at the side of the road, completely alone with her husband's body.

The paramedics' report wasn't linked to the recording, so Ingrid put in a request for it to be emailed over. She made a note of the cell tower the call had come through, then scrolled to find other calls from the same tower. She found a match and pressed play. It was the untriangulated call she'd already listened to, made an hour before Amita Harding's. This time, Ingrid paid careful attention.

"Emergency, which service do you require?"

No answer.

"Emergency, can you hear me?"

"Yes." The caller was female. She sounded young. Under fifty. Certainly not an old woman's voice.

"Which service do you require?"

The long pause again seemed longer this time. "Ambulance." The woman had an accent. European. It was impossible to be precise from the little she said, but the emphasis on the final syllable of 'ambulance' sounded eastern European. A Slavic language speaker.

"Where are you calling from?"

Ingrid strained but couldn't make out background noise before the call ended. Her heart beat a little harder. It was just possible, wasn't it, that the woman who'd hung up had witnessed the accident?

Ingrid listened repeatedly. Again, there was no sound that indicated rain or wind. She turned the volume up, trying to decipher the background noise at the end of the call, but sounds distorted on her computer's speakers. She scrabbled around in her gym bag for her headphones and listened for another time. Perhaps it was a man's voice. Could it be the last thing Matthew Harding said? Ingrid copied the recording, and sent it off to the FBI's audio lab for analysis.

She placed another forkful in her mouth, but the curry had gone cold: she'd spent over an hour eavesdropping on the calls. She opted for a swig of warm beer instead. It wasn't late, but she had barely slept. Her early morning cab ride out to the airport felt like it had happened weeks ago, not hours, and she struggled to keep her eyes open. Her computer emitted a dull ping telling her the open-source search had been completed.

The information was dense and she blinked hard to make sense of it. The database was an amazing resource, but it needed another iteration to be classed as user friendly. It outputted information in a way that would excite a math nerd, but the streams of poorly tabulated data made Ingrid's tired eyes swim.

She took another swig of beer and focused.

Kingfisher Holdings, according to data extracted from the Panama Papers, had links to the royal family of the Emirate of Jihar. The next document the database offered was the minutes of the Swanbury golf club committee meeting at which Sheikh Mohammed Al-Kareem was approved for membership. Other search results included gripes on a neighborhood forum about 'bloody Arabs' accompanied by a photo of a young man that the Bureau's imaging software had identified as the Sheikh's son, Samir. Ingrid smiled: even the super-rich couldn't hide behind their offshore trusts in the data age. She had found the owners of Uppenham Hall.

According to the Bureau's files, Sheikh Mohammed Al-Kareem was the third son of Jihar's elderly ruler and acted as the tiny nation's trade envoy, a job that had become more important since Jihar had been ostracized by the other Emirates for appearing too close to Iran and the Muslim Brotherhood.

Ingrid drained the bottle and shook her head at the screen. The chances that the Uppenham Hall's owners had witnessed the accident were slim enough; the chances they'd accept a call from the FBI could be measured in microns. After all her research, the person most likely to tell her who had been riding her bike was still Steve from the garage.

She logged into Facebook, hoping for a little red dot telling her she had a message from Portugal. The only notifications she had were prompts from Facebook informing her it had been weeks since she'd last posted anything. She navigated her way to Steve's profile, but instead of seeing him drinking a beer in the sunshine, an error message popped up. Steve had blocked her.

Ingrid's vision blurred momentarily. The curry lurched in her stomach. Why on earth would Steve block her?

It made no sense. They got on well. They had eleven friends in common. Why on earth would he...?

"Jeez." Ingrid let out a long sigh. How had it taken her all day to work it out?

Steve had been the one riding the bike. It must have been him. Ingrid thought about all the conversations they had had about her Triumph. He'd admired it from the moment it was delivered. And not only had Steve had access to her bike, he would have also had access to the security cameras in the garage.

Ingrid expelled all the air from her lungs, releasing a deep, low moan. She really had been dumb not to have made the connection straightaway. Ingrid hadn't known Steve well, but there had been plenty of times when they'd bantered about sports or motorcycles or how the Secret Service took themselves too seriously. He wasn't a friend, but he had always been friendly whenever she'd picked up an embassy car, or if he'd asked her to leave her keys in case he had to move the bike.

She slapped her forehead. He'd even had her bike key on countless occasions. He could have easily got a copy made. And he would have been able to repair whatever damage had been done in the accident. Now she thought about it, something had been different about her bike when she'd shown it to Thames Valley Police. She noticed it when she'd put her hand on the gas tank. He had resprayed it.

Ingrid's lip curled. Steve hadn't just taken her bike, he had killed someone and was trying to frame her for his crime. "Oh boy, are you going to pay."

She opened another browser window and looked up flights to Portugal. Thames Valley Police wouldn't know if she traveled on her Russian passport, would they?

7

The Monkeys and Peanuts bar was open from eight in the morning serving full English breakfasts for the expat community of Faro. You could order it with a mug of tea or a cold pint of lager, depending on the kind of day you had planned. Or the kind of night you'd had before. The radio was tuned to a British station, and a silenced TV screen above the counter showed BBC News with the subtitles on.

"You want another coffee?" the bartender asked.

She'd already had two, but after a fitful night on the couch in Marshall's office and an early morning train to Gatwick, she could use the caffeine. "That'd be great, thanks. And maybe one of those little custard tarts."

"You not been able to make contact with your friend?" he asked

"Not yet."

"She's probably sleeping it off."

Ingrid wasn't sure, but she thought his accent was from Birmingham. Apart from her taxi driver, everyone she'd spoken to since arriving in Faro had been English. Apparently, there was a considerable tax advantage for Brits basing themselves in Portugal. The streets had a surprising number of cars with UK license plates, and most of them were Audis, BMWs and Range Rovers.

The door opened, and Ingrid looked up from the newspaper

they had given her on the plane. It wasn't Steve, but it was someone who shared a lot of his characteristics. Slightly overweight, mid-forties, soccer shirt, earring and the kind of lumbering walk that proved humanity's evolution from apes. Her British friends would call him 'a right geezer'.

"Awwight, mate," he said to the bartender and took up residency on a stool at the bar.

Ingrid returned to her paper. She didn't really have a plan for tracking Steve down. The usual options were all out. Given she was in the country on a Russian passport in a fake name, she couldn't enlist the help of the local police. If she asked around and someone told Steve an American woman was looking for him, she risked him going on the run. And, of course, there was no option of calling on the embassy for help. Until she knew for sure that Steve had been the one to switch the CCTV footage, she had to assume he had accomplices inside Grosvenor Square. For now, Ingrid's plan was to overdose on good coffee and pastries and bide her time. If this was Steve's local bar, she was confident she was in the right place.

Her confidence paid off a little after half-past nine. Steve pushed through the door and nodded to the guy on the stool. Ingrid's veins flooded with adrenaline. He stared right at her.

Ingrid smiled.

Steve was back out the door before she got to her feet. She stood up quickly, knocking over the water jug on her table. She was at the door in two strides and pushed it open. Steve had darted through the tables in the beer garden and made it on the road. Ingrid gave chase and the tang of sea air stung her nostrils. "Steve!"

The road was a wide palm-lined boulevard that hugged the curve of the beach. To her left was the Atlantic Ocean, misty, milky and vast, and to her right was a succession of bars blasting pop music, tourist boutiques, cafés and rental car agencies.

Steve had the physique of a man who watched more sport than he played. He was panting hard after running forty yards. "I run five miles a day, Steve" Ingrid shouted at him. "Every day." She pulled level. "You want to stop before you collapse?"

He glanced over his shoulder at her, but carried on running for another few steps before accepting reality. "How did you find me?" He planted his hands on his knees and got his breath back.

"I'm a federal agent, Steve."

"Oh, yeah." His chest heaved with exertion.

"Sounds like you were expecting me."

He didn't answer.

Ingrid watched an outdoor fitness class on the beach while Steve remained doubled.

"I know about the accident, Steve."

Steve hauled himself upright. His face was pink from either sun or booze, or exertion. "What accident?" He wiped his forehead and nervously checked over both shoulders. "What accident?"

"Don't play dumb. You wouldn't have run if you didn't know why I was here."

He rolled his eyes skyward.

"And if I found you, the British police will too."

He kept peering down the street as if he was expecting someone.

She laid a hand on his shoulder. "Steve, why did you run if you don't know about an accident?"

A rickshaw driver pedaled up behind them, and Steve spun around. He was jumpy. Nervous.

"I know you killed a man."

His eyes widened.

"And I'm pretty sure it was an accident. But framing me? That was deliberate."

Steve blinked and swallowed repeatedly.

"I'm an FBI agent, Steve. Did you really think I wouldn't investigate?"

He shook his head slowly and closed his eyes. "I don't know anything about an accident, but I know I haven't killed anyone."

"They'll extradite you," Ingrid said.

He took a step back. "Nah."

"You'll be arrested."

His head swayed from side to side. His mouth twisted into a

snarl. "Nah. You're wrong. There's no extradition treaty with Portugal."

"True. But that only means extradition takes a little longer."

His palm slapped onto his bald head. His chest bellowed under his Tottenham Hotspur shirt. "Nah, you're wrong."

"Steve. I tracked you down. The police will come for you too. Going on the run only means you're going to get a longer sentence."

The muscles tightened in his neck. "Nah. This is all wrong. You got it all wrong." He looked at the traffic like he was going to throw himself under the next bus that came along.

"Steve, listen to me. I am not going to go to prison for killing someone when I know you did it."

He stared at the sidewalk and swore under his breath. "Shit. Fuck. Shitfuckfuck."

"But I can help you, Steve. You can come back with me and I can make it easier for—"

He looked at her, his desperate eyes blinking rapidly. "I never killed no one." Anxiety made his voice tremble. "And you are really fucking scaring me."

Ingrid tightened her grip on his shoulder. He was a big man, tall and broad, and he was desperate. Terrified. She genuinely thought he might run in front of a car. "Steve, come with me. Let's go back to the bar. Come on, come with me."

He didn't move.

She took a step backward, hoping to pull him with her, but he windmilled his arm and threw off her grasp.

"I've got to get out of here. This ain't happening." He turned sharply, but in two strides Ingrid was standing in front of him.

"If you didn't kill him, Steve, who did? You obviously know something."

His head shook rhythmically. "I don't know nothing. I promise you."

"A man was by killed by someone riding my bike, Steve. If it wasn't you, who was it?"

His eyes widened as if this was the first time he'd heard the news. Seagulls screeched overhead. Christmas music drained into the street from a nearby shopping mall.

He looked at his sneakers. "It could have been anyone," he said.

"Then why are you the one who suddenly quit his job and fled the country?"

He kept looking at the ground. "It wasn't me. I don't know who it was, but it weren't me." He was crumpling in front of her eyes. He had become oddly boyish, so much so she thought he might cry.

He wheeled back and couldn't stop shaking his head.

"Why could it be anyone? Steve, why?"

"Ah, my brain is spinning, man. This is not cool. This isn't what they promised." He looked up and down the street.

Ingrid needed to stay patient. "Why, Steve? I need to understand."

His head shaking morphed into tiny, repetitive nods. He sniffed. "There was a second key, weren't there?" He looked at her, expecting censure. When none came, he continued. "I mean, that was my fault, I admit that. I should have told you. You remember when your bike was delivered? Nah, you wouldn't cos you wasn't there. But I was. It was that actor, that one from the telly. He rode it in. Said it was a gift cos you'd helped him out. You remember?"

Of course, she did. Truman Cooper was a friend of the ambassador and Ingrid had done him a favor. The bike was a token of his thanks.

"I only ever gave you one key. Thought I could ride myself, see?" Steve blinked slowly. "But I was scared. It was a big bike, and it's worth thousands, innit, and I'm not insured so I only ever did it once or twice. But—" His voice snagged in his throat "—other people knew about the key."

Jeez, how many people had been riding her bike?

"Steve, I believe you. I do. But this is really, really important, okay?" She stared at him till he made eye contact. "I'm going to ask you one more question and you've got to tell me the truth. Understand?"

He couldn't hold her gaze. He kept looking over her shoulder. She turned to see what he was looking at. Just a few shoppers and a couple of guys chatting in the street.

"Do you understand?"

Steve was now staring at something behind her. She turned back and looked again. There was a man behind the wheel of a parked Audi TT, a phone clamped to his ear. Muscular, sun-darkened skinned, intense. His gold chain and signet ring glinted in the sun. He was either military or intelligence.

"Who is he, Steve?"

The man maintained eye contact with her as he buzzed up his window. The tinted glass shaded him from view.

"Steve?" Ingrid asked. "Who is that man?" She strode over to the Audi TT, breaking into a run when she heard its engine switch on. "Hey!"

The car was completely black—handles, hub caps, windows—making it more pretentious than sinister.

"Hey!" She leaned in to tap on the window just as it drove off, speeding down the boulevard. She threw her hands in the air and turned back towards Steve.

"Steve?"

He was nowhere to be seen.

8

Ingrid scanned the sidewalk. Joggers weaved in and out of shoppers, a woman dragged screaming twins by their wrists, but Steve had disappeared. She raced back to Monkeys and Peanuts and barreled through the door. He wasn't in there either.

"You seen Steve?" she asked the bartender.

He shrugged. "No, and I ain't seen your money neither."

She hadn't paid. She plunged her hand into her pocket and pulled out a crumpled twenty euro note. She placed it on the counter. "Now have you seen him?"

"Who's Steve?" he asked.

Ingrid bared her teeth in frustration before darting back out onto the sidewalk. He couldn't have got far. She checked left and right, but his Tottenham Hotspur shirt was not in view. She ran over the road, dodging traffic, and scanned the beach. Apart from the fitness class and a handful of dog walkers, it was empty. Ingrid looked back toward the bar and cafés, and searched for alleys and turnings. His best bet, she reasoned, was the shopping center.

She powered across the street and burst through the revolving door into the Palàcio mall. Mariah Carey's *All I Want for Christmas Is You* bounced out of the speakers. A maintenance worker rode a cleaning vehicle that left a wet snail trail across the tiled floor. She pulled up to get her bearings.

Ingrid was standing in the center of a three-story rotunda built around a waterfall cascading down from the third floor into a pool decorated with elves and wrapped gifts. Escalators zigzagged upwards, taking customers to circular walkways, wreathed in holly and ivy, leading them to upmarket stores and designer boutiques. Shoppers shuffled slowly, seemingly deaf to the peppy music urging them to buy more.

Out of the corner of her eye, something moved quickly.

Ingrid spun around and just caught sight of a man diving into a clothing store. She accelerated toward him, and chased him between racks and rails, but when she rounded a display of denim jackets, Ingrid pulled up sharply.

"Sorry."

The man didn't look anything like Steve.

Breathless, she rushed back out to the rotunda. Where the hell had he gone? Steve wasn't fit enough or fast enough to have got away. He had to be hiding. She scanned the storefronts and tried to think like a middle-aged, overweight Englishman.

"Come on," she said under her breath, willing Steve to make an appearance. The stores likely had rear exits; he could be anywhere by now.

She looked up. If she were Steve, she'd want to get to the top floor. She'd want a view of the entrance. Ingrid searched two tiers of balconies above her, expecting to see his pudgy face staring nervously down at her. When she couldn't spot him, she darted between distracted shoppers toward the escalator.

"Excuse me," she said. People turned and sneered but she pressed on, taking the stairs two at a time. "Excuse me."

A woman with several bags blocked the escalator. Ingrid couldn't get past. She hovered at her shoulder, desperate to leap over her shopping the moment they reached the second story.

Ingrid overtook the woman, barging in front to take the next escalator ahead of her. She heard shouting from below. She peered over the handrail to see what the commotion was on the floor of the rotunda. A group of people stared up. Ingrid followed their gaze. She twisted around to look at the balcony above her, just in time to see someone tumble over the banister and through the air, his arms circling as he fell. A collective gasp sucked the air out of the mall as they watched Steve somersault and hit his head on the edge of the fountain. His body slammed onto the marble floor. He didn't move.

Ingrid reached the top of the escalator and stumbled. Adrenaline flamed across her skin. She regained her balance and gripped the balcony handrail. She watched in horror as screaming shoppers circled Steve's lifeless body. No one was brave enough to approach him.

Ingrid raised her gaze and looked straight ahead, across the rotunda, to the spot on the third level where Steve had fallen. A man caught her eye, then quickly glanced away. He started running. Steve hadn't fallen. He had been pushed. Ingrid gave chase, speeding around the curve of the balcony, dodging shoppers gawking down at the tragedy below. The running man was athletic, well-groomed, and wore an expensive-looking sweater tight over his pecs. He shoved his way through a set of double doors and disappeared from sight. Ingrid kept running, determined to make up the forty yards he had on her.

She pushed through the doors and found herself in the emergency stairwell. Footsteps echoed off the bare white walls from below. Ingrid followed, taking the stairs so fast she fell against the wall. Her lungs sucked in air and she propelled herself downward.

A door opened below, drawing the Christmas music into the stairwell. She tore down the remaining steps and barreled out of the swinging doors. She was back in the rotunda. A muted crowd had gathered around Steve's body. No one was attempting CPR. One man was on his phone. Shop assistants stood at the threshold of their stores, unable to leave their stations, open mouthed with horror as George Michael reminisced about his last Christmas. A few heads turned as the well-built man dashed out of the mall.

Ingrid kept going and barged through the revolving door out into the salty air. She scoured the sidewalk and spotted his light blue sweater. She accelerated. She was thirty yards behind him. Twenty.

He dived into the open door of a waiting car. The driver of the black Audi TT didn't wait for it to close before speeding off. Ingrid stared as the car roared into the distance, clasping her head with both hands.

"Damn!"

Her mouth fell open and she breathed deeply. Her chest burned. What the hell had just happened? Dazed, she spun around, expecting hordes to tumble out of the shopping center in pursuit. The door revolved, but no one left the building. There were no police sirens. No wail of an approaching ambulance.

She was in almost the exact same spot where, just a few minutes beforehand, Steve told her about the second key. She pictured his expression when he'd seen the man in the Audi. It had been one of total fear.

What was it he'd said? *That's not what they promised.*

Ingrid started to run. If they had killed Steve, what would they do to her?

9

Bad weather created a backlog of flights at Heathrow and Ingrid didn't get back to London until late. She picked up a change of clothes at the airport and made her way to Marshall's office. His couch would do for a second night.

The FBI's offices were almost deserted, even though the Legal Attaché Program employed fifty-five people. Beneath the Attaché himself was a Deputy Special Agent in Charge and an Assistant Special Agent in Charge, and under them were Supervisory Special Agents running the counterterrorism and counterintelligence teams. As the criminal team only consisted of Ingrid and Jen, there was no need for an SSA. It was unusual for the place to be empty. Either a huge CT operation was underway, or everyone was at Christmas parties. Whichever was correct, Ingrid was grateful for the privacy. It would be hard to have the polite 'how are you getting on' conversations without giving something away about Steve.

It was impossible to tell if Marshall's office had been cleaned since his death. He had always been preternaturally tidy. Even after a ten-mile run, he rarely had a hair out of place. Ingrid caught herself smiling as she remembered how he preened over his hair, a perfect blond mop he maintained with vanity and lemon juice.

The delay at Faro airport had given her time to work out how she would bring Steve's killers to justice. She turned on Marshall's computer and logged in. While it creaked and whirred its way to life, Ingrid's gaze lingered on a framed photo of Marshall's sister Carolyn. A month ago, Carolyn had been a student at a London university embarking on her first adult relationship. Following Marshall's murder, she was now back in South Carolina and not straying far from her grieving parents' sight. Ingrid should call her and check in to see how she was doing. Ingrid pulled open Marshall's drawer in search of a Kleenex.

Needless to say, Marshall's drawer had plastic dividers creating neat squares for pens, loose change, thumb tacks and rubber bands. There was no emergency pack of tissues, but in one chamber was something that caught Ingrid's breath. A key chain of a little Scottish terrier. She had bought it for Marshall on their first weekend away. It had been a kitsch joke from a seaside gift shop after they'd walked for miles along a beach in Delaware and mapped out their life together, down to the pets they would have and the names they would give them.

"Hey there, T-Rex."

She was amazed he hadn't thrown it away when she broke off their engagement. She picked it up, tinkling three keys stamped with the brands Yale and Chubb. House keys, not car keys. She should probably offer to clear out his home as well as his desk. Ingrid reached behind her and slipped the bunch into her jacket pocket.

The computer emitted a self-satisfied murmur that announced it was ready for action. Ingrid dialed into the embassy's security logs. If neither she nor Steve had been riding her bike on November eighteenth, someone else in the building had taken it. Someone with contacts, influence and a network. Whoever was riding knew that Steve could name them, and they had forced him to leave the country. And when they feared he was about to squeal, they ensured his silence. Ingrid shuddered at the memory of Steve's head hitting the edge of the waterfall. She resisted the temptation to search for news from Portugal.

Doing so would leave a trail of digital breadcrumbs she'd have difficulty explaining.

Ingrid peered at the security logs from the eighteenth. The good news was the embassy was one of London's most secure buildings. No one got in without an employee pass, or a barcoded visitor pass from the security desk. The bad news was 1883 people had entered the building on the day in question.

She rested her chin on her hand and examined the lengthy list on her monitor. She flicked the mouse and watched the names cascade down the screen. It was going to be a long night. She didn't know who she was looking for, so she started by searching for her own name. The log showed her arriving at 08:02 and leaving at 17:40, almost exactly the same time the faked CCTV images had her exiting the garage. Was that a coincidence, or had whoever infiltrated the surveillance footage checked the attendance record first? Perhaps that had been doctored too.

She scanned the names on either side of hers, hoping to see one that would stand out, a flashing icon saying 'suspect'. Her eyes alighted on Marshall's name, and on Jen's. The ambassador's name leaped out as did a certain George Clooney's. She guessed it wasn't the actor, otherwise she'd have heard some gossip. Some names came in clusters. A run of Hispanic surnames, a batch of military ranks, a delegation of women. She clocked several Arabic names in a row and checked it wasn't a visit from the Emirate of Jihar. Her eyes began to water. The list became a jumble of meaningless words that decayed further into random letters the more she looked. She needed a way of whittling 1883 names down to a single suspect.

Ingrid got to her feet and paced the room, just as she had seen Marshall do many times. She could visualize him, a hand in his pocket pulling his shirt tight across his abs, the other pushing his hair out of his face, peering out of the window at Grosvenor Square below. She stood where he used to, and looked down through the murky, rain-smeared windows to the street. A sad-looking Deliveroo scooter weaved between the black cabs that always circled the embassy.

Bingo.

Scooter riders didn't need a permit in the UK, just a certificate of basic training. But to ride a motorcycle like hers, you had to train, and you needed to pass two tests to get a license. Ingrid didn't know what percentage of the population had motorcycle permits, but her instincts told her it was less than ten percent.

Jen normally did the data analysis for her, and it made Ingrid appreciate her assistant even more. She really was going to have to make things up with Jen and made a mental note to find those pink pearl earrings. She checked the date in the corner of the screen: she had almost two weeks to buy them before Jen's last day in the office.

Two weeks? Ingrid hoped she'd have left the country by then.

Ingrid cross referenced the attendance log with DMV and DVLA records on both sides of the Atlantic and found 122 people with motorcycle licenses. *Nice work.* Inside half an hour, she'd shrunk her list of suspects by ninety percent. But that was still too many people to interview on her own.

To shrink the pool further, she overlaid the remaining 122 with convictions for DUIs and dangerous driving. It was the kind of methodical police work she'd never seen a cop do on TV, but after another hour her list had just eleven names on it. Now she was in business.

Nine of them worked in the building, two were visitors. Only five were on site between 17:00 and 18:00 on the eighteenth. She allowed herself a smile. She had narrowed 1883 down to five in just over two hours. There was something very sweet about hunting down a killer when he had absolutely no idea she was coming for him.

Ingrid created files for her final five and pulled up the personnel records for the ones who were on the staff. She scrutinized a photo of Angela Dees, a twenty-three-year-old payroll clerk who lived, according to Google Street View, in a rundown housing project at the far end of the Central Line. The idea that this young woman whose Facebook posts were about *Love Island* and cavapoos was involved in the cover-up of a hit and run was somewhere between unlikely and preposterous. No, she was looking for someone with the means and motive, someone who could access the embassy's surveillance systems and have the reach to get Steve killed in Portugal. She was searching for someone with a network, and someone with a reputation to protect. That left her with two suspects.

Man, she loved her work.

Marcus Williams, twenty, was the son of the ambassador, Frances Byrne-Williams. Ingrid had worked a little with the ambassador, mostly on the case that had resulted in her being gifted the Triumph, and it seemed unlikely a woman dedicated to public service would have raised a cavalier killer. Her son's online activity displayed the expected mix of Ivy League studies, sporting achievements and internships with senators. While he had a smug expression and oozed a strain of entitlement that made Ingrid bristle, he only had an A1 license that limited him to riding bikes below 125cc. Ingrid's Triumph had a sixteen hundred engine. Which led her onto suspect number two.

Carlos Estevez was part of the Marines' diplomatic corps and was one of twenty-three Marines working in the London embassy. While civilians did most of the security, certain functions were fulfilled by Marines who could carry weapons on embassy premises.

Ingrid stared at Estevez's file. He was twenty-six, from Texas, and had served in Afghanistan. On Facebook, Ingrid found a photo of him straddling a Honda Rebel. On one forearm was a tattoo of a vintage Enfield. If he liked retro-looking bikes, he was likely to be sweet on her Triumph.

Estevez had access to the surveillance systems, a license to ride, and an international military network to call on. Ingrid pushed her chair back and smiled. She had found her man.

10

"Hey. You're in already." Jen hung up her coat.

"Morning." Ingrid wasn't about to reveal she had slept in Marshall's office again. "You have a good night last night?"

Jen's face twisted with awkwardness. "Oh, yes, thanks. It was, like, just a few drinks." She took her seat and switched on her computer.

Ingrid didn't know where she stood with Jen and was not about to pout at being left out. "You must have a lot of people you want to catch up with before you go."

Jen didn't answer. Things were not normally stilted between them.

"Listen, Jen. I'd like to take you out for a meal before you get on a plane."

Jen stuck out her bottom lip. "That'd be nice." Jen's eyes were glued to her screen, studiously avoiding contact with Ingrid's. "We might have to make do with a cocktail at the ambassador's ball. I saw you got an invitation."

"You're going?"

"You sound surprised."

Everything Ingrid said was upsetting Jen. "No, excited. We get to hang out." Though the truth was Ingrid had no intention of going.

"Jack needs to be there."

"Getting ready for the role of a diplomat's wife?"

"I guess. Though I was thinking, once we're back in the States I might, like, join the diplomatic corps myself."

Ingrid smiled. "You'd be great at it! I'd send you straight to the UN. Put you in charge of global peace." She'd gone too far. She sounded flippant. Jen would think she was mocking her. "You know if you need any kind of reference, I'd be happy to write one."

Jen didn't look at her. "Thanks."

After several minutes of silence, Ingrid got to her feet. "Listen." This was going to be uncomfortable. "About the other day."

Jen kept her focus on her computer.

"I'm real sorry. I've been pretty messed up, but that's no excuse for... for not saying goodbye." Ingrid thought she was handling it fairly well. She plunged her hands into her pants pockets and leaned against her desk. "Not my finest hour. Anyway, like I say, I'm sorry."

Jen's fingers hovered over her keyboard. She was as still as a photograph.

"So, if you, um, if you have a blank evening in your diary any day soon, I'd like to buy you dinner. Say thank you for being amazing these past few years."

Jen remained frozen.

Ingrid slunk back behind her desk. "You know I'm going to miss you, right?"

Jen was the person she had spoken to the most, and spent the most time with, since she'd been in London. She was the one who had supplied cough drops and Tylenol and tampons and found her keys when she'd mislaid them. Jen was family.

Jen's lips puckered. "Thank you." Her fingers blitzed the keyboard for a few seconds before she delicately ran a nail under one eye and carried on.

Ingrid returned to the profile of Carlos Estevez on her screen. According to the Marine working the overnight security desk, Estevez would start his shift at eight. The Marine Diplomatic Protection Corps, she'd discovered, was considered a prestige move in a regiment where there weren't many routes to promotion. Marines who worked in the embassy weren't avoiding deployment into conflict zones, they were dedicating themselves to the regiment for the long haul.

An email pinged into Ingrid's inbox. It was from the Bureau's forensics lab in West Virginia. 'Please find attached the report you requested.' Ingrid checked the time. It was three in the morning on the East Coast. Someone was working late. Or sleeping in their office. It was the analysis of the 999 call. She double-clicked the attachment, her mouth suddenly dry. The entire document was only seven lines long.

Length of recording: 19.04 seconds.
Location: internal, no engine noise detected.
Languages spoken: English and Arabic.

Voice 1: [CALL HANDLER] female, over 45. Language: English. Accent: regional English (Manchester). *Emergency, which service do you require? Emergency, can you hear me?*
Voice 2: [CALLER] female, under 35. Language: English. Accent: Central Asia native. *Yes.*
Voice 1: [CALL HANDLER] *Which service do you require?*
Voice 2: [CALLER] *Ambulance.*
Voice 1: [CALL HANDLER] *Where are you calling from?*
Voice 3: [BACKGROUND] male, under 35. Language: Arabic. Accent: Gulf native. Translation from Arabic: *Where is he?*

Ingrid found the recording and listened to the call again. Jen threw her a disapproving look that said, 'Couldn't you use headphones?' The man's voice was nothing more than a rumble. It was incredible what voice recognition software could do. She exhaled hard.

"What?" Jen asked.

"Oh." Ingrid hadn't realized she'd been audible. "That hit and run?"

69

"The one you were, like, arrested for?"

"I may have just found a witness."

"Cool."

It was better than that. She had two witnesses: a central Asian woman and an Arabic-speaking man. The chances that two 999 calls within an hour of each other from the same rural cell tower weren't related was unlikely. And it was even less likely the Arabic speaker wasn't connected to Uppenham Hall. She needed to get beyond those gates and find out what these two people knew about the hit and run. If they could confirm a man was riding, she was in the clear. Ingrid put in a liaison request to the Metropolitan Police asking for records of the cell number that had made the call.

She checked the time and stood up.

"Where are you off to?" Jen asked.

"I've got a case to crack."

"You do?" Jen sounded surprised. "Normally you bombard me with, like, a zillion research requests."

Ingrid smiled. "I gotta learn to cope without you sometime."

Ingrid took the stairs down to the lobby, and then navigated the familiar route to the embassy's gym, the smell of chlorine guiding her along the final corridor. Her source on the security desk had assured her Carlos Estevez would finish his work out about now.

It was a busy time of day for the gym. All the treadmills were occupied with employees surgically attached to their headphones, and the noise of fifteen motors and thirty feet hitting the rubber was loud enough to make her wish she had her own headphones. She winced at the smell. The air conditioning had never been up to the job at peak times.

Ingrid had deliberately chosen the time and place to confront Estevez. If she was right, he was behind two deaths. He had killed Matthew Harding, and his military contacts had silenced Steve Thompsett. Ensuring their encounter had plenty of witnesses lessened her chance of becoming his third victim.

She spotted Estevez easily. He was slim, muscular and very serious-looking as if considering an extremely complicated math problem. His hair was tightly cropped and his gray T-shirt clung to his firm pectorals. Compact and contained, he had the perfect build for martial arts.

Ingrid made eye contact with him in the mirror as he performed a sequence of bicep repetitions with a free weight. She was relieved he didn't seem to recognize her. She grabbed a five-kilo dumb bell as a precaution and continued walking in his direction. He slowed his reps as she approached, then stopped when she held his gaze.

"Can I help you?" He hadn't broken a sweat.

"I am Special Agent Ingrid Skyberg."

His features didn't move. He held the weight aloft, his elbow bent, showing her the motorcycle tattoo on his forearm.

"You heard of me?" Ingrid asked.

He checked over her shoulder. "Nope."

"I work for the Federal Bureau of Investigation. I'm part of the Legal Attaché Program."

He sucked his teeth. He didn't like having his session interrupted.

"I'm based here in the embassy. Fifth floor, if you ever want to find me."

He kept glancing behind her, giving the impression he had been expecting someone else.

"You should know that, this technically being American soil, I have the power of arrest in this building." She raised an eyebrow for emphasis.

He lowered the weight. "What gives, Agent?"

She nodded in the direction of his tattoo. "You like bikes?"

His features tightened. "What of it?"

"I ride a Triumph Thunderbird."

"Nice."

"Blue gas tank."

His eyelid twitched.

"Parked downstairs. Maybe you've noticed it?"

He stood a little straighter. "Ma'am."

Ingrid turned. The ambassador had emerged from the changing room. Ingrid had only ever seen Frances Byrne-

Williams in her tailored suits and a full face of make-up. Journalists often described the fifty-eight-year-old as 'matronly', but in Lycra and without the war paint she appeared lithe and friendly.

"Carlos," the ambassador said. "Good morning." She looked at Ingrid. "We've met, haven't we?"

Ingrid felt the prickle of nerves in the tips of her fingers. "Yes, ma'am. I'm Special Agent Skyberg. I assisted your friend Truman Cooper a few years back."

"The actor?" Estevez said.

"Oh yes, of course. He still mentions you, you know. Lovely to see you again." Byrne-Williams turned to Estevez. "Ready when you are."

"Yes ma'am."

Frances Byrne-Williams raised both eyebrows. "Well?"

"Ah," Ingrid said. "You're training the ambassador?"

Estevez puffed out his chest.

"Ma'am, I'm sorry. I need to speak to Estevez for a moment. I have some news about a mutual friend."

Estevez's thick eyebrows knitted. "Maybe start on the treadmill? I'll be right with you."

Byrne-Williams smiled at them both and left. She turned back. "Agent? Did you get an invitation to my party? Truman and Tom are coming, and I am sure they would love to see you again."

"Yes, ma'am, thank you. I did. Very kind to invite me."

"Well, it's my last hurrah, so to speak. I want to thank everyone who's been of assistance while I've been in post." She waggled her fingers, still full of rings despite the impending workout, and left them alone.

Ingrid took a step toward Estevez and leaned in. "You might want to call for a replacement."

He eyeballed her. "Why?"

The people around them slowed their routines and gawked, sensing tension in their postures.

"You know Steve Thompsett?"

"I don't think so."

"Steve from the garage?"

His eyes narrowed.

"Steve who let you have a key to my bike?" She lowered her voice. "Remember him now?"

"Uh-huh. A bit."

Ingrid studied his features. She was seeing confusion, not fear. "He was killed yesterday."

Estevez took a step back and crossed his arms. "You're telling me this because?"

"I think you know who killed him."

He maintained eye contact. His face was motionless.

"Where were you on November eighteen, corporal?"

He blinked slowly. "Not a clue."

"Corporal, I suggest you take this a little more seriously otherwise I will have to arrest you on suspicion of murder."

His jaw tightened.

"You need to phone for a replacement to train the ambassador. And then you need to come with me."

11

Estevez walked into the men's changing room and Ingrid followed.

"You can't come in here."

She tilted her head in an 'oh yes I can' way but compromised. She held the door open and stood at the threshold, watching him as he pulled on track pants and a hoodie. When he was dressed, Ingrid ushered him into the empty yoga studio. The lights flickered on automatically.

"Corporal Estevez, I need to remind you that you are on American soil. You understand that means I can arrest you?"

He dropped his gym bag, its contents jangling with keys and loose change. "Yes, ma'am."

"Let me ask you again. Where were you on November eighteen? I am an FBI agent, corporal. Lying to me would not be in your best interests."

"I have no idea, ma'am."

"You can call me Agent."

"Yes m—, Agent."

Under the harsh strip lights, Estevez appeared younger than his twenty-six years. If he were an actor, he would easily be cast as a teenager. He lifted his tee to wipe his face and revealed an impressive rack of abdominals.

Ingrid rolled back her shoulders. "Think hard, corporal. November eighteen. Less than a month ago."

His eyes scoured the floor. "Honestly, I do not know. What's November eighteen got to do with the guy from the garage?"

"I'll ask the questions."

He raised his hands in mock surrender.

"You keep a diary, corporal?"

"No." He was struggling not to end every sentence with 'ma'am'.

"Hand over your phone."

He crouched down and pulled it from a side pocket of his bag. He handed it to Ingrid.

"How do you unlock this?"

He swiped a code and Ingrid searched his apps for a calendar on his surprisingly old Samsung handset. "You don't have a diary on this? No calendar?"

He shrugged. "Nope."

"Really? Don't they come as standard on all phones?"

"Probably, but I need the storage for my music. I delete all that system junk."

Ingrid clicked on the music app. He had seven hundred and forty-two albums.

"I keep that phone as it has, like, two hundred and fifty gig. New phones don't have that kind of memory. Not that I can afford, anyway."

Ingrid kept hold of the phone. "Okay, let's try this another way. Why were you in Buckinghamshire last month?"

"Um." A flicker of doubt flitted across his face. "I don't know how to answer that."

"What don't you understand?"

"I don't know where that is, and I don't wanna lie, so…"

Ingrid was going to have to try a different tack. "When did you last ride my Triumph Thunderbird?"

He blinked rapidly. "Um, ah…"

"I know you've been riding it, corporal."

His shoulders hunched a little. "I thought it was that guy's. Steve's. You said he died."

"I said he was killed. Why did you think it was Steve's bike?" One of the strip lights above their heads started to flicker.

Estevez swallowed rapidly. "He saw me admiring it—it's a sweet ride—and said I could take it."

"How generous of him."

"I guess."

"And he just let you have it?"

"No." His forehead puckered. "He charged me fifty bucks. Fifty pounds. For a day."

Ingrid slapped a hand against her thigh. "He was like your personal Hertz?"

"Yeah, I guess."

Jeez. "And how often did you rent it from him?"

"I dunno. Six, maybe seven times. How did he die?"

How had she never noticed? Had Steve always topped off the gas? Or fixed the odometer? "What did you use it for?"

"Day trips. Sight-seeing. Taking girls out." He pulled a face. "Chicks dig bikes."

"You don't have a ride of your own?"

"Not in London, no."

Ingrid inhaled slowly. "I'm going to ask you again. When did you last ride my bike?"

"Um, let me think."

He was sweating more now than he had in the weight room.

"I honestly don't know. I remember it was sunny."

"Where did you take my bike?"

He rubbed his nose. "Listen, I don't know England all that well. I just rode out of London for a while. Went to see some countryside. You know what it's like. You amp up the tunes, get the bike into fifth and you look for some nice curves. You been there, right?"

She had. Going for a run sometimes gave her too much time to think, but going for a ride? That was like meditation. You're concentrating so hard on the road you can't think about anything else. "You head east? West?"

"I couldn't tell ya." Corporal Estevez moved from foot to foot, as if the floor was hot. "Listen, you said something about

arresting me for murder. I'd kinda like to know the details."
Either he really was innocent, or he'd been expecting her for
weeks and had been rehearsing his performance.

"On November nineteen, my bike hit and killed a man. I
know damn well I wasn't riding. And until you can tell me
where you were, you are my number one suspect."

His pupils dilated. "For real?"

"For real."

He picked up his bag. "Then you better come with me."

Carlos Estevez led Ingrid out of the embassy and around
the corner to a house shared by the twenty-three Marines
stationed in London. It was raining hard, making it feel like the
temperature had dropped below zero. Neither of them wore a
coat.

He fumbled for his keys then opened the polished oak door to
a five-story residence that, under different ownership, would be a
boutique hotel or an aristocrat's London home.

"You live here?" Ingrid asked. "Really?"

It had to be the highest value frat house in the world. It was
like something out of *Downton Abbey*. Dark paintings hung in
gold-leaf frames on the entrance hall walls, and the balustrade on
the staircase was polished mahogany. No wonder Marines
wanted to work for the diplomatic protection units. In days gone
by, the house would have smelled of roasted partridge and
Virginia tobacco, but now the aroma came from the fallen regiment of beaten-up sneakers that lined the baseboards.

On the second floor, the drawing room was strewn with bean
bags and gaming consoles. The drapes were drawn and it
smelled worse than the hallway.

"In here."

Ingrid strode over to the window to let some light in.

"Hey!" In a darkened corner, a Marine rolled over creating a
rustling sound on his bean bag. "Pull the drapes."

Ingrid yanked them open even wider.

"Who is that?" Shielding his eyes, the man peered at
her. "Oh."

Estevez cleared his throat. "She's with me."

"Oh," he said again, rubbing his eyes. "You got lucky, huh Charlie?"

Estevez didn't answer.

"Well, she's hot." The guy got to his feet. He was wearing boxers and a tee with a white stain down the front. Ingrid guessed she should be glad he wasn't naked. "Though ain't she a bit old for you?" He staggered out into the hallway without another word.

Now there was enough light in the room, Ingrid saw it was furnished with antiques and cut-glass light fittings. Two outsized televisions obscured a huge marble fireplace. Ingrid knew the ambassador's official residence—a vast mansion within the boundaries of Regent's Park—had been given to the US government by the Woolworth's heiress Barbara Hutton. She wondered if this jaw-dropper of a house had also been a gift. Or an asset seized for non-payment of taxes.

Estevez stood at a long, low desk laden with several computer monitors. It resembled the check-in desk for budget backpackers. Behind him was a poster-sized calendar and a poster of a Miley Cyrus in a low-cut swimsuit.

"This the office?" she asked.

"The mess room." He looked up at her. "You wanna see the schedule? I got the schedule for you." He gestured at the screen in front of him.

Ingrid crossed the waxed wooden floor, her damp sneakers squeaking with each step. The screen filled with the multicolor patchwork of a spreadsheet.

"I'm orange," he said, pointing at a line on the matrix, "and that's the eighteenth." He stood a little more upright. "I was working."

Ingrid leaned in. "Working where?"

Estevez looked blank. "Duh. The embassy, obviously."

"Front desk? Main gate?"

"Um." He grabbed the mouse and clicked on the appropriate orange square. "Sixth floor. The ambassador's suite. You could probably check the security footage."

Ingrid turned slowly and looked at him. Had he doctored

CCTV from the ambassador's office too? He was either innocent or cunningly brazen. "Says here your shift finished at six p.m. Where d'you go after work?"

"How the heck am I supposed to remember that?" A vein pulsed visibly in his neck.

The Marine with the stained T-shirt wandered back in. "So, you're not screwing her then?"

Ingrid pulled out her badge. "You might want to fuck off."

"Back off, Daley," Estevez said.

Daley looked at Ingrid's ID. "Fucking Bureau." He sauntered off again.

"I have an idea," Estevez said. "Something that'll prove where I was."

Ingrid was intrigued.

He shut down the roster and wandered over to the TV screens. "I was probably playing a game. My username should come up in the history." He picked up a console and switched on the TV. Ingrid didn't follow. She was still staring at the monitor. The roster had been replaced by the computer's screensaver. It was the US Marines' insignia. Written below it was their motto: Semper Fidelis. Where else had she seen that recently?

Ingrid's thoughts homed in on the roadside flowers that had been left for Matthew Harding.

12

Jen looked up from her screen. "You're soaked."

"I'll dry."

"Apparently it's going to snow tomorrow."

"You remember the last time it snowed?" Ingrid said, "London shut down for a week."

"You'd think the amount the Brits talk about the weather they'd be better at, like, dealing with it."

Ingrid pushed the wet hair off her face. "Well, it's not a patch on a Minnesota winter."

"Nor a California one." Jen propped up her chin on her hands. "You bought a new laptop?"

"Not exactly."

"D'you steal it?"

"Um. Kinda."

Ingrid filled Jen in on her interview with Carlos Estevez and how she had confiscated his hardware without the necessary paperwork. She wasn't even sure if, outside the United States, she was authorized to seize property, but as the gaming console hadn't provided him with an alibi, she'd insisted.

"What are you working on right now?" Ingrid asked.

Jen looked sheepish. "I have some spare capacity, if that's what you're asking."

"Can you go through these?" Ingrid pointed to the phone and

laptop. "And find out what Estevez was up to on November eighteen and nineteen?"

"You know I'm not an expert, right?"

"Sure."

"And we have a department that does this stuff for real."

"I do. But without the paperwork, I'm figuring I should do this on the QT. Plus," Ingrid failed to suppress a smile, "You're probably working on the seating plan for your wedding, so…"

Jen wrinkled her nose. "You better hand them over then."

If his devices gave Estevez a bone-dry alibi, Ingrid was going to need a witness who could confirm a man had been riding on the morning of the hit and run. She had to speak to the woman who had made the 999 call and searched for her files from the day before.

"Ew." Jen looked appalled.

"What?"

Jen held out Estevez's phone. "Porn."

Hardly a surprise. Ingrid stared at the phone number on her screen and prepared what to say. She couldn't be sure the woman who'd called 999 had seen the accident, but she'd been in the right vicinity at the right time. Ingrid knew nothing about the phone's owner except that she had cared enough to phone for an ambulance, but not enough to make sure one was dispatched. Ingrid tried not to judge. Shock can make people behave in odd ways.

She lifted the receiver on her desk phone, took a deep, calming breath, and dialed.

It didn't even ring. It went straight to a message that said 'this number has not been recognized'. Ingrid put down the handset and closed her eyes. Never had an unobtainable number felt so ominous. Had the same people who got to Steve also found the owner of the cell?

"Earth to Ingrid."

Ingrid looked up. "Hey."

"Just passing," Lexi Traynor stood in the doorway, her smile wide and bright. "You were miles away."

"Sorry."

"How you doing, girlfriend?"

Ingrid presumed she called everyone 'girlfriend' and smiled back. She gestured to the chair in front of her desk.

"I heard from Thames Valley Police." Lexi sat down and crossed her legs. Nothing about her appearance suggested she had been caught in a downpour or stepped in a puddle. She was, as ever, immaculate as she smoothed her fitted skirt over her runner's thighs. Not even a chip in her nail polish. "It was kinda strange."

"Strange how?"

Lexi's eyebrows narrowed. "They asked a couple of times if you'd ever been known by another name."

Ingrid's eyes immediately darted to the drawer containing her Russian passport.

"I said it was possible you'd been married or something like that."

"Nope, never married," Ingrid said, recovering her composure. "Odd they didn't call me."

Lexi tilted her head to one side. "Had the same thought myself."

"They say when I can get the Triumph back?"

"You'd know better than me how long forensics take."

"Weeks, in my experience."

"You gonna be okay without your passport that long?"

Heat flashed over Ingrid's face. Was Lexi fishing? Did she know about Portugal? Did the cops? "I reckon I can prove it wasn't me. Hopefully get it back in a few days."

"Well, that'll be nice. You can go home for Christmas," Lexi said.

Jen spluttered and the two other women looked at her. "Trust me," Jen said, "Christmas with her mom is not something Ingrid looks forward to."

Lexi turned to Ingrid. "For real?"

"Jen's worked with me for four years. She knows I don't even jingle half the way."

"Oh, gosh, me neither." Lexi flashed a wicked smile. "I got me two weeks in Barbuda."

"Ooh, nice."

"A bit of scuba, a lotta crayfish and whole heap of couples' therapy, if you know what I mean!" She let out a dirty cackle and got to her feet. "Say, d'you hear the news?"

"What news?"

"About that guy who worked in the parking lot downstairs?"

The hairs on the nape of Ingrid's neck stood to attention. "Which one?"

"The guy you were asking about. Steve something-or-other." Lexi stood a little taller, firmly planting both stilettos into the threadbare carpet.

"Steve?" Ingrid thought she was keeping her voice nice and even.

Lexi sucked her teeth and raised her brow. "He died."

Jen peered around her computer. "Who's Steve?"

"He, um, was the chief mechanic," Ingrid said. Was her expression displaying enough shock? "Ran the garage and the parking lot."

Jen's bottom lip protruded. "Don't think I ever knew him. Was he ill?"

Ingrid looked to Lexi to answer.

"No. They say he fell off a balcony." She made eye contact with Ingrid. "In Portugal."

Ingrid's insides constricted. "That's awful."

"I just thought it was so… coincidental, you know?" Lexi said. "I'm not sure I ever met him either, but two days ago you were looking for him and today I heard he'd died." She picked a thread off her jacket. "I just hope you don't ever come looking for me, you know what I'm saying?"

Ingrid still couldn't make eye contact. "How did you find out?"

"My boss mentioned something. Don't know who told him, but y'all know how quickly news flies around this building." She reached out and tapped Ingrid's desk to get her attention. "To be honest, I'm surprised you hadn't heard already."

Ingrid did a one-shoulder shrug. "Jen will tell you, I am always the last to know everything."

Jen took a break from typing to chime in. "Totes true. Ingrid still doesn't know the twist to *The Sixth Sense*."

Lexi's eyebrows moved toward her hairline. "For real?"

"Seriously," Jen said.

Lexi turned for the exit. "Remind me not to ask you to join my quiz team."

"Though," Jen said, "she is excellent on sports."

"I'm also very knowledgeable about sauvignon blanc and vodka."

Lexi hovered in the doorway. "Good niches to know." She winked before gliding out into the bullpen.

Ingrid slackened with relief. Was Lexi's drop by as casual and spontaneous as she'd made out? Flustered, she forgot she'd already called the cell phone and dialed it again, only to get the 'number not recognized' message a second time.

"Hey," Jen said. "You heard anything about who's getting Marshall's job?"

Ingrid turned away from her monitor. "You do remember the conversation we just had? The one about me being the last to know?"

"Oh, sure, but, like, well…"

"Yes?"

"Well, see, I heard, or rather Jenna heard, and she works for the Legat himself, that well…"

"Yes?"

"Well, that you were going to get it?"

Ingrid frowned at her. "Sure, right. Because I'm so good at paperwork."

"So, it's not true?"

Ingrid shook her head. "It's news to me."

Jen's shoulders softened. "Oh."

They both returned to their work until, less than a minute later, Jen piped up. "That's what I thought. I didn't, like, think you'd walk out on me if you were getting a promotion and everything." Jen waved Estevez's phone in the air. "Is there a specific time of day you're interested in?"

Ingrid opened an old bottle of Evian water. It smelled so

musty she screwed the cap right back down. "Yup. After five o'clock. Anything that suggests where he was or who he was with."

"Okeydokey."

Ingrid wandered out into the central bullpen and got a drink from the watercooler. She glanced over at Marshall's office door. It was still preposterous that he wasn't behind it, working out ways to make her life more difficult or sucking up to the bosses in DC. Her vision shimmered with disbelief, the floor apparently a little less solid than it had been moments before. Ingrid took a gulp of the cold water, then filled up her cup.

Back at her desk, she picked up her notes from the night before and scanned her hastily scribbled profile of Marcus Williams, the ambassador's son. She'd circled '125cc'. Something Estevez said sprang to mind: 'chicks dig bikes'.

If you could only ride a little bike, she reasoned, wouldn't that make the prospect of riding her Thunderbird more enticing? If you were out to impress, you weren't going to do it on something that was only two steps up from a bicycle. Ingrid opened up her file on Marcus Williams and reminded herself of his smug, privileged face. He even had a Wikipedia page. What twenty-year-old who wasn't a child star has that? He'd probably set it up himself. She clicked.

Williams's academic achievements and sporting awards were listed and a brief biography explained he had been born in Louisiana, the second son of Frances Byrne-Williams and Roy Williams.

Roy Williams. Ingrid knew that name.

The next click revealed Frances Byrne-Williams' ex-husband —they had divorced in 1998—was the founder of an investment firm based in Greenwich, Connecticut, and had a net worth of $3.8billion. Williams senior had made his fortune speculating on currencies and commodities and now used his wealth to buy political influence. His own Wikipedia page showed him shaking hands with two presidents: one American, the other Chinese.

Ingrid interlocked her fingers behind her head and peered at the screen. Marcus Williams wouldn't be the first rich boy to have his parents try to cover up a misdemeanor. She thought of all those frat boys accused of sexual assault whose sense of entitlement and access to five-hundred-dollar-an-hour attorneys had seen them avoid jail. Their only punishment was a lifetime of Google returns sullying otherwise golden futures.

An image search for Williams returned a photo of the tall, well-built young man squinting into the setting sun, a honey-color landscape of tall grass and scrub behind him. There was a rifle in his hand and the carcass of an elephant at his feet. Hunting hogs in Maryland was one thing, but an elephant? Ingrid felt sick.

Then she read the caption. *Worst thing I ever saw. Volunteering with anti-poaching charity Tusk in Tanzania. Who does this?*

She had been too quick to judge. Maybe he was one of those Princeton princes who planned on running NGOs before more decades of public service in Congress. Nevertheless, Marcus Williams needed to be ruled out. If she did things officially, Ingrid risked a diplomatic incident. She had only bumped into his mother a couple of hours ago. Maybe now was the perfect time to casually bump into her again, and this time start a conversation.

The floor above was much grander, and the ambassador's suite smelled of beeswax polish and cut flowers. The sixth floor always reminded Ingrid of an old cruise ship with wood-paneled walls, shiny floors and art deco wall lights. She reached the reception area and was surprised to find the ambassador's office empty.

She reached over the reception desk, looking for paper and pen so she could leave a note.

"Put your hands up."

Ingrid did so and turned. A Marine stood directly behind her. His Beretta M9 was aimed squarely at her head.

13

It was almost dark by the time Ingrid arrived at the Sir Steve Redgrave sports complex in Oxford. She would have made it in daylight hours if it hadn't been for the security breach in the ambassador's suite. Frances Byrne-Williams's computer had been accessed illicitly, and the Marines had shut down her office to investigate.

Under the circumstances, Ingrid swiftly reconsidered the wisdom of asking the ambassador for help reaching out to her son. She spun the Marine a story about needing Byrne-Williams's advice on a gift for a friend. Aware he was a likely ally of Estevez, she didn't want to give anything away about her investigation into the accident on Greenacre Lane.

Marcus Williams was judicious about what he posted on social media, but his friends were less discriminating. It hadn't taken Ingrid long to discover that Marcus Williams would be spending his afternoon at the rowing club. The first hour of the drive out to Oxford in a Hertz Toyota Prius was familiar. It was only after she passed the turnoff for Burnt Oak that Ingrid covered new ground. Despite Jen's prediction, there was no sign of snow; there was even a brief break in the rain.

Oxford looked like the tourist version of England. Lots of ornate, lion-colored buildings set around green lawns and populated by people carrying books or riding bicycles. Home to one of the nation's most prestigious universities, Oxford had long been a staging post in the career of successful Americans seeking a master's degree to embellish their résumés with.

Ingrid drove around the parking lot until she saw what she was after—the motorcycle bay—and pulled in next to it. There were only two bikes, a scrambler covered in mud and a Suzuki Marauder, a black beetle-like ride that aped the curves of a Harley. Or a Triumph. She already knew from checking the records that it belonged to Marcus Williams.

She got out of the Prius and the December wind instantly scoured the inside of her collar. She pulled it tight against her neck. The Marauder, complete with matching panniers and top box, was spotless, suggesting either that Williams had cleaned it that morning—or more likely had gotten it cleaned—or that it was parked undercover. There was just one blemish on it: the L-plate he was legally required to display until he got his full license.

Ingrid got back in the warmth of the car to wait. She reached for her phone and checked her emails. Nothing from Thames Valley Police. Nothing from Lexi Traynor.

"Ooh."

The dialing history of the number that made the 999 call had been sent through. Making sense of the document on a five-inch screen wasn't easy, but Ingrid determined it was an unregistered phone. It had probably been paid for with cash and can add minutes using vouchers. With more manpower she could find out where those vouchers had been purchased, and if they had miraculously been bought with a credit card, it might be possible to identify the owner of the phone. But she didn't have the manpower, and the chances were slim anyway.

The next page revealed the numbers dialed by the phone. Apart from the 999 call— which was the final call made from that number—every call was made to a number with a 993 prefix. Ingrid didn't recognize the country code, but a quick web search revealed it was for Turkmenistan.

"Wow." She marveled at the accuracy of the Bureau's audio

analysis that had predicted the woman was from central Asia. "Spot-on."

Ingrid zoomed in. Every call was made to the same number in Turkmenistan. "Ooh," she said again, sensing this would make it very easy to identify the caller. Ingrid wasn't about to dial the Turkic number—she didn't speak the language and without further research she risked scaring off a witness—but she had a new lead, and that got labeled as progress.

Ingrid looked for a pattern in the calls. The phone wasn't used often, and most calls were under two minutes. However, every week there was one longer call, usually around ten minutes in duration, always on a Thursday afternoon between two and four o'clock. The short calls all came via the cell tower used for the triple nine call, but the lengthier calls were made from a different location.

The next page of the report gave the GPS coordinates of each call. All the short ones were made from inside the grounds of Uppenham Hall. She typed the coordinates of the longer calls into Google Maps just as a commotion erupted outside the sports center.

Six tall, well-built men in their twenties tumbled into the parking lot, slapping each other on the back and shouting loudly. Rowers. She rolled down her window and listened.

"No fucking way."

"Not fucking happening."

"Well, we'll see about that." The last accent was American.

She opened the door and walked slowly in front of the car, stopping to linger next to the motorcycles. The group moved toward her, bleeping open their car doors as they walked.

"Look," one of them said. "Marky Mark was right. Girls do like bikes."

"Well they're not going to sleep with him for his looks, are they?"

Marcus stepped away from his teammates, his helmet in hand. He smiled at Ingrid. "Hi." He had the confident swagger of a man who had never once doubted his place in the world.

"Hi," Ingrid said.

"See you at Jasper's, yeah?" one of them yelled.

"What time you getting there?" Marcus shouted back.

"Depends how long things take with Michelle."

"You'll be early, then."

Male bonding banter had not moved on since Ingrid's university days. Marcus pulled on his helmet.

"You like bikes?" He fiddled with the chin strap

"I do."

"Well, if I had a spare helmet, I'd take you for a ride."

The leather on the right arm of his jacket was shredded, the kind of damage you get when you come off your bike and skid for several yards.

"I ride a Triumph," she said, instantly regretting it.

"Cool. Is that a Chicago accent?"

"A Thunderbird." She watched him closely.

He straddled his Suzuki. "Sweet." He gave her a big cartoonish smile. "I've ridden one of those."

You don't say. Ingrid made deliberate eye contact. "Beautiful petrol blue."

His eyes widened momentarily before he plunged his key into the ignition. An unmistakably flicker of panic had brought his flirting to an end. He pressed the starter button and flipped down his visor. He nodded before riding off.

There was a noticeable wobble as he pulled out of the parking lot.

14

Ingrid took a detour on the drive back into London. The GPS coordinates of the longer calls made by the unregistered phone led her to the town of Bishopsgate, about five miles west of Burnt Oak. The town's main street had the expected mix of Indian restaurants, florists, coffee shops and dry cleaners, seemingly the only businesses immune from the march of Amazon.com.

The satnav took her through Bishopsgate, past a train station emitting commuters returning from London, and out the far side of the town. After half a mile, the electronic voice told her that she had reached her destination. She was in a retail park with outsized versions of supermarkets, pet stores and DIY outlets. Ingrid parked and hoped to see something that would tell her why the woman from Turkmenistan visited every Thursday. She opened the compass app on her iPhone and checked the coordinates. She was a fraction of a degree out.

Crossing the parking lot like a water diviner carrying a rod, Ingrid moved carefully among the vehicles to the precise location. She was being guided to a branch of Tesco, one of the UK's biggest supermarket chains. It certainly made sense of the call pattern. The woman phoning Turkmenistan must do her weekly shopping on Thursday afternoons. It was Wednesday, but given she was there and someone might know something, she stepped inside the sliding doors. Glad of the warm air coming from a vent above her head, Ingrid took in the scale of the store. It was bigger than a terminal building at a decent-sized airport. A Christmas song about mistletoe and wine piped out of speakers draped with tinsel.

There were maybe fifty checkouts, all with lines of fractious shoppers leaning on shopping carts filled with turkeys and last-minute gifts. Beyond them, aisle upon aisle sold everything from children's clothes to flat screen TVs to out-of-season strawberries and frozen pizza. She'd read once that some retailers make half their annual profits in the month before Christmas. On the evidence in front of her, she could well believe it.

Ingrid looked around for the customer service desk and joined the line of people with refund requests and complaints about two-for-one offers.

"Hi," Ingrid said when she reached the counter. "Could you point me in the direction of the manager's office?"

"You want to speak to the manager?" The customer service assistant wore a tight-fitting uniform, and an exasperated expression. A badge revealed his name was Rashid.

"Yes."

"So does everyone else. What about?"

Ingrid pulled a business card out of her pocket and he looked at it.

"Yeah?" His wasn't the normal reaction. Most Brits expressed either disbelief or excitement when she showed them she worked for the FBI.

"I need to speak to someone about a customer of yours."

He gestured at the frantic Christmas activity going on behind her. "We're kinda busy."

"This is important."

He rolled his eyes. "I'll try calling her." He picked up a phone. "I'll be right with you," he said to an elderly woman standing behind Ingrid. "Soon as I can." His head tilted to one side as he gripped the receiver between his chin and his shoulder. "That just a refund is it, madam?"

He processed the refund, handing the older woman some

cash, and then turned his attention back to Ingrid. "She's not picking up."

"But she's working? She's in the building?"

"No one's got any annual leave till the middle of January."

Ingrid went off in search of someone more helpful, but every time she stopped a member of staff re-stocking fridges or fetching a 'click and collect' order from the warehouse, she got the same bemused reply: we have hundreds of customers an hour; do you really think we'd recognize a woman who comes in once a week? It's not like Ingrid had a photograph, or a name, or a description. Her request to review their CCTV footage was met with above-my-pay-grade shrugs.

Ingrid would make a formal application to see the surveillance recordings when she got back to the embassy. She knew the exact time the calls had been made, so it shouldn't be too hard to find an image of a woman on a phone, even if there were twenty cameras to check. The problem with that option was that the request would have to be made via Thames Valley Police. Ingrid could just picture Detective Sergeant Hayes's sour expression. She could almost hear her saying quietly to a constable, 'Don't worry if this gets lost in your in tray'.

Her phone rang.

"Jen. Hi."

"First things, are you coming back to the office this evening?"

Ingrid browsed the racks of cheap clothing. She could use some more underwear. "Unlikely. I'm out in Buckinghamshire somewhere."

"You okay?"

"Yep, I guess."

"Okay then. You want what I found on Estevez's laptop?"

"Hit me."

"I mean. I'm not an expert and, like, I could be wrong—"

"Jen, it's okay. This isn't for the courts." Ingrid picked up a hat and scarf set. She could also use a pair of gloves.

"So... Before I start, I have to tell you this was very easy. Do you use Gmail?"

"No."

"You sound distracted."

"Sorry. You have my full and undivided." Ingrid kept her voice low. She didn't want people overhearing.

"Good. So, Gmail. They track everything. Like, everything, seriously. All I had to do was log into his Gmail account. And technically, I didn't even have to do that because he's, like, totally logged in all the time."

Ingrid couldn't work out from Jen's preamble if she had struck gold or not. She picked up a pack of socks and realized she needed a basket. "And? What have you got?"

"Is there a specific time you want to know about?"

"After work on the eighteenth."

"Because I can give you almost a minute-by-minute."

Jen knew how to spin out a tale. "Just give me the highlights."

"Jeez, there aren't many of them. He basically watched gaming videos on YouTube, googled 'what's faster an eagle or a dolphin,' and searched for pizza restaurants near Waterloo station. Oh, he also ordered a case of Budweiser from Amazon at five past seven."

"And what is faster?"

"Oh, I didn't—"

"Don't worry about it." Ingrid got in a long line for the self-service checkouts. Everyone else in Bishopsgate seemed exceedingly worried about running out of mince pies. "Can you tell where he was?"

"Yup. I can see his whole evening on a map. On a Google map."

"And?"

"The furthest he got from the embassy was a pub in Shepherd's Market, from which he checked a basketball result. So that moral of that particular tale," Jen said. "Is to always log out of your Gmail account. Or, like, totally check out your privacy permissions."

Jen's evidence was compelling, but it was the flash of fear Ingrid had seen on Marcus Williams's face that made her sure Estevez was innocent. "Good work, Jen. Thank you."

"Shall I send his phone off to the lab? You know, for like actual professional analysis?"

"Not necessary." Ingrid was nowhere near the front of the line and the Christmas music was getting under her skin.

"Anything else?" Jen asked.

"Um." The jingling bells were burrowing into her brain, interfering with her synapses as effectively as a drug in a laboratory experiment.

"You sure you're okay, Ingrid. You sound, like, underpowered."

"I'm at the checkout in Tesco," Ingrid said.

"Ooh. Glamor."

"Actually..."

"Yes?"

"I put in an ANPR request two days ago. Could you chase it for me?"

"Sure thing. They normally come back quickly, don't they?"

They did. And it was worrying that it was taking so long.

15

Ingrid decided to pay Uppenham Hall a visit while she was still in Buckinghamshire. She navigated her way to Greenacre Lane and found the unmarked turnoff to the property. Several days of rain meant the Toyota Prius struggled for traction on the dirt track.

The air was thick with a constant drizzle. Laden cumulonimbus clouds loomed over the landscape, making late afternoon feel like the middle of night, especially so far from any street lighting. Ingrid slowed down and wiped the condensation off the window. She scanned the dash for the defogger. Beyond the hedgerows enclosing the track, the flashlight of a security patrol bounced through the branches. A dog barked as she drove past.

The lane was shrouded in dense shrubbery, but gaps where trees had died revealed a fence topped with razor wire. She made it to the muddy turnaround in front of the iron gates she'd seen on her first visit. She killed the engine, buzzed down the window and listened. A bitter wind through the leaves drowned out every other sound.

It seemed unlikely this was the main entrance. If Uppenham Hall was as grand as its Wikipedia entry suggested, this had to be the tradesmen's gate. She turned the key and carried on down the track. It had to lead somewhere.

The land on the other side of the track from Uppenham was just fields. She couldn't see any other sources of light, or evidence of occupation. Her headlights glinted off a puddle and Ingrid slowed to navigate it. When she accelerated again, the wheels spun in the mud. She put the car into reverse and the wheels spun again.

Something inside her wilted. *Please, no.*

Ingrid had grown up on a farm. She'd been stuck in mud many times in her life and she knew that, without a 4x4, continuing to go forward was a mistake. She also knew that pushing the car out of the rut on her own was going to be impossible. Her intestines twisted into a fist. Sweat beaded the top of her lip.

More in desperation than expectation, she revved again. However, without traction, the car wasn't going to move. She slammed a palm into the steering wheel and killed the engine. She reflexively looked up at the clouds, hoping for a little divine intervention. At least it wasn't raining. She got out, her sneakers instantly consumed by the mud. It oozed inside her sock. It was just as well she'd bought a fresh pair in Tesco.

Ingrid leaned against the hood, planted her feet deep into the mud, and pushed. The car rocked backward, then forward. She breathed deep, leaned in again and pushed harder, her feet slipping as she did so.

"*Govno!*" In moments of stress, Ingrid still swore in Russian. Through the windshield, a rectangle illuminated on the passenger seat. She had an incoming call. She yanked her feet out of the mud, opened the door and reached in for the phone.

"Ingrid Skyberg."

"Ingrid, hey girl."

"Hi Lexi."

"Everything okay? You sound terrible."

"I'm kind of in the middle of… a situation."

"Intriguing. Listen. I just had a call from our friends at Thames Valley Police. They want to interview you again."

"Okay." A faint alarm bell started ringing.

"They've gotten the forensics back on the motorcycle." Lexi's voice was measured and calm, but the alarm bell got louder.

"Forensics never come back that quickly." The darkened trees seemed to close in over her. "I mean, never. They take weeks."

"Oh really?"

"Don't you think it's odd?" Several rain drops splashed down on the windshield. Just what she needed.

"Isn't it good news? Looks to me like they want to get this over and done with."

Ingrid's breathing quickened.

"Nine o'clock in the morning. Tomorrow."

Ingrid didn't know how to respond. This was not how investigations played out.

"You wanna ride out together?" Lexi asked. "They want us at the station house in a place called... Bishopsgate."

Ingrid clasped her scalp. "No. It's okay. I'll meet you there."

She ended the call, dropped the phone on the seat and shut the door. She slumped over the roof of the car and let out a groan. Her jaw trembled, but not with the cold. Too much about this investigation wasn't adding up. The doctored CCTV. The ANPR not coming back while the forensics were miraculously fast tracked. The groan became a moan as rage bubbled up from her belly and exploded through her system.

Matthew Harding's death wasn't just a hit and run, was it? She was being drawn into something she did not understand. Something so dark that Steve had been killed to protect it. She pictured Steve's falling body, and the terror on his face when he'd seen the man in the Audi. He had known what was coming.

The rain started to fall more heavily.

"Oh, great. Just great."

Rain would make it harder to shift the car, and she did not want the security patrol to find her. She braced herself against the hood, forcing her sneakers deeper into the mud. Her hands slipped on the wet metal. She wiped them on her jacket and gripped the radiator grille. She pressed her feet down and shoved hard. The car moved, but rolled backward. Ingrid let out a howl, then pushed again, this time driving all her fury up from her heels, right through her back and piling down through her shoulders. She kept pushing and forced the tires out of their rut.

The Prius rolled backward and relief erupted out of her body. Her muscles burned like coals but she didn't feel any pain, only elation. She rested against the hood for a moment to get her breath and looked up between the trees. She let the rain cool her hot cheeks.

Ingrid needed to get out of there before the track softened any further. She scraped the mud off her sneakers on the foot plate and got in behind the wheel. She put the Prius in reverse and started making her way back to Greenacre Lane.

Her neck ached from the strain. Reversing a strange car on a dark track with the threat of imminent discovery should be on a course at Quantico, she thought. Her heart pounded against the inside of her shirt.

She reached the turnaround outside the gate and performed a three-point turn. Ingrid rounded her shoulders to release the tension and exhaled. The relief was short-lived. A beam of light swung toward her from inside Uppenham's grounds. It wasn't a guard on patrol, it was headlights. Not wanting to get caught on the track, Ingrid reversed up a few yards, killed her motor and turned off her lights. Her options were hide or run, and she didn't like her chances outpacing a 4x4.

She had an oblique view of the gates and followed the swoop of the headlights as the vehicle neared. Her mouth was dust-dry. She swallowed. She could hear its motor now. Diesel. Breathless, she watched the headlights slice through the iron gates, which opened to release a small van.

Ingrid's jaw tightened.

The van turned toward Greenacre Lane. To Ingrid's immense relief, it didn't belong to a private security company. It was emblazoned with the logo of a company: Mayfair Events—Boutique Party Planners.

After a few minutes, Ingrid switched on the engine and put the Prius into gear.

16

Ingrid scoped out the main entrance to Uppenham Hall. On the other side of the estate, and accessed from a road running parallel to Greenacre Lane, it was much more impressive than the tradesmen's access. A stone gatehouse sat behind a pair of ornate wrought-iron gates through which Ingrid spotted an automatic roadblock. There was no obvious vantage point to surveil the entrance covertly. Given the chances of intercepting the Turkic woman or Arabic speaking man were somewhere between zilch and zero, Ingrid returned to Bishopsgate where she was grateful to find a room at the Ilex Hotel. There seemed little point driving back to London when she had an appointment at the local police station in the morning.

The Ilex Hotel was the sort of place guests at a nearby wedding would be checked into by the bridal party… if they had been invited out of duty instead of love. From the outside it looked like a residential home for the elderly, and inside the smell of disinfectant was redolent of county hospitals.

"Just the one night?" the man on the reception desk asked, looking down at her muddy feet.

"Correct."

"And would you like to include breakfast?"

"No, thank you."

Her room was directly above the front door with a view over

the parking lot. A row of shops on the opposite side of the street included a café that looked a far better breakfast option than the brittle bacon and stale croissants of a three-star hotel buffet.

The room sported floral wallpaper and a pink patterned bedspread. It reminded her of the venues married men took hookers in 1980s TV shows. She tried to ignore the squeaking floorboards from the room above and plugged in her phone to charge. She looked for a safe for her Russian passport and embassy ID. It wasn't in the closet and it wasn't under the bed. There was no phone to call down to reception, so she headed back downstairs. When she closed the door behind her, it didn't shut properly. She pushed it closed, but the lock wouldn't turn.

"Well, that's just excellent."

The man on reception was watching TV. He muted it when he saw her. "Everything okay, madam?"

"My door doesn't lock."

"Hmmm." He tilted his head to one side.

"And there's no safe."

"Oh no, we don't have safes in the room, madam. But I can keep valuables here if you like?"

There were no other rooms available, and the lock could not be fixed until the morning. He did offer to give her a complimentary breakfast to apologize on behalf of the management.

Ingrid ate in the Indian restaurant on the high street and marveled that—no matter how small the town—you could always get a good curry in Britain. In the big cities, Indian restaurants had incorporated tapas and haute cuisine, but in places like Bishopsgate they delivered the quintessential curry house experience, with the menu and recipes as reliable as if each restaurant was part of a chain.

Ingrid locked her valuables in the glove box of the Prius on her way back into the hotel and jammed a chair against the door in her room. She washed the bottoms of her trousers in the bathroom sink and draped them over the radiator, hoping they would be wearable by the morning. Her sneakers were probably ruined. She'd only bought them at the airport twenty-four hours beforehand.

Lying on the soft bed, Ingrid rehearsed the things she needed to tell Thames Valley Police in the morning. The doctored CCTV footage. The scratches on Marcus Williams's motorcycle jacket. The reports she'd overheard in the office about Steve in Portugal. It was all circumstantial. She still needed a witness who would categorically say a man had been riding. She absolutely had to find the woman from Turkmenistan.

She slept surprisingly well. In the morning, her trousers were almost presentable and the weather had even cleared up a little. Ingrid decided to leave the car and head to the police station on foot. She crossed the forecourt, grinding her sneakers purpose-fully into the gravel to help rub off the mud as she passed the Prius. The night manager had been good to his word about getting the lock fixed. A handyman's white van was parked near the forecourt exit, its doors open while its owner searched for his tools.

A smartly dressed man turned into the parking lot. The way his suit fitted suggested he worked out. She stepped to one side to get around him, he stepped in front of her.

"Excuse me," she said, without making eye contact.

"I'm sorry," he said as he blocked her path again.

Ingrid looked up at his face expecting to see one of those apologetic smiles the English were obliged to plaster on their faces during such encounters. But his features were set. His eyes fixed on hers and he definitely wasn't smiling.

Adrenaline flooded her veins. Footsteps crunched toward her from behind. Instinctively, Ingrid sharply raised her elbow up and back, but instead of landing a blow, the handyman grabbed her arm. His other hand covered her mouth. She kicked out at the man in the suit who grasped her ankle and held it.

Ingrid bit the hand over her face, forcing her attacker to with-draw it. "You fuckers," she said, her voice rasping in her throat

"Now, now," the suited man said. English accent.

Patronizing fuck.

He grabbed her other foot and the two of them tumbled her into the back of the van. Ingrid landed hard. Her face scraped along the floor. Her ankle whacked into the wheel arch and they slammed the doors shut before she could yell for help. The whole thing had taken less than five seconds.

The men jumped in the front and started the motor. They reversed sharply, then turned on to the road. Ingrid winced as they moved. Her cheek burned but there was no blood, and her nostrils watered with the sting of gasoline. She twisted around to inspect her ankle.

"Hello, Ingrid."

She wasn't alone. Two men sat on a bench and stared at her. Both thirties, both tall and broad and soldier-fit. She didn't reply. She didn't know how. What the hell was happening?

"I'm John. This is Paul. You've already met George and Ringo." Israeli accent. Expensive suit.

Bile leeched into her stomach and a shiver rippled over her skin. Ingrid blinked hard, attempting to focus, trying to compute what the fuck was going on.

The two men smiled at her. Paul—a giant in sweatpants and varsity hoodie—reached out a long leg and clamped a foot down on Ingrid's backpack. He dragged it toward him with his heel. Ingrid tried to grab it, but John kicked her arm.

"Play nice," John said. "Or you won't get to play at all."

John sat with his legs far apart, elbows resting on his knees, and his hands clasped in front of his face. On the little finger of his right hand was a signet ring. His tailored attire was in contrast to the inside of the shabby, second-hand van. The only light came from a small mesh grille through which George and Ringo's heads were visible.

Ingrid pressed her palms into the floor and curled herself into a seated position. A collar of heat gripped her throat. *Deep breath. Think.*

She looked for an exit. Three possible options. The grille, a sliding door on the side of the van, and the double doors at the rear. She couldn't see any weapons, but assumed they'd have them. She had no chance of overpowering them. *What are your options?*

Her phone. It was in her pocket. If she got the opportunity, she could press the top button five times and silently summon the police. And if that wasn't possible, at some point in the future the embassy would use it to track her. Back up would come. Eventually. *What else?*

Ingrid tried to remember the kidnap protocols, but her brain couldn't parse the memory. *Come on! What else?*

She hadn't been tied up. That was good. She could run if she got the chance, and Ingrid bet on herself to outrun anyone. *The moment the doors open, be ready to run.*

Paul plunged his tattooed forearm into her bag and searched around. "It's not in here." She couldn't make out his accent. Definitely not British or American. He tipped her backpack upside down, sending a snowfall of receipts, coins and tampons onto the floor of the van, the coins skating sideways as the van veered sharply left. She had no idea what direction they'd taken her in.

Be compliant. Be obedient. Don't make them angry.

"It must be on her," John said. "Get it."

Paul dipped his chin and sucked his teeth. Outside, Ingrid heard a siren. Had someone seen them abduct her? She pushed the thought from her mind as Paul leaned over.

"Give me your phone." It was a South African accent.

Be compliant.

Ingrid said nothing and reached into her jacket pocket. She felt the top button. Her finger circled it as she maintained eye contact with Paul.

Be obedient.

She handed it over without pressing it. The siren got louder and the van pulled over to let the emergency vehicle pass. No one was coming to rescue her.

"Aw," John said. "Did you think they were here for you?"

Paul grunted. "Unlock it," he said, handing it back to her.

Again, her finger pressed against the top button. She wouldn't get away with it.

Don't make them angry.

Ingrid depressed the home button, unlocking the phone with her fingerprint. Paul snatched it out of her hand.

"Email or message?" he asked John.

"Email."

"Who to?"

John shrugged. "Just reply to the most recent."

Ingrid had assumed they'd toss the phone out of the van to stop them being tracked. Or download its data to a laptop. What were they planning?

John pulled out a piece of paper from his pocket and handed it to Paul. "Word for word, okay?"

"Yes, boss."

Ingrid resisted the urge to ask questions. The signet ring meant she had a pretty good idea who she was dealing with and what they had planned. Now wasn't the time to get answers. All that mattered was staying alive. Her task was to stay compliant so that when she made her move, it came out the blue.

"What's this word?" Paul asked, showing John the scrap of paper.

John leaned over. "Overwhelming."

"The past few weeks have been overwhelming," Paul said, reading the handwritten scrawl out loud. "And I don't want to—" He showed John the paper again.

John peered at it. "Carry on. Should be two words." He turned to her. "Maybe you'd prefer to dictate your own suicide note?"

He waited for her to reply.

"No? Might make it more authentic."

17

"How much further?" John shouted.

"Almost there," came the reply. Another Israeli accent.

Her captors were most likely ex-Mossad. That was a problem. Even the CIA thought Mossad was the best secret intelligence service in the world. What was it Nick Angelis used to say? "The CIA gets cocky, and the FSB gets sloppy, but Mossad just gets the job done."

In the ten years Ingrid had been at the Bureau, the intelligence business had moved away from state-sponsored activity to private agencies working for oligarchs, Silicon Valley billionaires, movie stars and hedge fund owners. An ex-Mossad agent could pocket a million dollars in a few years in the private sector by gathering blackmail evidence on corporate rivals, or surveilling the wives of husbands wanting cheaper divorce settlements. Unshackled from the diplomatic burden carried by MI6 and other state agencies, these private security firms were answerable only to the almighty dollar. They had all the infrastructure of the old days, but none of the responsibilities.

The mix of Israeli and South African accents made it likely the Beatles worked for an agency called Red Box, an outfit known for equal measures of ruthlessness and effectiveness. They were more than capable of hacking into the embassy's CCTV footage, and they would certainly have contacts at British Transport

Police who could mislay an ANPR request. Bribing a forensics lab to speed up the report on her motorcycle was also within their purview. The muscles between Ingrid's shoulder blades fused into a solid mass.

The van shook as the road surface changed, throwing her across the plywood floor as the wheels dipped and wobbled. Paul grunted. His fingers had tapped the wrong letters.

"How's it looking out there?" John asked.

"It's clear," Ringo said. He wasn't talking about the weather.

Ingrid looked again for a weapon, any heavy object she could aim at a head, or a sharp one she could lunge at a chest. There wasn't even a tow rope. The only things that rattled as they bounced over the stony ground were the strewn contents of her backpack. Ingrid turned away from her captors and spat on the floor to leave a DNA trace for whoever investigated her death.

"You finished with that email?" John asked.

"Almost," Paul replied. "You really think she'd sign it off 'with regret'?"

They both stared at her. She tried to keep her face in neutral.

"Just her name," John said.

The van slowed. They would be stopping soon. The journey hadn't taken long. It was less than ten minutes since she left her hotel room. Ingrid closed her eyes so she could listen. She needed every piece of intel she could get. She couldn't hear a road. Or a plane overhead. No construction noises or industrial machinery. The only thing she could hear beyond the battered walls of the van was the squawks of seagulls. They were a long way from any coast. Where the hell had they taken her?

The driver screeched up the hand brake and the motor stopped. Ingrid prepared to run. She studied John and Paul. They were preternaturally calm. Her heart beat so hard she could feel her pulse under her tongue.

The front doors opened and footprints squelched outside as George and Ringo walked to the rear of the van. They yanked the doors open, flooding the van with daylight and the stench of a nearby landfill site.

Well, that explains the seagulls.

When Ingrid's eyes adjusted to the light, she saw that Ringo had pulled a tan-colored handgun out of a holster under his jacket. A Sig Sauer 17. She wouldn't be able to outrun a bullet.

"All done?" John asked.

"Sent it." Paul tossed Ingrid's phone to George, who pocketed it. George actually looked a bit like a Beatle with a messy mop of dark hair, a slightly confused expression and a gangly, gawky appearance. He wore cargo pants and a woolen jacket and was almost certainly not from a military background. More likely recruited from a tech firm. Of the four, he was the only one Ingrid could overpower.

"Right then," John said. "Let's get this over and done with." He turned to Ingrid. "Okay little missy, you want to come with us?"

She scowled at him.

"You're going to get out nice and slow, you understand? You try anything stupid and we will make this a lot more painful for you, okay?" John's eyes held hers, unblinking. "You know how this works. You saw what happened in Portugal, didn't you?"

Ingrid sneered at him.

John jumped out. His top lip curled as his leather loafers oozed into the mud. His designer pants were going to get ruined. He extended a hand toward Ingrid, but she did not accept his offer of assistance. If she got the chance, she'd need both hands to escape.

Ingrid shuffled over to the open doors and scrambled into a crouch position. Overhead power cables spliced a white-gray sky. In the distance, a swarm of seagulls circled a rising slope of fetid earth, garbage peppering the dark soil like fallen glitter.

"Come on," John said.

Ingrid heard the snap of rubber and turned. Paul's hands were now encased in blue nitrile gloves. Her brain felt as if it had come loose, swirling inside her skull like a carnival ride. Acid rose in her throat. She had to bury the rage and banish the fear. *The only thing that matters is staying alive.*

Ingrid jumped before Paul pushed her, and her feet splashed into a muddy puddle. Ringo gestured the Sig in the direction he wanted her to move. Once clear of the van's doors, Ingrid saw she was at an abandoned construction site. The concrete skeleton of a half-finished building loomed over them. Beyond it, deep piling rods stuck out of the ground like bamboo canes in a giant's vegetable patch. Stacked shipping containers—some kind of site office—lay rusted and forgotten. In the neighboring field was a dilapidated caravan and miserable looking pony. Up ahead she spotted a galvanized steel gate breaking an otherwise impenetrable hedgerow of buddleia and bindweed. Apart from the hump of landfill, the land was flat. Electrified cables of a train track marked the far edge of the construction site. A vandalized realtor's sign proclaimed she was in 'Broughton Business Park, Buckinghamshire's new start-up hub'. The financing must have run out.

Keeping her head bent—a deliberately meek posture—Ingrid swung her gaze from side to side, scanning the landscape for her escape route. Fear rattled her jaw. *You'll get a chance. Wait for your moment.*

George shut the van doors and ran a couple of steps ahead. He pulled back a section of chain-link fence and climbed through the gap. John, taller, struggled with the same maneuver.

"Your turn," Ringo said, shaking the Sig at her.

Once through, the others followed. Ingrid looked up at the abandoned construction project and counted ten stories. A thick steel chain dangled from a pulley crane mounted on the roof, like a figurehead on the prow of a shipwreck.

Ingrid walked slowly, trying to buy herself some thinking time.

"Mind your step," Paul said, leading her into the building. Although there were no walls, the place smelled damp and the air was cooler. Sounds were amplified. Stone lintels and timber were scattered over the floor. A length of wood would be a good weapon, she thought, though it was no match for the Sig. John, George and Ringo followed close behind.

The structure had a rectangular footprint the size of three tennis courts. It consisted of nothing more than concrete floors held up by a forest of concrete pillars, their symmetry occasionally ruined by two elevator shafts and a zigzag of stairs. Their footsteps echoed off the hard, damp surfaces.

"Up," John said as they approached a staircase.

Ingrid suppressed a smile. The building was reminiscent of the multistory parking lots where she trained for parkour. A shoulder injury meant she hadn't practiced for a while, but if there was one place where the balance tipped in her favor, it was a structure like this. The open concrete staircases were perfect for cat leaps and monkey vaults. She would get her moment.

Stay obedient. Stay compliant. *Stay vigilant.*

Cable reels the size of dining tables littered the second story. Ingrid searched for a discarded wrench or an overlooked hammer, but John instructed her to keep climbing. The wind picked up, making the chain dangling off the pulley creak ominously. On the third floor she paused, pretending to be out of breath. She looked around, rotating her gaze from one missing wall to the other, searching for either an escape or a weapon. A sodden rope snaked across the floor.

"Up," John said again.

Paul bounced up ahead. His stride was so big he took the concrete stairs three at a time. He was the only one who had put on gloves: he would be the one to kill her. Ringo kept two steps behind her, aiming the Sig at her head. Ingrid took a deep breath and moved slowly. She wanted them to think she was beaten. That she was being a good little girl.

"What floor is this?" George asked. He also had South African accent but with a Californian lilt. Definitely a Silicon Valley alumnus.

"Fourth," John answered.

A random fact from a training manual flew into Ingrid's head: from the fourth floor, a human of average height, build and fitness has a fifty percent chance of survival. The chance decreases by ten percent with every additional story. Not that it mattered. If she survived the fall, the Sig would finish the job.

A concrete mixer and stacks of reinforcing steel mesh had been abandoned on the fifth floor. Not the weapons she was hoping to find. However, even if she saw a heavy tool lying around, they weren't straying far enough from the staircase for her to retrieve it.

You've got elbows. You've got fists. Fingers that can gouge out eyes. Feet that can trip people up.

Ingrid stopped looking for a weapon and concentrated on identifying a means of escape. She counted the steps between floors. Thirteen, approximately eight inches each. What was that? Ten feet per story? Something like that. She paused at the next level to give herself a chance to examine the elevator shafts. The light was dim and the shaft was thirty yards away, but she reasoned it probably had a car inside it. Builders erected the elevator shafts first to take materials to the upper stories. That meant there would be cables inside them, and cables were a great exit route if you were trained in parkour.

"Might as well take her to the top," John said.

"Cold, isn't it?" Ringo said.

Ingrid hadn't noticed. Stress acted like a form of hypothermia, shutting down her extremities, pouring her energies into core cognitive functions.

"Isn't this high enough?" Paul asked.

"Why not do it at the top?" John answered. "Let's make sure."

On the eighth floor, planks of timber were stacked up, ready for workers who would never come. A flock of starlings erupted from the stack, their dark wings battering the air, hinging themselves upward and out beyond the confines of the building, expertly dodging the iron hook dangling down from the end of the rusted pulley.

Ingrid stopped. There were only two floors left. The timber might be her best opportunity. She could vault over it, gain a second on them and bounce down the other stairwell or dive into the elevator shaft and hope to grab a cable.

Hope to.

"Move it," John said.

The four of them seemed very relaxed about their impending crime. Even Silicon Boy.

"I said move it."

Ingrid made a show of catching her breath.

"Now!"

Ingrid glanced at the wood stack but did as she was told. Whatever opportunity was on the ninth floor, she would have to take it. The sweet stench of the landfill itched her nostrils and made her insides heave. At least she thought it was the stench. She counted the steps. One… two… three. Paul had already reached the ninth floor. His hulking figure blocked her path. Six… seven…

Ringo was still holding the Sig. Even with his physique, his biceps had to be fractionally fatigued by now, his fingers incrementally chilled. She would have a second, maybe two, before he took the shot. She hoped it would be all she needed.

Hoped.

Nine… ten… eleven… Ingrid skipped the twelfth step and went straight for the thirteenth. She accelerated, catching Paul by surprise, and sprinted past him. She was three strides away and had covered twenty yards by the time John reached the top of the stairs, twenty-five by the time Ringo did.

Ingrid drove her feet into the concrete and accelerated toward the elevator shaft before Ringo fired.

Footsteps stampeded behind her. "Get down!" She couldn't tell who was talking, and she wasn't going to turn to find out.

A shot tore through the air, its explosive sound bouncing off the bare concrete

"You fucking idiot." John's voice. "It's not going to look like suicide if she's got a gunshot in her back is it?"

Ingrid neared the shaft. It was a pitch dark inside. Momentum propelled her forward. There was no stopping now.

Two more strides and she saw the shaft was empty. No cables, just a sheer drop of ninety feet. She was running too fast to stop. Ingrid leaned to one side, shifting her weight and curving her trajectory away from the opening. She leaned more, steering her body toward the concrete wall that enclosed the shaft. She leaped up, planted a foot on the wall and somersaulted backwards before landing and rolling. Paul grabbed at her jacket as she got to her feet, but Ingrid struggled free and powered away from him. She ran toward the edge of the building. She had twenty strides before she reached it.

Her focus narrowed on the line where the concrete met the air. She blocked out everything else. All that mattered was the line. She adjusted her stride. There was no margin for error. Four, three, two… She planted her left foot and drove the ball of her right down onto the edge, launching herself outwards, her legs circling over the drop below. Her eyes zeroed in on the steel chain hanging down from the pulley. Both hands reached out for it. Ingrid grasped at the metal, her hands slipping on the wet steel until they grabbed onto the hook.

She was falling. Time was passing too quickly. She was rattling right down. Her weight had activated the pulley and the ground was rushing up to meet her like a fist. With no counter-weight, she was dropping fast. Too fast. The landing wouldn't kill her, but it would sure as hell break her legs.

She prepared for impact, lifting her knees and getting ready to roll.

The chain tugged up sharply. Her icy fingers gripped the hook. She was suspended two floors up. She looked up. Ringo and Paul had jammed the pulley.

"What are you waiting for?" John shouted. "Get down there!"

Ingrid checked below. The mud was littered with concrete slabs and mesh sheets of rusted steel. Her old injury tore in her shoulder, radiating pain across her back. She couldn't hold on. Heavy footsteps ricocheted inside the building.

Ingrid picked a spot on the ground and let go, dropping into a debris-free patch. She softened her knees and rolled sideways, distributing the force. She pushed her fingers into the cold, wet mud and heaved herself up into a squat. She staggered upright and took a step. The right ankle was okay. The left ankle was okay.

Now run.

18

If she ran back to the road, they would hunt her down in the van and make her the next hit-and-run victim. The galvanized steel gate was approximately one hundred and fifty yards away. It had to lead somewhere. Ingrid ran to it.

Beyond the gate was a wide overgrown path enclosed by two tumbling hedgerows. Twining weeds curled around the gate. It hadn't been opened for at least a year. It couldn't lead anywhere important, but it was too late to change her mind.

She dared to check behind her. The Beatles still hadn't emerged from the building. Ringo would have taken up position, though. She would be in his crosshairs. If she stopped she was dead. Ingrid vaulted over the gate and landed on soft wet grass. It clung to her ankles as she powered on, putting as many yards between her and her pursuers as she could. A train rumbled in the distance.

The grass thinned in places to reveal a covering of gravel. It looked like an access road, the sort that led to electricity substations or telephone exchanges. Dead ends, usually.

The track curved a little. She ran hard and stayed as close to the hedge as she could, hoping the foliage would obscure her. Her lungs were starting to burn, but she had to keep moving.

The gate rattled. She didn't look to see who it was. It didn't matter. All that mattered was staying alive. She had a lead of two hundred strides. Even a trained marksman with a moving target only had a thirty percent chance of a clean kill. *Just keep running*. The path curled around a bend, shielding her from whoever was chasing. The grass petered out and her sneakers slipped on the gravel. There was something in the ground up ahead. What was it? She couldn't make it out.

A square access hole cover.

Ingrid snatched a look over her shoulder, crouched down and grasped the ring in the center of the heavy steel lid. The muscles tightened in her neck as she strained her entire body to move it. It gave a little. She leaned backward and it came loose with a searing, screeching scrape revealing a dark cylinder below. The gate clanged again. Now two of them were on the track.

"Where is she?" South African accent. Paul's voice.

Whichever Beatle was with him was too breathless to reply.

They would reach the bend any second. Ingrid looked at the hole, then looked at the hedge. A curtain of bindweed tumbled down over a thicket of brambles. The path ahead was long. When they turned the corner, they would take the shot.

Hole or hedge?

Hedge or hole?

Ingrid lifted up the mat of weeds and crawled underneath. Paul's footsteps vibrated the ground as he approached. She burrowed deeper, pressing herself under branches and brambles, her knees sinking into two winters' worth of leaves. Her lungs demanded air, but she only offered them shallow, quiet breaths. Fear skated over her skin.

Paul powered past, shaking the ground. A few seconds later, another pair of feet closed in on her. The footsteps stopped and Ingrid froze.

"Here!" George's voice

"What?" Paul called back.

"Down here."

Ingrid's breathing quickened. There was a tremor in her right hand. She daren't look. She daren't move. Was a piece of clothing visible? Between the twigs and branches she could see shards of daylight, a lead-light window of random shapes. The gray material of Paul's sweatpants.

"Look!"

The gate clanged again. Soon they would all be there.

"The drain, man," George said. "The cover's off."

Paul thundered, gravel crunching under his sneakers. "Really?"

"Well, where else is she?"

John shouted from down the path. "You got her?"

"No, mate," Paul yelled.

"You think it's a sewer?" George asked.

"What do you think?"

"I think it's a real good place to leave her phone."

"Do it."

John's footsteps were lighter. Probably something to do with the alligator skin shoes. "She down there?"

"Reckon so," George answered. He threw in the phone and it clanked as it bounced off the shaft's walls.

"What are you waiting for?" John asked.

"What, me? I'm not going down there," George said.

"Yes, you fucking are. Look at the size of you. We're not gonna fit, are we?"

"What am I supposed do when I'm down there?"

After a pause, John said, "Hold her head in the shit till she drowns."

"What about the suicide note?" Paul asked.

"They're not going to find the body for so long we don't have to worry about that. Get down there."

They scraped the steel cover across the ground, grinding it over the metal lip with a howl that stabbed into Ingrid's ears.

"What if it's a trap?" George's voice. "What if she just pulled that open to make us think that's where she went?"

No one answered.

"We're all standing here like loons while she's already a mile away."

"Or she's hiding," John said.

Ingrid swallowed hard. Her face was almost numb.

"Yeah, she could be hiding," George said, a tinge of excitement in his voice at the prospect of not having to go into the sewer.

"Okay," John said. "You, go down there. You, you get the van. See if you can find a map of the sewers. Try and work out where she might surface and drive there."

"What are you going to do?" George asked.

Ingrid heard the double click of a magazine being loaded into a semi-automatic. "I'm going to check around here. She might not have gone far. We meet back at the gate in thirty minutes."

Gravel scattered as they moved in different directions. George's feet performed a slow, musical scale as he hit the rungs inside the shaft, each step a note lower than the last. But it was John's prowling footsteps that Ingrid tuned into. He'd guessed right, and he had a gun. He kicked the undergrowth. He moved slowly, deliberately. He was listening.

Ingrid's pulse throbbed in her spine as the muscles stiffened in her back. Her thigh twitched. She had the beginnings of a cramp. The shoulder muscle she had torn on the pulley blazed.

"Where are you, you little bitch?"

He wasn't moving away. It sounded like he was circling.

"What can you see?" he shouted to George.

"Fuck all." His voice echoed up the shaft.

Ingrid glimpsed the gray of John's suit through the branches. "Use the flashlight on your phone." His voice was amplified. He was crouched over the hole. "Is it dry?"

"What do you think?"

They had sent the wrong man down the drain. The others were military. They'd been through worse. Much worse. They would have sat for days in damp jungle camps or hidden in silence in storm drains until the enemy passed. The tech boy wouldn't be able to hack it.

Something rustled in the bramble and Ingrid stiffened. It rustled again. Her mouth fell open. She needed more air, but she dare not make a noise. Ingrid swallowed. She had to control her breathing. Little in, little out. Something moved again. Ingrid couldn't turn to look. Her vision narrowed. She gasped.

It was a wren, bouncing down from a branch and hopping over the leaves.

Ingrid clenched her fists and held her breath. Had John heard her gasp? Why was he so quiet?

George's metallic percussion emanated from the drain. He was making his way back up.

"What are you doing?" John shouted. He had moved further away.

George clanged up to ground level.

"What are you playing at?" John shouted

George inhaled noisily. "Jesus, if she's down there she deserves to live."

Ingrid flinched at the sound of a heavy crack.

"Fuck you, Goldie."

So, John's name was Goldie.

"You not even going to give me a hand up?"

"Don't forget to put the cover back. If she is down there, let's make it impossible for her to escape."

Ingrid listened as their footsteps receded. She let her breathing deepen. She unclenched her fists. After a few more minutes she adjusted her position, crunching the leaves beneath her knees then straightening her legs. What had John said? A rendezvous at the gate in thirty minutes. She could wait them out.

She checked her watch. Nine forty. She needed to let Lexi know what had happened. Not turning up at the station house was a breach of her bail conditions. A warrant would automatically be issued for her arrest.

Ingrid exhaled slowly. She couldn't tell Lexi, could she? The Beatles had known she was about to talk to Thames Valley Police. Someone had told them, and that someone could have been her lawyer. An agency like Red Box would have spies everywhere, and either the Prius or her charge card had led them to the Ilex Hotel. Until Ingrid knew who the mole was, she couldn't speak to anyone.

If there was a silver lining to George throwing her phone into the sewer, it was that no one could track her. Just in case they could trace her via her Apple Watch, Ingrid loosened the strap and dropped it on the ground.

From now on, she was on her own.

19

When she was confident the Beatles had left, Ingrid crawled out of her hiding place. She made her way back into Bishopsgate along the railway track to make sure she stayed out of view.

Her shoulder felt bad. The muscles over her scapula were too painful to touch, let alone massage. She needed painkillers. And not the kind you could buy over the counter. On the outskirts of town, she spotted the monolithic metal cubes of the retail park. The blue and red Tesco sign called to her like a beacon.

Ingrid was covered in mud from the knees down. Her jacket had gotten ripped on the brambles. She looked like a vagrant. She checked her pockets: the car key, a bank card that she could no longer use and just under fifty pounds in cash.

Ingrid elicited several disapproving stares from the other customers in Tesco, but with the cash she had she was able to buy track pants and a sweatshirt, underwear and socks, and a pair of sneakers that were reduced by seventy percent, presumably because they were lime green. After a can of heat rub and pack of the strongest pain meds she could find, Ingrid had just enough left for a coffee and a pastry. She applied the rub, took the medicine, changed her clothes, and discarded the ruined ones in the restroom. Afterward, she settled into a chair in the in-store coffee shop. She needed to make the drink last. She had over two hours to wait.

The Costa Coffee concession was in a gallery overlooking the supermarket floor, giving her a good view of the aisles below where couples fought about turkeys and rivals clawed special offers out of each other's carts. With every sip of her long black, Ingrid found a new way to despise Marcus Williams. She hated the arrogance that had led him to believe he could ride a bike he hadn't trained for. She detested the entitlement that let him think he could take any motorcycle he wanted. His confidence that his father's money would make every problem disappear enraged her. But it was his lack of regard for human life—for Matthew Harding's, for Steve's, for hers—that she truly loathed. The belief that his existence counted for more than other people's, that he could commit a crime—that he could actually kill someone—and not have to face the consequences infuriated her. And, oh boy, did she want him to pay.

Daddy's billions wouldn't go nearly so far in jail.

The size of the operation to protect Williams stunned her. Ingrid pictured him on Greenacre Lane moments after the accident, phoning his father and requesting help. Daddy had probably told him to sit tight, to get the bike out of view, and to wait. He then called the same firm he used to get intel on rivals, dirt on employees, or accusers he wanted to silence. Within hours Red Box would have gotten the bike repaired and taken it back to the embassy. Then they infiltrated the security systems and either bribed or incentivized Steve to give up his life in London. Compromised contacts inside the police and forensics services were subsequently leaned on to frustrate any future inquiries.

And when their coverup had been threatened with exposure, they had murdered Steve. Then they had tried to kill her. The damage to Williams's reputation, and to his father's investments, was so grave that no price was too high to prevent the hit-and-run becoming public knowledge. The desire to expose the conspiracy, and put Williams and his father in jail, burned white hot. She needed the witness to talk to her. She needed the Turkic woman's testimony not because it would clear her name, but because it would ensure Williams spent the next two decades in jail.

When the time came, Ingrid returned to the ladies' room and made herself look as presentable as she could. She dampened her hands to style her hair, adding a little volume with the hot air hand dryer. She picked off twigs and leaves from her jacket and dabbed at the mud with handfuls of wet toilet paper. There was nothing she could do about the lime green sneakers, but she was satisfied she plausibly passed for a woman popping into the supermarket on her way home from the gym. Ingrid wanted to look as normal, and approachable, as possible.

The main entrance to the store comprised two sets of automatic sliding doors. Between the two sets were seasonal items: bags of logs, kindling, Christmas tree stands, and those red-leaved plants that Ingrid could never remember the name of. To prevent the December weather encroaching into the store, the entrance was pumped full of hot air. Ingrid had been lingering in the hot zone for almost thirty five minutes before she saw what she was looking for. Or rather, who she was looking for.

The diplomatic license plate—easily identifiable by the D in the middle of numbers on either side—belonged to a hearse-like minivan with blacked-out windows that matched its paint color. It was a Thursday, it was between two and four in the afternoon. That minivan had definitely come from Uppenham Hall. With anticipation flooding her veins, Ingrid stepped out into the cold.

Ingrid waited next to the shopping carts and watched the vehicle park. A tall, thickset man in his thirties got out of the driver's door. He was of Mediterranean or Middle Eastern appearance and checked something on his phone as he walked to the side door. He tugged it open, sliding it back to reveal two women inside. As best Ingrid could tell, they were in their twenties, maybe their teens. One was Asian, possibly Filipino or Thai, the other Caucasian. They both looked at him like they hated him.

Ingrid observed them as they trudged into the store. The women collected a cart each and set off around the aisles. The man headed to the café where Ingrid had just spent the last two hours. In the vegetable section, they grabbed sacks of potatoes, armfuls of carrots, and bags upon bags of onions. Ingrid scooped up a basket and popped in the odd zucchini while she shadowed them. Whenever they reached the end of an aisle, the women made eye contact with the driver who looked down on them from the café. Ingrid wondered what he would do if they took too long to get through a particular section. The Thai girl had a large bruise on her left cheek.

Ingrid didn't speak Turkmen, but most people from former Soviet states learned a little Russian at school. When the Asian girl was fetching frozen fish from another aisle, Ingrid approached the girl she thought had made the 999 call.

"*Privet*." Hello.

The girl turned sharply, her large brown eyes flashing with terror.

"Do you speak Russian?"

She shook her head.

"English?"

Her head shook again. The girl's features trembled.

"Don't be afraid. My name is Ingrid. I want to speak to you about the motorcycle accident you saw."

The girl threw several bags of pasta in her cart and moved sharply away. Ingrid let her get to the end of the aisle, saw the man in the café nod to her, and then followed the girl down the next aisle.

"Do you remember the accident?" Ingrid asked. All she needed was for the girl to be sure a man had been riding. If she could identify Marcus Williams that would be even better.

"Please, leave me alone."

Ingrid smiled at her. "I need your help."

"I cannot help you." She picked up two jumbo packs of toilet paper.

"But you saw the accident?"

The girl's eyes were imploring Ingrid to leave her alone. She checked over her shoulder to make sure they weren't being watched. "What accident?"

"A motorcycle hit a man, a runner." Ingrid talked quickly and quietly. "On Greenacre Lane."

The girl kept walking, collecting a twin packet of kitchen roll from a high shelf. She shook her head. "No. No accident."

The Thai girl appeared and smiled at her. She pulled her friend away from Ingrid and the two girls bowed heads briefly, checking their list. Was she just saying she hadn't seen an accident to make Ingrid go away? Ingrid approached her again in the soft drinks department. The girl recoiled from her, but her desire not to make a scene, or get into trouble, meant she did not say anything.

Ingrid grabbed the other end of her cart. "But you dialed 999."

She swallowed slowly. Her jaw tightened. Her head moved, almost imperceptibly, from side to side. "No," she managed. Tears threatened her eyes. "I see nothing."

Ingrid sensed she was reliving something. The way she flinched when Ingrid had said '999' was the giveaway.

"Katja."

Ingrid turned. The driver was at the head of the aisle, tapping his wrist. Katja's features crumpled with fear. She tugged the cart hard to release Ingrid's grip and hurried toward him. Ingrid ditched her basket of zucchini, deodorant and peanuts and went in search of the stationery section. She tore a page out of an exercise book and clicked a pen with a unicorn top. The ink wouldn't run. She licked the nib and tried again.

She wrote out her name and was about to add her cell number when she remembered about the sewer. She wrote down the switchboard number at the embassy and slipped the paper into Katja's cart when her handler was checking his phone. Ingrid didn't know for sure if Katja was a domestic slave, but her haunted eyes were the hallmark of a woman living in fear and subjugation.

Ingrid needed her as a witness. And that meant Ingrid had to free her.

20

Ingrid had three pounds and twelve pence in her pocket. She couldn't use her charge card for fear of being tracked, and she didn't have a phone. Her embassy ID and Russian passport were in the glove box of the rental car. At least she hoped they were. The Beatles could well have seized the Prius, or the hotel management might have towed it for overstaying. But if it was there, then it was possible Red Box didn't know about it and it was her ticket out of Bishopsgate. She walked toward the Ilex, checking regularly that she wasn't being followed.

Ingrid approached the hotel with caution. The Prius was still there. The van her abductors had used wasn't, but that didn't mean the Beatles weren't sitting in other vehicles, or working on the scaffold above a convenience store that had a view of the Ilex forecourt.

Almost directly opposite the hotel was Biddy's Café. It had a vintage sign from the 1940s and a menu offering baked potatoes —a staple of the British lunch, Ingrid had noticed—and bacon sandwiches. Ingrid did a walk-by to assess who Biddy's customers were. The gang of school kids taking up one table were unlikely Beatles fans, and the women in the corner animatedly pointing at a glossy gossip magazine probably hadn't been in the military or trained by Mossad. She went in. It was only after she'd been looking at the yellowed plastic menu above the counter for two minutes that she remembered how little money she had. Thankfully, a carton of apple juice was only eighty pence.

Ingrid took a seat at a Formica-topped table away from the window and positioned herself so she could observe the forecourt of the Ilex. The schoolkids—a mix of boys and girls—compared survey results for an end of term geography project. Ingrid couldn't let their spikes of laughter disrupt her concentration. She had to be absolutely sure no one was watching the car before she drove it away.

The street lighting flickered on, helping her to a better view of the cars on the forecourt. It was bounded by a low brick wall with a gap that wasn't quite wide enough for two cars to get through. A faded sign said 'Residents Parking Only'. Poking over the top of the wall was a laurel hedge with more gaps than an eight-year-old's smile.

Three other cars were also parked at the Ilex. In the driver's seat of a white Jaguar XE was a man who could be the fifth Beatle: thirties, lean, well-groomed. Anyone who could afford a Jaguar would be staying at a much nicer hotel than the Ilex, instantly raising her suspicions. A telephone engineer working at a junction box near the street was also toned and tanned. He seemed far more concerned with getting tools from his van and replacing them than actually using them. He could well be a member of an elite security operation. Returning to the Prius was too risky.

Ingrid had almost finished her juice when a Range Rover Vogue swung into the Ilex's forecourt. It was too dark to be sure what color it was, but the way the street lights bounced off its paintwork, it was either brand new or recently cleaned. Ingrid shuffled in her seat to get a good view of whoever got out.

The Range Rover took a long time to park, first trying one space, then another, rolling back and forth to fit precisely between the lines. The driver's door opened, and a woman climbed out. A short woman with long, reddish blond hair. Ingrid's jaw fell open.

It was Jen.

Shales of ice ghosted over Ingrid's skin. What the hell was Jen doing there?

"Oh, God, no."

Ingrid felt something rip inside her. Was Jen the embassy mole? *Please, don't let it be Jen.* Yet, it would explain why she could afford such a nice car on her clerk's salary. Ingrid's nostrils burned with the promise of tears. *No, not Jen.*

Ingrid's head shook slowly. She thought about how she had hurt Jen by not saying goodbye. Did Jen know about the Russian passport? Was the reason she hadn't been invited to Jen's leaving drinks because alcohol might loosen her tongue? God, it was all possible, wasn't it?

"No." Ingrid wiped away a tear. "I know you. It couldn't be you."

Jen closed the car door and surveyed the hotel. Ingrid checked the telephone engineer. She scrutinized the Jaguar driver. Neither gave Jen more than a cursory look. More importantly, Jen didn't appear to be looking out for them. She hurried inside the Ilex.

The school children scraped their chairs back and noisily negotiated who needed to pay for what. Ingrid tried to block them out. She rested her chin on her hands. If Jen was the mole, the Red Box operatives would have acknowledged her in some way, wouldn't they? Ingrid had worked with Jen for over four years. It simply wasn't possible that the bright, friendly, naïve Jennifer Rocharde was an enemy agent. She was sure of it.

Ingrid scanned the café. On the counter were flyers for local events. A jazz night. A Christmas fair. She grabbed a handful of them.

"Could I borrow a pen, please?"

The server handed her one, and she scribbled a note on the back of a flyer. She intercepted the schoolkids as they tumbled toward the door.

"Which one of you wants to earn two quid?"

"Two quid?" They rolled their eyes in unison. Two pounds didn't even buy them a phone top-up.

"Really, none of you?"

One boy wriggled nervously. "What have we got to do for it?"

Ingrid gave him her best smile. "Take these flyers and stick one on every windshield of the cars in the hotel parking lot."

A girl sniggered. "It's a car park, actually."

"And a windscreen," said another.

Ingrid kept talking to the boy. He was little and his clothes didn't fit. "But this one,"—she showed him the one with the note —"you gotta make sure goes on that Range Rover."

"Is that all?"

"That's all. And if you've got any left, put them under the wipers of all the cars on your way home."

The boy took her money and the fistful of flyers. Ingrid watched nervously as he crossed the street. He went straight for the Range Rover—she should have given him better instructions to make it less obvious—but then did as he was told and put the other flyers on the windshields of the other cars. The guy in the Jaguar shooed him away. Ingrid could only hope he didn't notice the boy wave to her as he started down the street, drumming up trade for January's Weight Watchers meeting as he made his way home. Ingrid prayed she hadn't just wasted the last money she had.

21

Jen stepped inside Biddy's Café. Her hands covered her open mouth at the sight of Ingrid. For several moments, she was frozen. Nervously, Ingrid got to her feet and smiled.

Jen's head started to shake, slowly moving from side to side. Tears glistened in her eyes.

"Any table you like, love," the woman behind the counter said.

Jen still didn't move. Ingrid pulled out a chair for her, and Jen took a tentative step toward her. Then another. "I thought you were dead," she said, her voice faltering.

Jen's shoulders shuddered. Ingrid grabbed them and embraced her. "I'm sorry. I'm so sorry." The shuddering became deep, uncontrollable heaving. All Ingrid could do was hold her until it subsided. "Come on, sit with me."

Ingrid ordered them drinks. A filter coffee for her and a hot chocolate for Jen who could not stop crying.

"But you sent me that email." She blew her nose on a paper napkin.

Ingrid explained she hadn't written it, that they had forced her to unlock her phone.

"Who?" Jen asked. "Who made you?"

"A private security agency." Ingrid told her about the

building site and the pulley and the sewer. Jen listened with disbelief.

"Why? I don't understand."

Ingrid tried to piece it together, and told Jen how she was being framed for killing Matthew Harding, and how they wanted to silence her before she named the real killer.

"You know who it is?"

Ingrid nodded. "It's best if I don't tell you, though."

Jen's eyes widened, but she didn't disagree. "And was that why you were leaving the country in a hurry?"

Ingrid was taken aback. Jen was still bruised by her disappearing act. "No, I hadn't even heard of Matthew Harding until I got to Heathrow."

"So why, then?"

Ingrid needed to give her an adequate explanation. "I, um, I." It all seemed so distant now. Irrelevant almost, even though it was only three days beforehand. "I felt my life was a total screw-up."

Jen nodded. "And then it, like, got screwier?"

"The screwiest."

The two friends smiled, and Jen reached out and placed her hand on Ingrid's. Ingrid grabbed Jen's fingers and squeezed. She hadn't realized how much Jen had meant to her. "I'm sorry," she said. "I didn't mean to hurt you."

Jen's eyes brimmed over. "In your defense, though, you had, like, been through a lot."

Ingrid pressed her lips together. "True, that."

Neither of them spoke for over a minute. They just stared at each other and kept holding hands. The server brought over their drinks.

"Thank you," Ingrid said.

Jen sipped her hot chocolate. "At least now I know why I couldn't get a trace on your cell. The police wouldn't even try, you know?" She wiped her nose again. "They said you were an adult. That you weren't, like, a risk to the public or anything. They said there was nothing they could do. Hardly a surprise. Jeez, you know that better than anyone." Jen couldn't stop talking. "I'm just so glad you paid for your hotel with a card. That's how I found you."

Warmth surged inside Ingrid as she watched Jennifer ramble. She was so impressed with how Jen hadn't crumbled.

"Penny said I should go home, you know, that I should take the rest of the day off—"

"Wait." Ingrid had to interrupt. "You told people I'd emailed you a suicide note?"

Jen nodded. "Uh-huh."

"How many people? Which people?"

"Um, Penny, Maisie, Rhiannon, some of the other girls in the bullpen." She tipped her head back. "Oh God, now I have to tell them you're not dead, and, like, I'm a total idiot for believing the email."

"Oh, Jen." Tears stung at the corner of Ingrid's eyes. "You are so not an idiot. You're the most tenacious, brilliant woman I know, and I am just so damn grateful they emailed you and not... and not my mother." Ingrid slapped her hands against her cheeks. "My mom hasn't been told, has she?"

"I, er, no. I don't think so. No one at work would call her. They'd, like, totally think I'd already done it."

They both smiled.

"They totally would." An awful notion occurred to Ingrid. "Were people surprised?"

"What do you mean? Like, of course they were."

"But they all thought it was plausible I was suicidal?"

Jen considered that for a second. "I guess... After Marshall..."

Ingrid sighed. "Don't tell me people think I am still hung up on him! Please!"

The door to the café opened suddenly, letting in a blast of December air. Ingrid's insides lurched. Her heart thundered. She turned to face the door, her eyes bulging.

The man was too old to be a Beatle. He waved at the server and smiled. Ingrid exhaled and her abdominals relaxed. She turned back to Jen. "You know, I don't think you should tell anyone."

"What?"

"That I'm alive. Someone wants to kill me, right? So it's not a bad thing if the people who want me dead think I didn't make it out of the sewer."

"For real?"

"Yep." Ingrid paused. "At least I think so."

"What if someone asks questions?"

Ingrid pulled a face. "Dunno. Tell them you call the cops every day, asking if any bodies have turned up. Tell them you've got an alert with all the morgues."

Jen leaned in. "It's not like they're going to check themselves, are they?" The faint smile on her lips told Ingrid that Jen liked the idea of being in on the conspiracy, being part of a team.

"No one can know we're in contact though, you understand? And I mean no one. There's a mole in the embassy and if anyone figures out you can lead them to me, you'll become a target too."

Jen puffed out her cheeks and took several breaths. "Understood."

"You're sure?"

Jen nodded.

"You really up for this?"

"I'm sure." Jen chewed her bottom lip, a tic that meant she had something bad to say.

"What is it?"

"There's something else. About you being dead."

Ingrid looked at her sideways. "What?"

"Well," Jen dropped her voice to a whisper. "There's a rumor."

"What kind of rumor?"

"See, so, well… Apparently—like, I totally don't have this confirmed or anything—there was a security breach. In the ambassador's suite." Jen paused and narrowed her eyes. "And well, someone said that you were seen snooping around her office—"

Ingrid fell back against the wooden chair. "And people think it was me?" She rolled her eyes to the ceiling. "Guess it's easy to blame the dead girl."

Jen settled the bill and Ingrid left Biddy's first, in case

anyone was following her. She walked briskly away from the café until, several minutes later, Jen's Range Rover slowed. Satisfied she wasn't being tailed, Ingrid jumped in and they headed back to London, taking a route that avoided the freeway.

When they passed through a small town Ingrid asked Jen to park.

"Have you seen someone?" Jen asked. "Are we, like, being followed?"

"No, but I need you to go in there." She nodded in the direction of a convenience store, its strip lights casting a blueish glow on the damp sidewalk. "Have you got cash?"

"Not much, but there's an ATM across the street. What's going on, Agent Skyberg?"

Ingrid explained. They needed a way of communicating without anyone knowing. The best way to do that was to buy two cheap cell phones with cash.

"I should leave the office more often," Jen said when she got out of the car. "Way more exciting than the things you normally get me to do."

Ingrid watched Jen cross the street and use the ATM. Her eyes followed her to the store to make sure no one was following. Ingrid hated putting Jen in danger. If anything happened to her, she would never forgive herself. Pearl earrings were hardly a sufficient token of gratitude, but Ingrid was damn well going to find the right pair.

Jen re-emerged clutching a paper bag. Back in the car, Jen handed over a phone and her charge card. "Figured you could use this."

Ingrid looked at the black plastic rectangle and read the name in embossed silver letters: Jack Tucker. "This is your fiancé's?"

"Don't worry, he never checks the statement. That's totally my job. The PIN is the last four digits."

Ingrid considered it for a moment. The chances of the Beatles linking the usage of Jack's credit card to her activity were seriously small. "Obviously you can claim it all back on expenses."

"You could probably use this car too."

Ingrid knew Jen's fiancé earned good money and came from a wealthy family, but surely he'd miss a brand-new Range Rover?

"I can always tell him it's getting repaired. He totes would never know."

"Thanks, but I don't think it'll be necessary. Can you arrange for the Prius at the hotel to be collected though?" Ingrid got the key out of her pocket and placed it in the cup holder in the armrest between them.

"No problemo."

"And you can make sure everything in the glove box is squirreled away?"

"Sure thing."

They went through the protocol for using the burner phones. "The key thing is to keep it turned off as much as possible. Only turn it on when you're several hundred yards away from your own phone," Ingrid said.

"But what if it's an emergency?"

"I'll send a carrier pigeon."

They approached the outskirts of London, and when they reached a landmark Ingrid was familiar with, she asked Jen to let her out.

"Here?"

"Yep. Anywhere it's safe to pull over."

They were on a four-lane highway with parking restrictions. Jen checked her rearview mirror and indicated, immediately eliciting a blast from someone's car horn. She corrected and kept driving.

"There's no rush. Just somewhere near here."

"What's around here?"

Ingrid thought about telling her. "It's probably best if you don't know."

A few hundred yards further along, Jen nosed the Range Rover into the curb.

"You sure about this?"

"Yep."

"Well, I guess I can keep tabs on you with the credit card."

"And don't forget to switch the phone on once a day."

"Got it." Jen smiled. "This is kinda fun."

"Apart from the bit where people want to kill me."

"Yep, apart from that bit."

The two friends embraced, and Ingrid stepped out into the London drizzle, strangely elated by the fact no one knew where she was going or what she had planned.

22

Ingrid had never been there on foot before, and she'd certainly never started from the Uxbridge Road, but she eventually found her way to Magdalen Avenue. She stood outside number ninety-six for several minutes reassuring herself it was empty. When she had dug into her pocket to give Jen the key to the rental car, she had also felt another set of keys attached to a small plastic dog called T-Rex.

Ingrid had never understood why, as a single man, Marshall had rented a house in the suburb of Ealing. A sleek, city-center bachelor pad would have been much more his style, but she could picture him calculating the price per square foot and multiplying by a factor related to the number of Tube lines or proximity to Heathrow. Whatever his reasoning, he had ended up living on a tree-lined road surrounded by neighbors with trampolines in the gardens and booster seats in their station wagons.

Ingrid had hung around long enough for the busybodies to notice. She couldn't delay any longer. The front yard was only a few feet deep and in a couple of strides she was standing under Marshall's porch, activating the automatic light. She turned the key in the lock and opened the door, pushing aside a pile of mail.

The smell hit her immediately. Three weeks beforehand, she had left the house with Carolyn to make the awful journey home with Marshall's body. It was understandable they had forgotten to put the trash out. The same mistake in summer would have seen the place infested with flies.

Marshall's place was a typical Victorian row house. It had what a realtor would describe as 'good proportions' and 'original features'. Ingrid closed the door behind her, stepped over the mail, and walked down the dark hallway toward the kitchen at the rear of the property. To her left was the stairway leading up to the bedrooms, and to her right was the living room where she and Carolyn had sat in numb silence in the hours after Marshall's death. A wave of sadness hit Ingrid with such force she had to place a steadying hand against the wall.

She reached the kitchen and tried not to inhale. She removed the trash can liner and put it out in the back yard. Leaving it out front might attract unwanted attention from neighbors. Ingrid didn't want anyone to know she was there.

It was so cold in the house that her breath misted as she checked the cabinets for food. Regimented boxes of rice, packs of buckwheat noodles, and spice jars filled the shelves. Marshall had loved Asian cuisine and had been a half-decent cook, obsessing over where to get the best salmon for sushi or shiitake mushrooms for gyoza. His culinary flair had been one of the better things about living with him, though it always left Ingrid with a stack of dirty dishes. In another cabinet, Ingrid found fitness supplements, vitamin pills, protein powders and herbal tinctures.

"You thought you'd outlive us all, didn't you?"

Behind the next door she discovered neat rows of canned beans and tomatoes. It was as if he had been prepping for the apocalypse. Or a 'no deal' Brexit.

Ingrid closed the refrigerator as quickly as she had opened it.

There was a pool of brown liquid where a lettuce used to be and the milk had gone rancid. The embassy must have assumed that Carolyn would have taken care of the house. Ingrid hoped no one remembered to do anything about it anytime soon. With any luck she could hide out at Marshall's for as long as it took. The deep freeze revealed plastic containers of labeled leftovers.

She selected the one that read katsu salmon and put it in the microwave.

She wandered the house, eating straight from the Tupperware. They had left the drapes drawn, thinking it would be better for security at night while the place was empty. Ingrid figured that meant she could risk putting on a side lamp in the living room without anyone noticing number ninety-six had a new occupant.

It was like looking at a crime scene. A surge of grief shuddered through her body as she thought about all the places where Marshall's DNA could still be harvested. There would be a blond hair on the back of the couch, skin cells on the X-box console and traces of his sweat on the unwashed sheets.

Nobody really dies anymore.

Ingrid let out an involuntary sound, somewhere between a howl and moan, and sank into an armchair. She put down her dinner; her appetite suddenly gone. Grief had slammed into her like a truck. For the first time, she experienced the *permanence* of Marshall's death, and the irrevocable nature of the loss shimmered at the edge of her thoughts. For several minutes, grief subsumed her as she mourned a man she had both loved and loathed.

Footsteps on the sidewalk wrenched her out of the fog. Fear flooded her body. She zoomed back to the rough hand over her mouth, and the smell of gasoline in the van. The memory of the building site, the terror of the undergrowth; her limbs trembled.

The footsteps stopped. Ingrid's ribcage tightened. She scanned the room, checking escape routes, assessing hiding places. Shouting. A woman's voice. An argument about… Someone was cheating. Someone else was ending it. It didn't matter; they hadn't come for her and she let go of the tension. She slumped against the chair and inhaled deeply, the desperate air stabbing her lungs.

The screaming went on for many minutes. Ingrid didn't want to intervene, and she certainly wanted to avoid having to give a statement to the police, but if someone was threatening violence, she needed to be able to assess the situation. She climbed the stairs and entered Marshall's bedroom at the front of the house. She pulled back enough of the drapes to get a view of the street.

A woman stood in the doorway of the property opposite, screaming at two people on the sidewalk. She threw something at them. It looked like a PlayStation and Ingrid followed its trajectory as it rattled along the road. It tumbled to a stop beside a motorcycle parked under a streetlamp. A Harley.

Marshall's Harley.

Devastated anew, Ingrid let the drapes fall shut. She turned and, in the darkness, saw something flash in the corner of the room. A green, glowing light. Marshall's modem.

"Dear God, Marshall, I could kiss you." She smiled. "And believe me, I never thought I would say that again."

In the gloom, she made out the rectangle of his monitor. Beneath his desk was the tower of his computer. She switched on his lamp.

"You're kidding me."

Next to the keyboard was Marshall's iPhone. As if in a fever, Ingrid opened a drawer for the charger. She held her breath as she plugged it in. She waited for the empty battery symbol to appear. It dinged and came to life, swirling heat across her skin.

This was too good to be true.

She turned on Marshall's computer. It emitted a cymbal sound followed by a series of clicks and whirrs. The monitor was still dark, though. She groped its underside for the on button. Either her heart had stopped or her breathing had. Her face felt numb. Her chest was tight. Then the screen illuminated and Ingrid collapsed into Marshall's chair. Her head fell into her hands. Her shoulders heaved with relief, but when she raised her gaze disappointment sucked a moan out of her lips. A cursor blinked in the empty password field.

It had been too good to be true.

There had been a time when Ingrid and Marshall had known each other's passwords. She cringed to remember they had even shared a Hotmail account at one point. She hadn't given it too much consideration when he'd set it up, but came to suspect it was one of the ways he had exerted control over her as their relationship deteriorated.

She stared at the cursor. Ingrid placed her fingers on the keyboard. It was worth a try, wasn't it? She typed in his old password: un_GU355A8L3. He'd thought it was very clever.

The egg timer spun and Ingrid swallowed to lubricate her parched mouth.

The screen flickered.

She was in.

23

Marshall's computer was arranged as neatly as his hair. No stray documents, just tidy rows of labeled folders. Photos. House. Finance. Family. Rocco. Marshall had named all of his bikes Rocco. She'd never known why.

The internet connection was slow, but she logged into the embassy servers remotely and checked her emails. Her breath misted into a blueish fog in front of the bright screen. Still nothing on the ANPR hits. Still no response on her request to see Marcus Williams's phone records. Nor had anyone higher up the food chain authorized the unfreezing of her undercover diary. Ingrid was about to send an email to the Legat's secretary to ask him to do just that, but remembered she was meant to be dead. However, the Bureau could still be useful in other ways.

In cases where the FBI needed plausible deniability, they occasionally employed private security firms. That meant someone in DC would have compiled an extensive dossier on the Beatles' employer. She navigated her way to the right database and found detailed assessments of the biggest operators in the private security industry. Top of the list was Fortnum Security, the organization that employed her friend Nick Angelis, if 'friend' was the right word for someone who frequently infuriated her. Ingrid made a mental note to call him. The last time she'd seen Nick, he'd looked uncharacteristically unwell.

Ingrid shivered. It was cold. She opened a chest of drawers in search of a sweater and some thick socks. A memory surfaced of the apartment she'd shared with Marshall in DC when she'd often worn his clothes. They had been good together once.

She glanced back at the screen filled with reports and spreadsheets. It was going to be a long night. She would need fortification. She returned downstairs to see what liquor Marshall had in his retro cocktail cabinet. He claimed to have found it for twenty pounds at Greenwich market, but it had probably come from a vintage boutique in Ladbroke Grove for ten times as much. Aperol. Vermouth. Cassis. Angostura bitters. Triple sec. Maybe Marshall entertained more than she'd realized. However, he had also been the sort of man who would practice making cocktails in case he got the chance to impress a boss or a woman he brought home. She pictured him making a perfect whisky sour, adding the lemon peel twist, and then drinking it alone. As far as she knew, Marshall hadn't made any friends outside the embassy since he'd been in London. In fact, apart from old school friends, she'd never known him to socialize with anyone who wasn't good for his career. She poured herself a tequila—a large one— and headed back upstairs.

She pressed the home button on Marshall's iPhone as it charged. It required his fingerprint or a four-digit code to unlock. She took another gulp, hoping the alcohol would burn away the memory of being forced to unlock her own phone in the back of the van. The blaze of the tequila stung her eyes.

How many attempts did she have at guessing his four-digit code? Three? Ten? Marshall's birthday would be too obvious. His mom's birthday? His lucky number had been 21. She tried 2121, and the screen shook, telling her to try again. She had to think carefully before another attempt. She couldn't blow it. A familiar number like Marshall's was unlikely to trigger the interest of anyone monitoring the Criminal Division's phones. But a new number, especially an unregistered number like the burner in her jacket pocket, would immediately raise a red flag.

Ingrid put down the iPhone and returned to Marshall's computer. She scanned the list of the Bureau's approved private security firms. Based on its reliance on Mossad agents, she was satisfied her hunch about Red Box was correct. She opened a browser and visited the firm's corporate website.

It was sleek and minimalist. A red box in the middle of the screen spun, increasing with each rotation until it filled the browser. A corporate slogan appeared: Your ally in a hostile world. The 'about us' section talked of veterans from the world's elite intelligence units offering 'solutions' to business and litigation challenges. Never had the words elite, solutions and challenges been more sinister. She clicked on the personnel link. None of the men—and they were, without exception, all male—were the agents who had abducted her, but several of them all wore the same signet ring.

Ingrid needed to find a link between Marcus Williams and Red Box. The most obvious tie was his father, Roy. A Google search offered a link to a report by a journalist based in the Ukraine. It was too long to read, so she did a File/Find command for Roy Williams's name. He was listed as an investor in a failed bank. Ingrid scrolled around, scanning for salient details, until something made her stop. A photo. Above a caption that read 'Red Box executive Arnie Goldfarb' was the smiling face of one of the Beatles. He had more hair in the photo, but it was definitely John. Goldie. That's what George had called him.

Now she knew his name, Ingrid compiled her own dossier on Goldfarb. His online presence was discreet, but combined with the Bureau's intel, she found enough information to be confident of a link between his resumé and Roy Williams's business interests. Further digging revealed a string of unfortunate accidents— food poisoning, brake failure, anaphylaxis—that had befallen those who had obstructed Red Box's operations. Throwing Steve off a balcony fitted a pattern.

Fueled by the tequila, Ingrid compiled a mental a list of the things she needed to put Marcus Williams on the stand for killing Matthew Harding. If she could prove that, the entire Williams edifice crumbled.

Number one. The real CCTV footage. Ingrid wasn't hopeful— it would almost certainly have been destroyed—but there was a chance the embassy used a shadow server where the actual footage might be found. She also needed to get the footage of her leaving the parking lot analyzed. A small shift in the light, or a millisecond missing from the log, would prove it was doctored.

Number two. The ANPR data. Clearly, Ingrid wasn't going to get anywhere requesting the hits on her own license plate, but if she applied for data from the vehicle that left the embassy immediately before she was supposed to have left, the cameras might have picked up Williams riding her bike in the distance. She started composing an email to Jen, asking for all the traffic camera footage from around the embassy, but stopped herself. An email from a dead woman was a very bad idea. And given how far Red Box's tentacles had already reached, it was possible such a request would alert someone on their payroll. Given they had tried to kill her, Ingrid was not going to put herself or Jen in danger. Ingrid needed another way of making DS Hayes believe Marcus Williams was in the saddle. It was time to call her for a favor.

On Marshall's nightstand, squatting like a black plastic toad, was an old-fashioned telephone. Not so ancient it had a dial on the front, but old enough for the handset to be connected to the base with a coiled wire. She picked it up and was comforted by a dial tone. A call to directory assistance gave her the number for Belgravia police station. Ingrid asked to be put through to Detective Sergeant Cath Murray.

"Hey there, stranger," Cath said. "Nice to have you back in the country."

There was something so normal about hearing Cath's voice that it made the events of the past few hours even more incomprehensible.

"Thanks." Ingrid knew she sounded weary. "Can you spare me five minutes?"

"Are you okay?" Her tone was genuinely sympathetic. "You need some company?"

"That's a lovely offer, but that's not why I'm calling."

"Not a social call, then?"

"Sorry."

"Okay," Cath said, sounding more business-like. "But before we get on to that, just let me know how things went back home."

They played on the same soccer team and were more than co-workers, but they hadn't quite made it as far as drinking buddies. Ingrid was touched Cath was asking about the funerals.

"And how are things now you're back?"

Ingrid looked at her empty tequila glass. How the hell was she supposed to answer? "Fine. Listen, could you possibly chase something for me?"

"I can try."

Ingrid explained she didn't want the ANPR request to come from her, or the embassy, and Cath knew not to ask why. Ingrid gave her the date, time and location she was interested in.

"You want me to check London Transport as well?"

"They have something better than ANPR?"

"They do in London."

Every bus in the city, Cath explained, was fitted with several cameras, and they were much better at identifying drivers—and riders—because they were lower to the ground and in amongst the traffic. There was also a chance it was a database Red Box hadn't thought to infiltrate.

"Leave it with me," Cath said. "Should have something for you tomorrow. Or the day after. Are we going to see you at footie soon?"

"I don't think I'm going to make training this week."

"See you next week then, yeah?"

The two friends said goodbye and Ingrid went downstairs to pour herself another tequila. In the hallway, she passed the thermostat for the central heating. She considered putting it on, but feared the steam jetting out of the boiler flue on the side of the house might attract attention. Better to be cold than discovered.

Back at Marshall's desk, she was immensely relieved to discover that Facebook automatically logged Marshall in. If Red Box was monitoring her activity, masquerading as Marshall should buy her a bit of time. She searched for Marcus Williams's carefully curated page and looked again at his photos. The future senator was styled as the sports jock, the academic, the volunteer and the dutiful son. She wasn't going to find anything useful in his own posts, so Ingrid checked out his friends. Hopefully they would be less careful.

She took a good slug of tequila and examined the names and faces. None of his friends immediately stood out, so she went back to the beginning and worked through them alphabetically. She examined everyone's timeline to discover where they had been on the eighteenth and nineteenth of November. All she needed was one of them to leave a comment about the excellent round of golf they'd played at Swanbury, and she was close to putting Marcus Williams in handcuffs.

After fourteen friends, Ingrid was still only on the Ds. Her vision started to blur. She either needed caffeine or sleep. She opted for more tequila, this time bringing the bottle up from the living room. She opened iTunes and searched for some beats to keep her awake. Marshall's most recently played album had been the soundtrack to the TV show *Nashville*.

"Aw. Really?"

Ingrid wasn't in a country mood. She wanted drums and guitars. She scrolled until she saw Kings of Leon, then found a pair of headphones in Marshall's drawer to make sure the neighbors wouldn't hear. The liquor burned through her synapses and the relentless music kept her focused. She was half way through the Fs when she realized she was singing, and onto the Js when she suddenly stopped. Ingrid blinked hard, making sure she wasn't imagining things. She looked again.

"Yes!" She raised her glass to the screen. Alcohol usually increased her tendency to talk to herself. "Yes!"

Jamie Jefferson, a fellow student at Oxford, the cox on the rowing team, had posted a photo of himself and two friends. They were in a damp-looking field under a gray sky. They had their arms around each other. Two were holding cocked shotguns, the other was proffering a grouse. The caption read: Awesome day at Sammy's place. Ingrid wrinkled her nose. The geolocation tag was Bishopsgate.

"Boom."

She poured another tequila and enlarged the image. There

was no one in the background, and she didn't have the right software to see if the reflection in one of the boy's glasses would reveal a faint image of Marcus Williams behind the lens. But if a judge put Jamie Jefferson under oath, he would only have two choices: perjure himself or place Marcus Williams in the vicinity. And if Jamie wouldn't, one of his two smiling friends would.

Ingrid pushed back in the chair and ran her fingers through her hair. They snagged on a knot that she tried to unpick. She hadn't looked in a mirror since the restrooms in Tesco, and her hair had been a bird's nest then. Ingrid kept staring at the screen, certain she was looking at her Get Out Of Jail card.

"Oh, you doofus. Call yourself an FBI agent."

The obliging Jamie Jefferson had tagged Sammy. She wasn't sure why she hadn't clicked on his name immediately. The tequila, probably.

Samir Karim.

Karim. *Karim.* Why was that ringing a bell? *Ah.* The spelling was different. Kareem. "As in Sheikh Mohammed Al-Kareem." She inhaled deeply. "Please tell me you're related."

24

Ingrid opened her eyes. It took her several moments to work out she was in Marshall's bed. She rolled over to check the time on her phone. Her shoulder was stiff and head hurt, but possibly not as much as it might have done given the empty bottle of tequila on Marshall's desk. Where was her phone?

"Ah."

That was why it wasn't there. Terror rippled through her veins as she remembered what had happened. The air outside the duvet was cold. She wanted to stay in the warm, but she needed water. And something to eat. And painkillers. She pushed herself up to a seated position, stirring the bile in her stomach, and slung her legs over the side of the bed. She had slept in the track pants she'd bought at the supermarket and was slightly impressed with herself for buying such versatile clothing.

Ingrid rubbed the sleep from her eyes and crossed the room slowly. She reached the window and pulled at one of the drapes. Through the slender, bright gap, she checked to see if anyone was watching the house. It was Ealing, she told herself; everyone drove a nice car, but as best she could tell, neither the Audi, the Mercedes nor the BMW contained an ex-Mossad spy. Which was just as well: fighting for your life is always harder with a hangover.

She pulled on the socks and sweater she'd worn the night

before and staggered to the kitchen. Marshall was a coffee snob, so it was not a surprise to find a bag of artisan beans blended to an Italian recipe. She poured them into a grinder and flinched at the noise when it crunched into action. She found his Moka stovetop coffee maker—he always insisted it made far superior coffee than a French press—then opened the refrigerator.

"Ew."

She'd forgotten about the rotting vegetables and furry milk. Her stomach heaved, thrusting a painful jab through her abdomen. In the freezer she unearthed some frozen fruit and ice cream. An unopened bottle of apple juice lurked in a cabinet. Black coffee and a berry smoothie. It was almost healthy. She took a swig of each and trudged back to the bedroom. She stopped halfway, her attention seized by a photo of Marshall and Carolyn, aged twelve, in front of the Gateway Arch. Ingrid had taken the picture, but could not remember why they went to St Louis? An aunt? A sports game?

Ingrid sat down at the desk and picked up Marshall's fully charged phone. He had three new messages. Not bad for a dead guy. It still demanded a code. She bit the inside of her lip. Maybe Carolyn's birthday was worth a go? The keypad shuddered and told her to try again. How many chances did she have left?

The monitor flickered into life, revealing details of her investigation from the night before. Eighteen browser windows were open, all displaying a different Facebook page for one of Williams's friends. None of them put Marcus on the hunting trip to Uppenham Hall with Samir Karim who, it turned out, was also on the rowing team. Either it was an extremely unlikely coincidence that Marcus Williams was riding on Greenacre Lane just a few hundred yards from his teammates' day out, or he had been very good at making sure he wasn't photographed.

Everything she had on Williams was still circumstantial. A prosecutor would persuade a jury she'd gathered evidence as part of a vendetta to clear her own name. Who knew what Williams's teammates would say under oath. Would the influence of his father's billions and political contacts be enough for them to perjure themselves? The fact was, she still needed Katja.

Ingrid took a slug of coffee. The good news was that Katja was still alive, which had surely meant Red Box didn't know she'd witnessed the accident. And if they didn't know about her, then they couldn't ensure her silence. The bad news was her only witness was too petrified to talk.

Ingrid checked her emails. "Bingo."

The analysis of the number Katja had been calling in Turkmenistan was complete. Ingrid started to perform a fist pump, but found she needed her hand to stifle a yawn. She clicked on the email. There wasn't much information, just the address associated with the number and the name of the account holder who lived in a small town on the shores of the Caspian Sea. Satellite imagery showed it to be a residential street with very few cars, usually a sign of an impoverished neighborhood. An image search returned photos of the town's mosque and a nearby quarry as the local highlights.

With the same number being dialed at the same time of the week, Ingrid's instinct was that Katja was calling home. But if she was right about Katja being trafficked, there was a significant risk the calls were to whoever had smuggled her into the UK. Victims were often conned into making journeys with the promise of jobs that would repay the loans they'd been forced to take out to cover their travel costs. It was unlikely, but possible, that the regimented call pattern indicated she was phoning to make a repayment. Ingrid stared at the number. It either belonged to Katja's parents or her tormentor. Calling it could put Katja's life in even more danger. She needed to think a little more before picking up the phone.

Ingrid wandered into the bathroom. Marshall's hairs were still in the sink, his toothbrush still in the holder. It hadn't been used in a month. How gross would it be if she…? Her teeth were sticky. Her tongue was furry. She turned the hot faucet—why did the Brits still have the hot and cold separate instead of mixers?—and held the toothbrush underneath the flow. A minute in scalding water was as good as disinfectant, right? Her teeth felt much better after a good scrub.

Ingrid lingered in the shower for a long time. At first, she mulled over the wisdom of calling the Turkic number, then she simply didn't want to get out. It was warm inside the shower cubicle and she hadn't thought about what she would wear.

"Come on, Skyberg. It's cold, but it's not Minnesota cold."

Wrapped in a towel, she entered Marshall's walk-in closet. He didn't have a lot of clothes—he threw things out the moment they started to sag—but they were all well-made, if a little dull. She'd never even seen him wear a colored sock.

Ingrid pulled on a pair of slacks that she belted over a crisp white shirt, hoping the *Annie Hall* style was back in fashion. She looked like she was waiting tables. Ingrid looked at her feet. The one thing she had never borrowed from Marshall were his shoes, and the only pair she owned were the lime green sneakers she'd bought the day before. Even with two pairs of socks she couldn't make Marshall's size thirteens fit her size nine feet.

"Ooh, I wonder…"

Ingrid padded down the hallway to the room Carolyn had used. Under the bed were several pairs of Converse and a pair of brand-new Dr Martens boots. Carolyn either hadn't had space for them in her suitcase, or she had decided her parents would find news of her sexuality difficult enough to come to terms with without her—and Ingrid could just picture Marshall's mom saying this—'flaunting it for the whole world to see'.

The DMs were a pinch too small, but they would do.

She was cold. She needed a sweater or a cardigan. On a shelf in Marshall's closet was a neatly folded rainbow of cashmere sweaters worthy of a window display. She grabbed a cream one before rushing back to the desk. She'd had an idea of how to get into Uppenham Hall, but something made her return to the closet.

The moment she opened the door, she forgot what it was.

She peered at the sweaters and the shoes and the suits. What was it? What had she seen? It wasn't the shirts. It wasn't the woolen coat. She had the sense the thing she was interested in wasn't clothing.

It was the suitcase. Out of the corner of her eye, she'd spotted the case had a built-in lock. She kneeled down and examined it. It read 2112. Ingrid pressed the zip pulls into the lock and rolled the barrels, locking the case. She then thumbed the barrels back to 2112 and the case unlocked. So that was Marshall's code. Somehow, she'd known it would involve the number 21.

Alarmed that she still knew Marshall so well, she ran back to his desk and grabbed his phone. She tapped in the code and held her breath until the lock screen was replaced with the regiment of apps on his home screen.

"Oh, Marshall. If only you'd been this helpful when you were alive."

25

Ingrid didn't speak Turkmen, and the inconvenient fact she was supposedly dead meant she couldn't make use of the Bureau's translator services. She hoped six decades of Soviet control made it likely whoever answered would understand a little Russian.

She checked the time and was shocked to find it was almost eleven thirty. With the drapes drawn and the quietness of the suburban street outside, she'd thought it was much earlier. Turkmenistan was five hours ahead of London. Afternoon was a good time to make the call.

Ingrid's palms moistened as her fingers hovered over the keys. It was almost certainly Katja's family, right? The odds of the number belonging to the trafficker were minimal, weren't they? Heat radiated from her pounding heart. After a deep breath, Ingrid keyed in the digits.

A woman picked up after a few rings.

"Hello," Ingrid said in Russian, "I am calling from England—"

The woman talked over her. Ingrid didn't understand what she was saying, but heard loud and clear that the woman was anxious. Her syllables tumbled over each other, her pitch seesawed. The static on the line didn't help, but Ingrid was eventually able to work out the woman was repeating the same word. Wait.

"Do you speak Russian?" Ingrid asked.

The woman responded in Turkmen. Ingrid was unable to decipher any of it.

"Do you speak English?"

She waited for a reply.

"England," the woman said, still sounding panicked. "England. *Da.*"

Ingrid heard shouting in the background. Then footsteps. A male voice. Should she hang up?

"Yes?" The man sounded old.

"Do you speak English?"

"Little."

"Do you speak Russian?"

"*Nyet.*"

"I am calling from England—"

"Katja?"

Ingrid exhaled so hard her breath was visible. "Yes, I am phoning about Katja—"

He dropped the phone. He had a frantic conversation with the woman. Ingrid had no idea what they were saying.

"Hello?" he said.

"Hello."

"Five."

"Five?"

"Yes, five." There was a long pause. "Minutes. Five minutes. Please."

There was a clunk as he put the receiver down more gently this time, followed by a flurry of footsteps and doors opening and closing. Ingrid could no longer hear the woman, but thought she could detect the man muttering to himself.

Ingrid strolled to the window and checked the road through a gap in the drapes. A gangly youth in exercise gear loped down the street, taking a keen interest in the parked cars as if he was looking for one to steal. Or maybe he was checking his reflection in the windows. She scrutinized the houses opposite and satisfied herself none were hosting a Red Box operative on surveillance duty.

She looked at the phone. The call had so far lasted three minutes. Now and then, she heard a noise at the other end of the line. She felt like a NASA engineer waiting for Apollo 8 to reappear from the dark side of the moon.

A rumble came through from Turkmenistan. A squeak of a door opening. Loud voices. Footsteps. Then silence.

"Hello?" It was a young man's voice. He was out of breath.

"Hello. You speak English?"

"Yes. Who is this?"

"I am calling from England." Ingrid chose her words carefully, mindful not to say anything that could put Katja in harm's way.

"Yes?"

"I need to speak to Katja."

Several conversations seemed to be going on behind him. "I see." There was a pause. "Is she okay?" His English was precise and slow.

"I saw her yesterday," Ingrid said.

He relayed this to the other people in the room who made jubilant sounds.

"Where is she?" he asked. "We hear nothing for four weeks. My mother very worried."

Ingrid exhaled. It wasn't the trafficker. "She is still in the same place."

"I see." His intonation suggested this was a phrase he had picked up from movies but did not properly comprehend.

"Do you know how I can contact her?"

He made some unintelligible noises. He was being bombarded with questions. "Sorry. Can you repeat?"

"I want to speak to Katja."

He spoke rapidly in Turkmen, silencing the conversations behind him. "But you saw her yesterday. I do not understand."

Ingrid took a deep breath. "My name is Ingrid Skyberg." She hesitated. "I work for the police." It was more straightforward than explaining she was employed by the FBI. "Katja was a witness to an accident—"

"Accident?" In the background, several people gasped.

"She is fine. She *saw* the accident. I need to talk to her."

"Ah, okay." Again, he spoke in Turkmen and the other voices sing-songed over each other.

"Do you have a number for her? A phone number?"

"No. She has very important job. Always working. She say not to call her." He paused. "She always call here. My uncle's house. Same time every week and my mother make sure she is here. But she not call for one month."

"Do you have an email address for her?"

"No. No email. She is okay, yes?"

"Yes, she is well," Ingrid said. If you call being scared and imprisoned 'well'. "When I speak to her, I will ask her to call you, if you like."

More Turkmen, more chattering.

"How you speak to her? You not have number."

He had a point. "I will find her. When I do, is there a message I can give her?"

He relayed Ingrid's question, and the conversations exploded behind him. "Yes, yes you must. Please tell her Krystyna, her sister, tell her Krystyna had baby. A girl. Xenia. You tell her this, yes?"

"Yes, I will tell her. And I will also ask her to call you."

She thanked him for his help and ended the call. To talk to Katja, Ingrid was going to have to get inside Uppenham Hall. She had already worked out how to do it. She opened a new browser and was about to start typing when a loud crash made her jump. Her breath stalled.

"What the?"

Ingrid pushed the chair back slowly, careful not to make a noise, and crept out onto the landing. She stood perfectly still and listened. Was someone in the house? A desiccated plant sat in a ceramic pot next to the banister. She picked it up and prepared to throw it at whoever came up the stairs.

She heard whistling from out on the street. She listened hard, her senses elevated, but there were no other noises coming from within the house. Still carrying the plant pot, she started down the stairs. Ingrid paused on the third step. A figure was visible through the frosted glass of the front door. How had Red Box found her so quickly? A trace on Marshall's phone? His landline?

The figure moved. Ingrid's mouth fell open. She waited.

A hand pushed an envelope through the mail slot. It fluttered down to the mat, landing next to a scattering of new mail. When the hand withdrew, the mail slot snapped back loudly. *That's* what she had heard. She almost dropped the plant pot with relief.

Back at the desk, Ingrid's pulse took time returning to normal. She stared at the open browser. What had she been about to search for? The shock of the mailman, or the remnants of the tequila, were slowing her thought processes.

"Ah, yes."

The party planner. There had been a name on the van that pulled out of Uppenham Hall. It'd had a London connection. Something upmarket like Buckingham or Kensington. Definitely a place.

Mayfair.

Mayfair Events. Ingrid had found and dialed the number before she'd worked out what she was going to say.

"Mayfair. Please hold." The woman who answered held her hand over the receiver and conducted a conversation with someone else. Ingrid couldn't decipher any words, only the tone: stressed. "Hi. Mayfair. How can I help you?"

Here goes.

"Hello there, I've been asked to liaise with you about the…" Ingrid stumbled, unsure what was going to come out of her mouth next. "…ice sculpture. For the party at Uppenham Hall." Did the super-rich still do ice sculptures, or were they very 2005?

"Uppenham Hall?"

"Yes."

"Oh dear. Hold on."

The line went silent apart from intermittent beeps. The 'oh dear' was worrying.

"Julie speaking." She sounded even more harassed. "You're calling about Uppenham?"

"Hi, yes, I've been told to coordinate with you about the ice sculpture."

"Oh yes?"

"Yes. When should we deliver it?"

"Nobody told me about an ice sculpture."

Ingrid stalled for time. "Oh. I'm sorry. Do you not want it?"

"Who ordered it?"

"Um." Should she say the sheikh did? "The name I have on the order here is Sammy."

"Oh, God. Please tell me it isn't rude."

"Rude?"

"It's not a giant cock and balls or anything, is it?"

Ingrid tried not to laugh. "No, no, it isn't. Nothing like that."

"Thank goodness. How quickly will it melt?"

Ingrid had to make something up. "It sits on a refrigerated plate. It's good for a few hours."

"Ah, okay. And where is it for? Entrance hall or dining hall?"

"Er. Entrance hall."

Julie made some notes, tapping her keyboard loudly. "Best bring it in last, then. Don't want it getting bashed. Shall we say four?"

"Today?

"Well, it's not going to be any bloody use to them tomorrow, is it?"

26

Ingrid wouldn't be able to rent a car without ID, even with Jen's credit card. She was going to have to take the Harley, which presented her with a minor problem. The waitress outfit was much more likely to blend in at a party than the motorcycle messenger look.

She found Marshall's bike gear in a closet under the stairs. He had different clothing for different seasons. Unfortunately, his winter riding jacket was made of safety-conscious white leather with lime green flashes.

"You were always such a poseur."

With the helmet, she looked like a Mighty Morphin' Power Ranger. At least his riding pants were predominantly black. She had no choice but to wear his boots, so she scrabbled around in his closet for his thickest socks and a backpack to put her waitress outfit in. She shoved Jen's credit card and iPhone into her pockets, then looked at the burner phone. Jen might try to contact her on it, so she tossed it into the backpack.

The battery on the Harley had gone flat, so she bump started it and sped out west towards Burnt Oak. It was good to be back on two wheels, though she was very glad of Marshall's thermal layers and his heated hand grips. Forty-five minutes later, Ingrid pulled up at the main gates of Uppenham.

The house itself was not visible from the road, just a stone gatehouse and the beginning of a driveway that curved away through a thicket of trees. A security guard stepped out of the gatehouse carrying a clipboard and trudged through the sleet to the locked gates. The way his jacket stretched across his belly suggested he had put on weight since he had been measured for his uniform.

"Collecting a package," Ingrid said.

He looked at his notes. "Got nothing for you."

"Perhaps I'm picking up from the main house?" she said, a little too hopefully.

He clenched his teeth together. "I doubt that very much. I'll call the house. See what it is."

Ingrid kept the engine running and held tight to the heated grips while she figured out a different ruse to get inside the grounds.

"Nope, nothing for you, I'm afraid." His tone was infused with the whine of someone trying to impersonate a posh person. "I suggest you contact your dispatch center."

"I think I know why it isn't on your list. I'm collecting something for Mayfair Events, not the homeowner."

"Is it to do with the party?"

"I guess."

"You want to try the rear entrance. It's right over the other side of the estate."

He gave her directions to the tradesmen's entrance Ingrid was already familiar with. On her way to the rear gate, she spotted a narrow turnoff that might offer a shortcut and took it. It was little more than a forester's track, and she was wary of getting the Harley stuck in mud. It was hardly a dirt bike. She found a clearing and decided to abandon her ride.

The map on her phone was little help, but she trusted her sense of direction. She secured the helmet on the handlebars and headed off on foot. The gloomy woods gave way to open fields that shimmered under a veil of frost. She hoped her unorthodox route would allow her to reach Uppenham's grounds without being seen by either a traffic camera, or a security patrol.

Ingrid unzipped Marshall's jacket. Walking in thermals and

leathers was an excellent workout, regardless of the temperature. The boots slipped and rubbed, even with the extra pair of socks, but she was thankful they were waterproof. An occasional roar of a speeding car on Greenacre Lane rolled up the valley, reminding her of the accident that had brought her here.

When a succession of headlight beams followed the same path at the far end of the field, Ingrid knew she had found the track that led to the tradesmen's gate. She hurried toward it but was prevented from reaching it by a thick tangle of bare elder trees and hawthorn bushes, all strangled by ivy. Her body temperature fell as she slowed to look for a breach in the bushes and she zipped back up. A vehicle rattled up the track, passing just a few yards from her, but there was no way of getting through the hedge. She walked a few hundred yards in search of a gap, and then a few hundred more in the other direction, but was still trapped in the field on the wrong side of the track.

Another vehicle approached and Ingrid stood still, fearful its headlights might glimpse her ridiculous jacket through the foliage. It slowed as it passed her, then stopped a few seconds later and applied the handbrake. She was closer to the gate than she'd realized.

A smattering of voices, a whirring of electric gates, and the diesel engine coughed back to life. She'd been so concerned with getting onto the track she had forgotten to think how she'd get through the gates. On the plus side, she hadn't heard any dogs.

Ingrid kept searching for an exit, a gate or a style. She was beginning to think she'd made a mistake and would have to retrace her steps and get back on the bike. Then she noticed the dark branches of a towering chestnut tree stretching up into the steel-gray sky.

Maybe she didn't need a gap.

Good motorcycle leathers were the modern equivalent of chain mail. She wouldn't want to test them against a medieval lance, but she'd once broken up a street fight without a flick-knife making it through to the skin. A couple of seasons of brambles and ivy were no match for her reinforced jacket. And the boots would withstand a fox bite if she trod on its lair.

Ingrid pressed into the wet, prickly foliage and got as close to the chestnut tree as she could. She reached up for its lowest branch and grasped it through the articulated riding gloves. Her injured shoulder complained, but she ignored the pain. She'd had worse injuries. She wedged a boot into a cleft in the bark and hoisted herself up. She straddled the branch and listened, making sure she hadn't sparked the interest of a security patrol. Ingrid pulled herself across the branches to reach the other side of the tree. Now she needed a way to climb down to the track without twisting an ankle.

Another vehicle came up from Greenacre Lane. She watched the high beams fracture through the branches. She didn't have time to clamber down before it got close. Marshall's white jacket was too visible. There was no way they wouldn't see her.

Govno!

She stretched out and lay flat on the branch, hoping to obscure as much of the white as possible from the driver's view. The vehicle was close enough now to hear it had a diesel engine. A truck, most likely. She gripped the wet branch with her thighs and tried to keep still. When the truck rounded a bend, she saw it was a box van, the kind with a flat roof. She held her breath as its headlights swooped in her direction. The driver changed gear and slowed to navigate a puddle as he passed underneath her. Ingrid took her chance. She released her grip and dropped down, clattering onto the van's roof.

If the driver noticed, he didn't stop. Ingrid pressed herself against the cold metal, lying as flat as she could until the driver came to a stop and scraped on the handbrake.

"Name?"

"Dixter. Dixter's the florist. Should be on your list."

Ingrid tried not to breathe, fearful the mist would catch the headlights and alert the guard.

"Back unlocked?"

"Should be."

The guard's footsteps squelched as he walked around the van. She felt the clunk as he unlocked the door. The van rocked to one side as he opened it. Ingrid closed her eyes. The scent of lilies drifted over her.

"You might want to take a look at this," the guard said.

Ingrid's heart froze. The driver shouted through his open window, "What is it?" His door cranked open, and he jumped down, the van swaying as he did so. Ingrid listened to his shoes squish into the mud.

"Oh, great, he said. "Julie'll be thrilled about that." He sighed heavily. "Maybe we can turn them into posies."

He stomped back to the cab, muttering about five hundred pounds worth of ruined roses. He slammed the door so hard Ingrid's steel-toed boot bounced onto the metal roof.

"What was that?" the guard asked.

Ingrid tried not to breathe.

"Probably something else falling over."

The gates opened, and the van made its way down the drive, snaking through the valley toward the house. After two hundred yards, Ingrid hoisted herself up onto all fours. She wriggled to the rear of the van and jumped. She rolled on impact and stayed low to the ground.

When the driver passed over the brow of a hill, Ingrid got to her feet and started walking.

27

Ingrid moved away from the driveway for the cover of the woods. The white leather jacket was designed to be visible. It would be impossible to hide if she got swooped by headlights of the next vehicle through the gates. Or a patrol guard's flashlight.

Ingrid studied Uppenham Hall from a vantage point on the hill above. Sited in a cleft in the valley, the stately home was almost perfectly square and had been constructed around a central courtyard. Built of huge slabs of stone, its austere Georgian facades were adorned with domed turrets in each corner, reminiscent of tiny observatories. Visitors arriving through the main gate would pass through undulating grounds dotted with dovecotes, ponds, Scotch pines and Henry Moore sculptures to arrive at a grand porticoed entrance. Several vehicles were parked in front of the Hall, two of which were illuminated by bright arc lights. Ingrid couldn't quite tell from such a distance, but they looked like racing cars.

To the rear, a kitchen garden of ordered vegetable beds was enclosed inside a rectangle of red brick walls. It sat in the middle of a lawn that stretched toward a cluster of outbuildings; stables, greenhouses and bothies. Another van descended to the house from the tradesmen's gate, its yellow high beams carving through a settling mist of twilight blues. The entire valley was fringed with woodland. The hoot of an owl drifted low across the landscape. It was magical.

The building had five stories. Only one light was visible on the top floor at the rear. A few more lights were illuminated on the third floor, but most of the activity appeared to be at ground level. The van parked next to the other tradesmen's vehicles near the open back door, which cast a rhomboid of light over the gravel driveway. Ingrid picked out a route through the folds in the hill that enabled her to creep toward the rear entrance without being seen.

There was no obvious security presence, but that didn't mean there wasn't one. On a private estate where grouse shooting took place, there was a high probability there were guards who would legally be carrying a shotgun. And they'd have dogs. A woman with a clipboard—arms flapping, voice audible a hundred yards away—came to the back door to monitor the unpacking of the flowers.

The florists ferried displays from the back of their van into the house, dodging and weaving their way past a team delivering Christmas trees. Ingrid walked briskly, purposefully, toward the open doors of the florist's van. She swiped a bouquet of lilies and held it in front of her face.

"Where do you want this?" she asked the woman with the clipboard.

"That looks like a dining hall one, thanks."

Ingrid stepped inside, wiped her boots on the mat and strode across limestone flags that had been worn and warped by the centuries. Her leather pants squeaked. The boots clomped. She was too audible as well as too visible. She followed wet footprints into the heart of the house, and when they petered out, headed toward the noise until she reached a galleried hall with two long dining tables. Draped in white linen and crowned with enormous candelabras, each table was set for forty guests.

"Ah. Far table please."

She put the display down and asked the woman, who appeared to be in charge, if there was somewhere she could get changed.

"Are you with Maclaren or Ferrari?" she asked.

"Um." That was not a question Ingrid had anticipated. "Maclaren."

"If you ask for Sophie, she'll point you toward the green room."

Ingrid gave her a smile. "And where can I find Sophie?"

"She's the blonde. You probably met her when you came in."

"So... Front door then?"

"Best place to find her."

Ingrid left the dining hall and followed a corridor that led into a ballroom where a team of people wrangled lights around a twenty-foot spruce. The tree team wore dark green uniforms, unlike everyone else in the room who sported black shirts embroidered with the word Mayfair. Clearly no one was part of the regular household staff. She wasn't going to find Katja here. Opposite the Christmas tree, an enormous screen showed a live feed of an empty motor racing circuit. A clock counted down to the start of a race. The captions were all in Arabic. A Mayfair employee blew up silver and gold balloons from a bottle of compressed gas. A banner stretched across a balcony announced 'The Inaugural Jihari Grand Prix'.

Ingrid had grasped a vague sense of the layout of Uppenham Hall from studying the outside building. She headed through the west wing in the direction of the portico at the front. The corridor was lined with display boards showing photographs of racing drivers and Formula One memorabilia. Her Mighty Morphin' Power Ranger outfit was fortuitously apt. However, her cover was more likely to be blown: if anyone asked her a question about Formula One, she wouldn't have a clue how to answer. She needed to find Katja, and that meant disguising herself as a member of the catering staff.

Ingrid reached the entrance hall at the front of the house. A Christmas tree rose out of the center of a pile of presents, each perfectly wrapped in coordinated colors. The boxes, undoubtedly, were empty. A blonde woman stood in front of two enormous oak doors talking frantically on her cell. Ingrid glimpsed the forecourt through the open doors and saw the two Formula One cars under a lighting rig she'd spotted from the woods.

Ingrid marched confidently through the cold entrance hall and found herself in a corridor in the east wing lined with dark lacquered doors. She found a cloakroom and slipped inside. In the unlit gloom, she made out the shapes of several empty clothes rails armed with coat hangers. A large leadlight window offered a view over the forecourt and the driveway beyond.

She peeled off the backpack, unzipped her leathers and changed into black slacks and a white shirt. She attempted to smooth out the creases and ran her fingers through her short hair. Not that there was much that could be done with it after the bike ride. Helmets were the reason bikers kept their hair long, even after they started to go bald. Ingrid transferred the iPhone and credit card to her pants pocket and placed the bike gear neatly in a corner, folding the white jacket inside out so it was less likely to attract attention.

Two doors further down, she found the ladies' restroom and set to work with damp fingers and the hand dryer to revive her hair and freshen her appearance. Satisfied she couldn't improve things further, Ingrid pushed out into the corridor.

If Katja went to Tesco every week to do the grocery shopping, Ingrid's guess was she worked in the kitchen. From her limited knowledge of English stately homes—gleaned from watching BBC period dramas with her mother—she assumed the kitchen would be downstairs and at the rear of the property. Ingrid returned to the back of the house through the east wing, completing a circuit of the central courtyard. It was less grand than the west wing, but the wide corridor was nevertheless lined with ancient obsidian carvings on marble plinths. They appeared to be antiquities from Babylonia or Assyria, but Ingrid wasn't about to stop and check. The woman with the clipboard at the back door marched toward her, furious about something, her red shoes slamming into the stone floor.

Ingrid avoided eye contact, put her head down and tried to look like she knew where she was going. They passed each other, and Ingrid relaxed. A second later, the footsteps stopped. Ingrid's shoulders tensed.

"Who are you?"

28

"I'm Anna," Ingrid lied.

"Are you busy?" The woman wore a heavy woolen coat over a red pussy bow dress.

"I can spare five."

"Great. There's been a cock-up with the menu. It's all hands on deck, I'm afraid."

"Lead the way."

The woman didn't introduce herself, but Ingrid recognized her voice from the phone. It was Julie from Mayfair Events.

"What's the problem?" Ingrid asked.

"The fish was supposed to be trout. Apparently, it's going to be salmon." Julie's voice had an insincere twang to it, as if she was constantly doing an impersonation of someone she didn't like. "Need to reprint the menus."

"Who messed up?" Ingrid said, following behind.

"The caterers."

"Oh," Ingrid's pace slowed. "The household kitchen isn't cooking dinner?"

"They couldn't handle eighty." Julie trotted down the corridor past the cloakroom. "I had to get someone in from London."

"Well, eighty is a lot." Ingrid could barely cook for one.

Julie pushed open a door and flicked on a light. "Where's your accent from?"

"The States."

"And who are you here with?"

"Oh." Ingrid didn't know how to answer. "The agency."

Julie sucked her teeth but didn't say anything. The room had several desks, maps and calendars on the wall and a massive whiteboard displaying some sort of timetable or schedule. The housekeeper's office.

"Okay." Julie plopped herself down at a desk and turned on a monitor. "Hmm." She looked for the actual computer. "You any good with these things?"

Ingrid wasn't useless. "I can certainly give it a go."

"Really?" Her features sharpened. "That'd be great because I simply don't have time."

She handed Ingrid a USB thumb drive, told her to find the file called 'menu' and replace 'trout' with 'salmon' and print off eighty-five copies.

"Printers are the bane of my life, so very happy to make that your problem."

"And where do you want them? Dining room?"

"It's a dining hall, darling." She pulled a face. "Yes, that'd be great. But can you then bring that USB thingy back to me? Rear entrance?"

"Sure. No problem."

Julie had only left the room for a second when she popped her head back through the open door. "What did you say your name was again?"

"Oh. Um. Anna."

"Thanks, Anna."

Ingrid got the computer working and plugged in the USB drive. She scanned the file names and clicked on the one labeled 'guest list'. It was odd she hadn't seen anyone of Middle Eastern appearance so far. If the Al-Kareems were having eighty people for dinner to celebrate Jihar hosting its first Grand Prix, she would have expected the sheikh, or his wife, or one of his children, to be overseeing the preparations.

Ingrid scanned the guest list, looking for the Oxford students she had stalked online. She didn't recognize any of the names, so she Googled a couple of them. A minister from the Department of International Development. An executive from an oil and gas engineering firm. Not Samir's college buddies.

She opened the menu file, substituted salmon for trout, then looked around for the printer. It was an old, beige plastic laser printer. She turned it on and a series of lights flashed on and off as it warmed up. She closed the office door and went back to the computer.

"Jeez."

Every single name on the list, she realized, was male. Outside of Freemason gatherings and frat houses, that had to be rare. Even the Vatican had a few nuns running about. Eighty men. She pitied the waitresses. Ingrid hit 'print' and picked the first sheet out of the printer tray to check it over. She read the menu as more copies were spewed out. After the dessert there was a course of 'Fun & Games'.

If outside caterers were taking care of the food, she wondered how the regular kitchen staff would be deployed Ingrid left the printer rumbling away and slipped out into the corridor to find out. Down one wall was a mural of a village cricket match that started on an English village green and ended in a dusty park somewhere with a much drier, hotter climate. White-faced players in white linens played against a team of dark-skinned boys in colored T-shirts and shorts. The story of the British Empire in a single painting.

She was looking for a way of getting down to the kitchen, but the only staircase she found led upward. Modest, by the standards of Uppenham Hall, she presumed it was used by the servants. Surely that meant she was close to finding the kitchen.

"Yes?" The voice came from behind her. It was high pitched, but definitely male.

Ingrid bit her lip and turned.

"Can I help you?" The man was tall and slender with white hair and whiter skin. If all stately homes were haunted, he was Uppenham's tweed-wearing ghost. The brace of rabbits in his hand suggested he was the groundskeeper.

"Hi." She gave him one of her friendliest, cheerleader smiles.

"I'm looking for the kitchen."

He pursed his lips and flared his elongated nostrils. "Are you now?"

"I think I took a wrong turn."

"I'll say." He nodded in the direction over her shoulder. "You were heading the right way. Once you see the suit of armor, you'll start to smell it. Follow your nose."

The parquet floor gave way to limestone slabs. It was either a sign she was moving into the working part of the house, or that sections of the building had been constructed at different times. A decorative recess in the wall was indeed home to a suit of armor, and beyond it a stone staircase spiraled downward. There was a definite aroma, but she wasn't sure it was cooking.

The ceilings below ground were much lower. The walls were fully tiled, reminding her of the older Tube stations in London. Shouting bounced off the hard shiny surfaces. There were so many voices she couldn't even make out if they were speaking English. She inched along the brightly lit corridor and headed for the cacophony.

A figure crossed the hallway, scurrying from one room to another. The sound of metal hitting metal sluiced right through her ears, making her wince. Footsteps approached quickly from behind; she turned to see a woman in tatty clothes hurry past. She carried an enormous stack of folded table linens. Ingrid followed her, and the closer she got to the kitchen, the more distinct the shouting became.

"You know what a fucking *bain-marie* is, you moron."

"I can't fucking find anything in this fucking kitchen."

"Well, I fucking told you we should have done all the prep off site."

There was a louder crash as another figure, this time taller and broader, stomped past the end of the corridor.

"I said spotless! You know what that means? Fucking do it again."

Ingrid reached the kitchen doors and peered in. She flinched as a cook slammed down a stack of aluminum baking trays. He looked up at her and sneered. She carried on walking, and was soon knocked sideways by a woman carrying a heavy, flat wooden box.

"Sorry," she said. It was the Thai girl from the supermarket.

"Hey," she shouted after her, but the girl kept walking, staggering occasionally as she struggled with the weight of the box. "Hi."

The girl was going to drop it. Her grip was failing. She adjusted her posture, but it was still slipping from her grasp. Ingrid ran to help but was fractionally too late. The box slid out of the girl's hands and smashed onto the tiled floor. An entire service of silver cutlery clattered over the tiles, sending an avalanche of noise down the corridor.

"It's okay." Ingrid put her hand lightly on the girl's shoulder. "I'll help."

She bent down and moved the box to one side, propping its lid against the wall. The girl, shaking with fear, kneeled down and they both scooped up the cutlery faster than they could put it back in the box.

"What the fucking fuck," someone called out. "What's broken now?"

"It's okay," Ingrid kept saying.

The girl said nothing, though up close Ingrid saw she wasn't a girl. She was in her thirties. She had a thin red mark on her cheek, like she'd walked into a very narrow post.

"Do you remember me?" Ingrid asked.

The woman didn't want to make eye contact.

"We met yesterday. In Tesco?"

The woman shook her head and kept pressing the cutlery into velvet-lined slots.

"I was talking to Katja." Ingrid passed her a handful of spoons. She held her gaze as their hands touched. The woman was trembling. "I want to help."

The woman took the spoons and stretched to reach others. A figure was approaching.

"I need to speak to Katja again. Where is she?"

The woman kept her eyes on the floor. "No," she said softly.

"I can help," Ingrid repeated.

A heavy black boot landed millimeters from Ingrid's hand. She looked up.

"Who the fuck are you?"

Ingrid clambered to her feet. "Hi."

The man was broad and tall. His chef's whites made his angry face appear very red. "I asked you a fucking question."

"Well, that's good," she smiled, "because I came here to ask you a fucking question."

He flinched. He hadn't been expecting backchat.

"Are you in charge of the food?" she said, standing a little taller. The Thai woman picked up the rest of the cutlery and closed the case. Ingrid bent to help her lift it.

"Who's asking?"

"I need to check about allergies." Sometimes, lying was fun. "We've got two people coming with shellfish intolerances. Wanted to be sure you knew."

The Thai woman wrapped her arms around the antique oak box and hurried away.

"Was it on the list?" the chef asked. An Irish accent.

"I'm sure it was. I just came to check."

He rolled his tongue over teeth. An enormous crash cascaded out of the kitchen. "What the actual fuck?" He turned to go back. "There are no crunchy little crustaceans, all right."

When he had disappeared inside the kitchen, Ingrid followed the woman through an open door to a room with a large table where three girls polished plates and paired cutlery. Katja wasn't among them, though they all shared her gaunt expression.

At the periphery of Ingrid's vision, a door opened half way along the corridor. The man from the supermarket stepped through it, stroked his face and headed in her direction. She turned and walked away, keeping her back to him, hoping he would think she was one of the many agency staff in the busy house. He entered the room where the girls were and shut the door.

Ingrid checked left and right, then retraced her steps. She reached the door the man had come out of and tried the handle.

It turned.

29

Ingrid found herself in an airless room the size of a toilet cubicle. A bulkhead light illuminated bare brick walls surrounding an old-fashioned cage elevator, like the sort bellboys got a dime for operating in black-and-white movies. She entered and pulled the concertina grille across. The control panel only had two buttons, up and down. She pressed the up button, and the cart rattled as it climbed. With nothing to break up the brick, it was difficult to guess how far she was ascending, but when it stopped, Ingrid opened the grille as quietly as possible and stepped into a tiny lobby between the elevator and another door. She stood still and listened.

Ingrid turned the handle slowly and opened the door an increment. She listened again. Through the gap she saw a narrow corridor. It had a low ceiling and its once-white walls were the color of cooked pasta. Cold air rushed in through the crack. It felt like she was only inches below the uninsulated roof; it was ten degrees cooler than the ground floor. She heard the scurrying sound of birds in the rafters. Birds, or mice. She had to be in the servants' quarters, right up in the eaves of the house.

She stepped as softly as she could, but the floorboards creaked. Every few feet she passed a narrow door. An open door revealed a bathroom with broken tiles and a dripping shower head hanging off the end of a rubber hose. It smelled of stagnant water and wet towels. She tried the handle of a closed door. The latch sprang open to reveal a deserted bunkroom. Six people shared a room no bigger than a sleeper carriage on a train. Hand washed underwear and socks were draped over the ends of the beds. There was no sign of anyone. All the staff were helping with preparations.

She stopped again and listened. The loudest sound was her heartbeat.

Further along the corridor, she heard crying behind one of the doors. She didn't have a cover story, so saying anything was a risk. What possible reason could she have for being where she was? Ingrid rested a hand on the egg-shaped door knob. The brass was cold to the touch, and it sent a shiver over her entire body.

"Hello?" she said quietly.

The crying stopped.

Ingrid looked down at her hand. Above the knob was a key operated Yale lock. The door fitted in the frame so poorly it rattled. "Are you okay in there?"

There was no reply.

"I'm looking for Katja," she said.

More silence from the other side of the door.

"Do you know where I can find Katja?"

Ingrid waited for a reply.

"Who is that?" The voice was halting and soft.

Ingrid leaned in closer. She swallowed. "Katja, is that you?"

Again, silence.

"Katja, if that's you, I've got some news for you."

"Who is this?"

"We met yesterday." Ingrid paused. "In the supermarket."

"Go away." Katja's voice was brittle.

"Can you unlock the door, please?"

"No."

Ingrid heard movement beyond the door, the rustling of fabric.

"I want to tell you about your sister."

The rustling stopped.

"Krystyna."

After a long pause, Katja responded. "Yes?"

"She's had her baby."

"Yes?" Her voice inflected upwards.

"Can you open the door, please?"

"No, I cannot."

"Please Katja." Ingrid leaned into the door, speaking as gently as possible.

"I do not have key."

Ingrid couldn't believe it. "You're locked in?"

No answer.

Ingrid checked the lock. It was just a simple latch. It would be easy enough to kick open, but she didn't want to create any noise. She reached into her pocket for Jen's charge card. She'd never actually used a card to open a lock, but she knew plenty of thieves who had.

Footsteps thundered up the wooden stairs. Someone was coming. Ingrid glanced both ways, then slid the plastic rectangle between the door and the frame. The lock depressed easily, and the door swung open.

Katja crouched on a small double bed, holding the comforter around her shoulders. She had a long red welt on her trembling face. Apart from the bed, the only other furniture in the room was a Victorian washstand, a wastepaper basket, and a wicker chair draped with clothes. In the corner was a riding crop. So that's how the girls got the marks on their faces. Katja pressed herself against the wall.

"Do you remember me?"

Katja nodded. Her eyes were red from crying.

"I can get you out of here."

The girl moved her head slowly from side to side. She wiped her nose with the back of her hand. Ingrid examined the lock from the inside. The knob that would normally open the lock had been removed, but the night latch still worked. Ingrid latched the lock in the open position and pushed the door to. She leaned against it and raised her finger to her lips. The footsteps outside got louder. The two women held eye contact as they listened to them approach. Ingrid couldn't breathe. She dug her heels into the floor and pushed her body against the door, bracing for it to open.

The footsteps grew louder still. Ingrid felt them vibrate through the floor. They were right outside. But they did not stop. Whoever it was carried on down the corridor, stomping furiously.

"I spoke to your brother," Ingrid whispered.

Katja looked confused.

"You used to call your family every week. From Tesco."

She nodded.

"But you haven't called them since you phoned for an ambulance."

Katja looked over Ingrid's shoulder at the door, as if she was expecting someone.

"My name is Ingrid. I work for... the police. I need to talk to you about the motorcycle accident."

The comforter slipped off Katja's bare shoulder. Ingrid suddenly placed the smell: sex. Ingrid picked up the clothes from the chair and gently put them on the bed. She turned to face the door. "I won't look." Ingrid balled her fists. She wasn't just going to get Katja out, she was going to make the bastard who'd done this pay. "Get dressed."

Katja shuffled behind her.

"Your sister had her baby. A girl. Xenia. She is doing very well."

Katja sniffed loudly.

"You can call them later, when we get out of here."

"I cannot leave," Katja said. "They will not let me."

Ingrid checked over her shoulder. Katja was dressed, so she turned around.

"And if they know I speak to you, they kill me." Tears breached Katja's eyes. "Please, go."

Ingrid moved toward her and kneeled next to the bed. "I will protect you." She held Katja's gaze until the girl blinked. "And I will make sure the people holding you are punished."

Katja's head wobbled, as if she had lost all strength in her neck muscles. "But I did not see a motorcycle. I cannot help you. They will kill me."

Ingrid ran a hand through her hair. "Katja. I am not going to leave you here. Even if you don't want to talk about the accident, I will still protect you. What they are doing is illegal."

"But there was no accident." She wiped away her tears.

"Then why did you call 999?"

Katja's shoulders heaved, and a sob shook her chest. "Ayana."

Ingrid was not expecting that. "Who's Ayana?"

30

Ingrid sat beside Katja and waited for the girl to speak. Her instinct was to put an arm around her, or to reach out and touch the girl's hand, but Katja had had enough of unwanted physical contact for one day, if not a lifetime.

"Tell me about Ayana."

Katja nodded she wanted to talk, but she couldn't stop crying to get the words out. Ingrid needed to be patient.

"Whatever it is, I promise I will help."

Katja wiped her face with her sleeve. "You are American, yes?"

"Yes."

"So, you are not police?"

"American police. FBI."

Katja screwed up her mouth. "So how can you help?"

Ingrid nodded. "I work at the US embassy in London. I work closely with the British police. I promise, whatever it takes, I will make sure you are protected."

"You have gun?"

This shocked Ingrid. "Not today. Not here. Tell me about Ayana."

Katja sniffed. Ingrid looked for a Kleenex for her. She saw several used condoms in the wastepaper basket, but there were no paper tissues.

"Ayana was new." Katja wiped her nose with her hand. "Only been here two weeks."

Ingrid didn't like her use of the past tense.

"She was young, fifteen. No, fourteen. From Kyrgyzstan." Katja froze at the sound of floorboards creaking. There was someone in the corridor. "He will come back," she said. "If he finds you here…"

Ingrid crept over to the door. The footsteps didn't get any closer. "Keep talking," she whispered.

"Ayana thought she was getting good job, but…" Katja gestured at the room. "She fight. She say it not right. So…"

Ingrid pressed herself against the door to prevent it from opening. "I'm listening."

"They have parties here."

"Like tonight?"

"Yes. And when the guests leave… most of the guests, they make us… you know…"

Ingrid nodded. "They make you sleep with the remaining guests?"

Katja wiped away another tear. "And they take photographs."

Ingrid clenched her fists to contain her anger.

"So, they say, oh you are just prostitute, you will be deported. You will bring shame on your family, you know?"

Tears pooled in the corner of Ingrid's eyes.

"But Ayana said 'no'. She said her family would know they had made her do it. They would tell the police, they would tell the TV people."

An icy draft scraped under the door. "What happened to Ayana?"

"One month ago, I was cleaning. On the family's floor, where their bedrooms are. There had been party the night before, and there is always a lot of cleaning. They like it all done before they get up. This man, this American man, one of the guests, he come out of his room and he ask for help." She paused, letting out another sob.

Ingrid resisted the urge to offer comfort. Her job was to let Katja talk.

"Ayana was in his bed. He is going crazy. He is saying 'oh no, oh no', you know?" Katja bit the corner of her lip. "I look at Ayana, I try to help. But… but she is already… she is already dead." Katja sniffed hard. "He ask me to call doctor, then he put his clothes on, put his boots on, he put his jacket on." She wiped her tears away. "She is dead and he just leaves. Just go. Ride away." She flicked her hand toward the small window. "I don't know what to do, but I call for ambulance, only… Samir, he come, he take the phone and he tell me I will get killed too if I tell anyone. This," she gestured to the room, the bed, the wastepaper basket with used condoms, "this is because I had a phone."

Ingrid shifted her weight and took Marshall's phone out of her pocket. "I promise to get you out of here."

"How?" She shrugged. "They will kill you when they find you. Bury you with the others."

Ingrid searched on her phone for an image. "Others?"

"In the woods. Girls who got sick. Girls who starve themselves to escape. Boys who are too much trouble."

"And Ayana?"

"Yes."

Ingrid held out the iPhone and showed Katja a photo of Marcus Williams. "Please take a look. Is this the man? The man who killed Ayana?"

Katja took the phone. "It is the man, but he did not kill Ayana."

"He didn't?"

"Bashir kill Ayana."

Ingrid was confused. "If Bashir killed her, why was Ayana in this man's bed?"

Katja shrugged. "Maybe they blackmail him too."

Ingrid fell hard against the door. Katja hadn't witnessed the accident, but she had seen so much worse. "And who is Bashir?"

Fear flashed across Katja's face.

"Is he the one who takes you to the supermarket? Who did this to you?"

"Yes."

"And he killed Ayana?"

"Yes."

"How do you know?"

"Oksana, one of us, she see him." Katja held her hands in front of her and mimed placing them around someone's neck.

"And this man," Ingrid pointed to the photo of Williams. "This man thinks she died in his bed? He thinks he killed her?"

Katja pushed out her bottom lip. "Yes."

No wonder Marcus Williams fled. No wonder he had an accident on a bike he wasn't trained to ride. The lengths he'd gone to in covering up the hit-and-run made sense now. He couldn't risk being caught for Matthew Harding's death because he feared he would also be charged with Ayana's murder.

Ingrid needed to think quickly. Assuming Ayana's body could be found, and traces of Williams's DNA were still retrievable, it still wouldn't place him at Uppenham Hall on November nineteenth. Only Katja's testimony could. And that meant Ingrid's first priority was getting Katja to safety.

"Katja," Ingrid said, "I am getting you out of here tonight."

"How?"

Ingrid didn't have a car. "There is a truck," she said, "it belongs to the florist. I will get you into it, and you will hide. When the truck is outside the grounds, I will make the driver stop and you will be free." She didn't even know if the florist was still on the premises, but she hoped her plan sounded convincing.

"Then what?"

"Then we call the police and they will take care of you, and they will arrest Bashir and—" Ingrid stopped. Someone was in the corridor. Someone large and heavy and angry. The floor shook as he approached.

Ingrid felt the door move as he put his key in the lock. It didn't turn because of the night latch. He took the key out. Ingrid thumbed the latch, locking the door, and stepped to one side, flattening herself against the wall. She looked at Katja and raised a finger to her lips. The girl's eyes widened with fear. Ingrid heard his breathing through the door.

He tried the key again. This time the lock turned and the door flew open, shielding Ingrid from his view.

"Get up," he said. His voice was deep and thunderous.

Katja pushed the duvet off and shuffled to the edge of the bed.

"Take off your jeans."

Ingrid nodded at the girl, telling her to obey his instructions. From the other side of the door, he threw something at her. A pink box. Wax depilation strips.

"You're a hairy bitch."

Ingrid almost gasped with shock.

"I told you to take your fucking jeans off, didn't I?" Ingrid couldn't place his accent, but wherever he was from, his London vowels meant he'd lived in the UK for a long time.

Katja fumbled with her zipper. Surely he would not make her do it with the door open? Ingrid held onto her breath, desperate not to give away her advantage.

"Faster."

The floorboard moved as he shifted his weight and Ingrid readied herself. She reached into her pocket for the bike key. He took a step toward the bed. He was almost six feet. Over two hundred pounds. His shaved head glistened with sweat.

Ingrid mirrored his next step, shadowing him as he crossed the room. He sensed her and turned. She thrust her fist toward his face, aiming the bike key at his left eye. He grabbed her wrist but she twisted her arm free of his grasp. Her knee made contact with his balls. As he fell forward, she clenched her hands together and rammed them up into his jaw.

"Run. Get out!"

Bashir wheeled back toward Ingrid and he reached for her head.

"Go!"

The girl was too scared to move. She hadn't even zipped up her jeans.

Bashir clasped the back of Ingrid's head. He brought his own down sharply, aiming his forehead at hers. Ingrid bent her knees to avoid the blow, but he ripped a fistful of her hairs from their roots. Ingrid reared up, cracking her head into his jaw. Pain detonated in her scalp, radiating outward as he stumbled backward.

"You fucking bitch, you're—"

He froze. He stood motionless. Only his mouth moved, opening slowly. His hands reached behind his head as Katja brought the riding crop down hard against his neck another time, slicing the flesh. His blood flecked Ingrid's face. She raised her right knee, slamming it into his groin. A third thwack of the crop landed on the side his face, sending him down onto his knees. Ingrid drove a Dr Marten sharply into his ribs. When he grabbed his sides, she kicked again to cripple his fingers.

Katja's eyes were bulging with horror. The crop still quivered in her grasp. She couldn't believe what she had done. Ingrid grabbed her arm and pulled her out into the corridor. Bashir kneeled with his head on the bed, dazed and unseeing. Ingrid picked up the chair and slammed it into the side of his head. He slumped forward and fell onto the floor. Ingrid rolled him over and reached into his pocket for his keys. She pocketed them and pulled the door shut. It would take him a while to get out.

"Come on," Ingrid said. "Let's go."

"It is this way." Katja led Ingrid away from the elevator. "We have to get the others."

"Others?"

"I cannot leave them here."

"How many are you?"

"Eight."

How the hell was she going to get eight of them out?

31

"We have to be quick," Ingrid said. "A few kicks and he'll break down that door. You get the others and I'll come and find you at the rear entrance."

They raced down the servants' staircase.

"No, too much danger," Katja said. "We meet in walled garden. We talk about this many times. We hide there till you bring truck."

"How long will that take?"

"I not know where everyone is. Half hour, maybe."

"We don't have that long. Five minutes, max."

They reached the bottom of the stairs where Ingrid had encountered the groundskeeper and headed to the back of the house. Katja went to the kitchen and Ingrid ran outside to find the florist's truck. The cold air whipped inside her shirt as she rushed toward the parked vehicles. None of the drivers were behind the wheel, and all the doors of the vans and trucks were locked. Ingrid hurried back into the house to find anyone with a key to any kind of vehicle. It didn't matter what it was. If it had gas in the tank, she would take it. She reached the dining hall where the table was set and the floral centerpieces had been installed, but the room was deserted. Where was everyone?

Ingrid ran on to the ballroom and found the serving staff already in position, holding trays of drinks. The first guests were imminent. The last thing she needed was to be asked to help, so she ducked back into the corridor and opened the next door she came to. She stepped into a side room, a library of some sort, and examined the keys she had taken off Bashir. None of them were car keys. Damn.

Voices drifted in from the passageway. The first arrivals.

"...of course, if I had shares in it, I might feel differently..."

"...ah, yah, well, the best time to buy..."

"...was ten years ago!"

Ingrid waited till they had passed and opened the door. She edged out into the hall and walked as purposefully toward the front entrance. She had a good idea where she could get a vehicle. The closer she got to the lobby, the cooler the air became. Up ahead, she saw where the corridor opened out into the reception area with the Christmas tree and fake gifts. Beyond it was the corridor in the east wing where the cloakroom was. Inside the cloakroom, she was counting on finding a car key inside a pocket of a discarded winter coat. Pleasantries and greetings drifted down the passageway as the host welcomed more guests.

She couldn't walk through the lobby with the family there, not with Bashir's blood slashed across her shirt and a clump of hair missing. She needed to create a distraction. She searched for a fire alarm button to press but couldn't spot one. The chatter stopped and two guests left the foyer and walked toward her. She couldn't let them see her up close, so she tried the handle of a door and slipped inside another darkened room.

Ingrid leaned against the door and breathed heavily. Katja would be gathering the girls. Bashir would have broken the door down. She didn't have time to hide. The moment Bashir or anyone else noticed the girls were missing, the chance to get them to safety was gone. When the guests had passed, Ingrid checked the room for a fire alarm panel, and when she didn't see one, she opened the door. She peered down the corridor at the lobby. How the hell was she going to get on the other side without being seen?

Her options were limited. Run all the way back through the house and approach from the other wing? No. It would take too long and the risk of being caught was too high. Jump out a window and break into the cloakroom from the outside? Out of the question. There was only one plausible option: speed.

Ingrid ran hard toward the entrance. She fixed her gaze on the opposite corridor and accelerated. If she was quick enough, no one would have time to stop her. She didn't glance at the sheikh and his acolytes. She kept her focus front and center. Lactic acid seared into her quads.

Ingrid saw the wrapped boxes under the Christmas tree too late. Her toe clipped one as she leaped over it. It wasn't the empty prop she'd imagined and she clattered to the ground, her knee slamming hard into the stone floor. Stars pricked her vision. Pain exploded through her leg.

"F—" Somehow she stopped herself from swearing. She grabbed her left knee and squeezed her eyes shut. This hurt. This really hurt.

"What are you doing?"

Ingrid opened one eye and saw a man standing over her. She recognized him. Samir.

"What are you doing? Can't you see we have guests arriving?" His accent was upper class English. He was wearing a long white kandura robe and headdress. He did not offer her a hand to get up.

Ingrid couldn't speak. She panted hard.

"And what the hell is that?" Samir pointed to the blood on her shirt.

"I'm sorry—" she managed

"Ah! There you are." A woman's voice. One Ingrid had heard before. It was Julie. "What on earth happened to you?"

Ingrid thought about Katja, about how the girls would be assembling in the walled garden, and how she only had minutes to reach them before the plan was ripped apart. She needed to get out of there.

"I'm so sorry, Mr Al-Kareem," Julie said. Ingrid summoned the strength to get onto all fours. She immediately lifted her left knee off the ground. The pain was worse than an electric shock. "I can only apologize."

"Get her out of here."

Ingrid stood up slowly and tested her knee. It could take her weight. She looked down at the box she had kicked as if to scold it. "I need to clean my shirt," she said and turned toward the cloakroom.

"And fix your hair," Samir shouted.

Julie followed. "What on earth were you playing at?"

Ingrid didn't answer. She couldn't go to the cloakroom now. She had to get rid of Julie. Ingrid limped toward the office. "After you left, someone else asked for help," Ingrid said, her breathing still labored. "So, I left the menus printing."

"Who? Who asked for help?"

Ingrid pushed open the office door and hobbled to the printer. She scooped up the menus and handed them to Julie. "I was running to get you these. I hadn't forgotten."

Julie looked at the stain on her shirt. "Christ! What happened to you?"

"It's nothing."

"It clearly isn't. What the hell happened?"

Ingrid gestured to the stain. "It's animal blood. Somehow the meat got delivered to the front door." Not a bad lie, she thought. "I helped carry it to the kitchen.

"Meat? At this hour? That should have been here hours ago. Another bloody cock-up."

Ingrid picked up the USB drive. "Don't forget this."

"Oh, gosh. Yes." Julie turned for the door. "Do you have another shirt?"

"Yes," Ingrid lied. "I always bring a spare on jobs like this."

"Oh, that's good. Don't suppose you've got another pair of shoes as well?"

Ingrid peered down at the DMs. "You have a problem with these?"

"Hmm." Julie jutted out a hip. "They're not very on brand, if you know what I mean?"

Ingrid needed to end this conversation. She had to get to Katja. "Not sure I could have carried a leg of lamb in stilettos."

Julie tilted her head. "Good point."

Ingrid waited for Julie to leave. *Please, just go.*

"But perhaps you should stay in the kitchen tonight?"

Yes, let's send the young girls in the unsafe footwear into the lion's den and keep a woman in her thirties with combat skills and sensible shoes out of sight. Excellent idea. "Of course."

When Julie had left, Ingrid went straight to the cloakroom. The knee was sore, but it worked. A young woman was hanging up a coat.

"Hi," Ingrid said.

The girl's eyes popped at the blood on Ingrid's shirt. She raised her hands to smooth down her hair. "Julie is asking for you. Apparently, you are needed in the kitchen."

"Oh."

"Do you want to give me that?" Ingrid motioned for her to hand over the coat.

"Oh, um, sure."

The young woman left, and Ingrid plunged a hand into the coat's pocket and felt for a set of car keys. Empty. She checked the next coat on the rail and felt a jolt of elation when her fingers hit metal. She stepped over to the window where she had a clear view of the cars on the forecourt.

"Good evening."

Ingrid spun around. Two men, clearly father and son by their receding chins, were removing their overcoats.

Ingrid smiled at them. "Good evening, gentlemen. May I?"

She took their coats, still flecked with mist, and wished them a pleasant evening. When they had left, she checked their pockets. She searched all the coats and returned to the window with two keys to try.

The lever to open the window moved so easily she almost over balanced. She aimed the key fobs at the parked cars. The lights illuminated on Range Rover, sending a jolt of lightning through her system. Ingrid was about to jump out the window when something in the corner of the room caught her eye. The white flash of Marshall's bike gear. She grabbed the jacket and trousers and bundled them into his backpack, then slung it over her shoulder. She had to help her left leg get onto the window sill and lifted it through the open window. She jumped down into the flower bed, driving a spike of pain up through her knee. When the agony subsided, she reached up and closed the window.

The bright arc lights on the F1 cars made the surrounding lawn appear pitch black. It was impossible to see anything beyond them. She skirted wide, and when she was sure another car wasn't coming down the drive, Ingrid scurried through the blackness to the Range Rover. She climbed inside.

32

Ingrid put Marshall's phone in the holder on the dashboard, and it immediately lit up. It was five fifteen. She fumbled the key into the ignition, but didn't turn the engine on. She needed to think.

If Katja was right about Ayana not being the only body buried in the grounds of Uppenham Hall, making a carload of trafficked girls disappear was well within the Al-Kareems' capabilities. They might think twice about killing an FBI agent, but the moment they discovered everyone thought she was already dead, they'd murder her too. Ingrid scrolled Marshall's contacts and found her number at the embassy. If Uppenham Hall's security team intercepted the escape, she would press dial. Her desk phone would not be answered, and that meant there would be a recording of the crime that the Sheikh's private army could not easily erase.

Ingrid watched a car make its way down through the valley and park in front of the residence. A Lotus Elise. When the driver was inside the Hall, she turned on the engine, but not the headlights. She pulled slowly away from the forecourt and when she was a hundred yards from the house, veered off the driveway and onto the lawn. Keeping her distance from the building, she drove over the grass to the back of the Hall. With all the activity within the house, and the security operation focused on the

EVA HUDSON

perimeter, she was counting on no one noticing a blacked-out car moving slowly through the grounds.

She made out the rectangle of the walled garden in the deepening gloom and steered toward it. She crossed over the tradesmen's track and circled over to the rear of the high brick walls. Ingrid positioned the Range Rover behind the walls so it would not be visible from the house and killed the engine. She looked around the car. Four or five of them could squeeze onto the back seat. Another in the front, and two in the trunk. It was doable. She took a deep breath and opened the door.

The grass was wet under foot and it was starting to snow. Thick blue mist curled in the folds of the valley. Ingrid reached a gap in the high walls and stepped inside the kitchen garden. Pale stone paths extended between geometric vegetable beds protected by willow barriers. Bare fruit trees stretched their branches flat against the walls, and long clear plastic tunnels, like giant sea creatures, shimmered in the sharp breeze. Ingrid's deep breaths clouded in front of her face. An owl hoot stirred the air. The girls were nowhere to be seen.

The hairs rose on the back of her neck and fear prickled her skin. Marshall's shirt was no barrier against the cold. Where were they? Had Bashir found Katja? Ingrid took a few steps forward, her feet slipping on the worn stone. Something shifted at the edge of her vision and she twisted sharply. A figure stood at the end of a path. It was too murky to tell who it was, but the timid posture suggested it was one of the girls. Ingrid waved. The figure did not wave back.

Ingrid walked toward her. After a few paces, she saw the girl had dark skin and long hair. She wore a toweling robe instead of a coat. Ingrid waved again. The girl didn't move. Ingrid stopped and looked around, suspicious she was being lured into a trap. In the darkness, Ingrid made out other figures. She couldn't see their faces, but she recognized their postures as nervous and insecure. Ingrid picked up speed.

"Hi." She kept her voice low. "Are you all here?"

The dark-skinned girl shook her head.

"Where's Katja?"

Three girls stepped out from behind a bay tree. Katja was not among them. Ingrid waved at them and beckoned them to come forward. She reached out a hand to the girl in the robe. A steaming puddle spread beneath her feet. The girl was too petrified to speak.

"It's okay," Ingrid said. "It's going to be okay."

The others shuffled toward her. Two more emerged from behind a bench. "Where's Katja?" she asked again.

"She go for Chantana," one of them said. "She will not leave her."

"Katja's in the house?" Ingrid asked.

The girl nodded.

It was too risky to wait. She should take these six girls and get them to safety before Bashir raised the alarm, before anyone in the household questioned where the girls had gone. But she couldn't abandon Katja. Ingrid would not leave her to a fate like Ayana's.

"Do any of you drive?" she asked.

They all shook their heads.

"Okay then. The car is just over that wall. Wait in it and lock the doors. If I'm not back in five minutes, there is a phone in that car. You press the button on the top five times really quickly it will call the police. Understood?"

One girl nodded.

"Now, go."

Ingrid inhaled the cold night air and hurried down the path toward the Hall. She stood in another gap in the walls and observed the house. The lights were all on at ground level and a drumbeat of kitchen pans was audible through the open windows. The rear door was open and unguarded.

She sprinted over the lawn, knowing the white shirt made her visible against the dark grass. The wet grass clung to Marshall's slacks. Near the horizon, where silhouetted trees met a blue-black sky, a dot of light bounced around. A patrolman. Ingrid accelerated.

She neared the open door just as a figure appeared in the doorway. She pulled up sharply. Her heart pounded painfully. A second figure joined the first. Ingrid checked left and right, but there was nowhere to hide. She was target practice. Her chest heaved as they stepped out of the cowl of the door. They staggered down the wide stone steps and onto the gravel, their arms around each other. It was Katja and Chantana, the Thai woman from the supermarket. Ingrid ran to them.

Chantana's eyes were swollen shut. Her lip was split and blood drooled over her chin. She was close to collapse. Ingrid put an arm around her shoulders and another under her buttocks and scooped her up.

"It's this way." They dashed quickly between the walls and into the secrecy of the kitchen garden. "What happened?"

"Bashir," Katja said, her voice breaking. "He find us."

"He could have killed her."

"I know."

Chantana was so tiny, and so light, Ingrid was able to carry her easily. Her eyes lolled in their sockets. She was barely conscious. Katja opened the trunk and Ingrid lay Chantana down on the gray carpet, the trunk's interior light revealing the horrific extent of her injuries. The girls on the back seat gasped.

Ingrid swallowed. "How did you stop him?"

Katja's face hardened. "I had knife from kitchen."

Ingrid's eyes widened and Katja held her gaze. Ingrid placed a hand on Katja's shoulder and. "Get in. I'm taking you both to the hospital."

Katja scrambled into the trunk, positioning herself awkwardly beside her semi-conscious friend. Ingrid closed the trunk and walked slowly around the car, taking a moment to compose herself before climbing in behind the wheel. She checked over her shoulder. Five terrified women stared back at her.

"Are you ready?" she asked.

None of them could answer her. Ingrid drove over the lawn and maneuvered the Range Rover on to the track, then headed toward the tradesmen's gate.

"Go faster," the girl in the passenger seat said, but Ingrid kept the car in third gear and avoided revving the engine. When she was over the brow of the hill, she flicked on the headlights, illuminating flakes of falling snow.

"Faster."

How was she going to get the girls through the gate? Whatever happened, she couldn't let the guard look inside the car.

"Please hurry," Katja said from the back. She sounded desperate.

Ingrid glanced over her shoulder. "Get down, as much as you can. You too," she said to the girl in the front seat. "Down."

Ingrid switched on the hazard lights and changed down to second gear to increase the noise of the engine. She flicked the switch that operated the lights, making them dip and rise. The gate came into view. The guard, draped in a waterproof cape that clung to him like wet paint, turned toward them. Ingrid pressed her palm into the horn, blasting it and blasting it to make him know this was an emergency. It was the closest she could get to a siren and blue flashing lights. He raised both hands, telling her to stop.

She depressed the accelerator, making the engine roar. He needed to know she wasn't going to do as he asked. He dropped his hands and stepped to one side. He pressed a button on the gate post and the gates swung open. They opened inwards but were moving too slowly. Ingrid was going to smash into them. She was going to impale the car. She gripped the wheel and eased off the accelerator. They were still going to hit the gate. Ingrid squeezed the brake and the wheels slid on the wet road surface. The girls screamed.

"Come on!" Ingrid willed the heavy steel gates to move faster. She risked totaling the car and hurting everyone inside. She had to slow down. It didn't matter if the guard saw the girls.

"Come on!"

The guard looked at her, his mouth agape. She kept flashing the lights, but there was nothing he could do to speed up the mechanism. Ingrid slowed further. Her mouth was parched. Her heart had stopped.

Ingrid accelerated the moment the gap was wide enough. A crunch of metal reverberated through the car as the side-view mirror crushed into the gate and sheared off. Ingrid steered sharply left and onto the track. She checked the rearview mirror and when the guard wasn't in vision, she inhaled. The 4WD handled the mud and the ruts with ease, and she powered down towards Greenacre Lane.

Ingrid leaned over and typed 'hospital' into the satnav.

33

Ingrid rubbed her knee and shifted uncomfortably on the plastic seat in the hospital waiting room. Chantana had been taken in for surgery, and two of the other girls were being assessed for symptoms of advanced malnutrition. The others sat blank eyed, staring at uncertain futures. Ingrid had to leave before the police arrived. There was still a warrant out for her arrest, and she couldn't spend the coming hours in custody when she needed to track down Marcus Williams.

Ingrid put on Marshall's leather jacket for warmth and stepped out of the Accident and Emergency unit's main doors. She limped a little bit, still wary of putting too much weight on her left leg. A group of smokers were pacing up and down as they fed their habits, some of them attached to drips on wheeled stands. Jen's number was in Marshall's contacts.

"Hello, this is Jennifer Rocharde, I am unable to take your call, but you can try my cell…"

Ingrid called Jen's cell. It went to voicemail. It was six in the evening. Maybe Jen was on her way home from work? She called again, and this time left a message.

"Jen, it's me. I really need your help and I need it right now. Can you call me? I'm on Marshall's number."

The Al-Kareems, she realized, had used the same technique on Williams that they had on Katja. They had probably filmed him having sex with Ayana, who was underage, and then threatened to show his family if he didn't comply with their wishes. To be absolutely sure he did their bidding, they had gone a stage further and killed Ayana and let him think he was responsible. It was a classic recruitment pincer move used by intelligence agencies. If you can't dig up the kompromat, you create it. The question Ingrid needed to answer was why Marcus Williams was so damn important to the Emirate of Jihar. Ingrid exhaled hard. The son of one of America's most senior diplomats had, most likely, been recruited as an asset for the Emirate's regime. She needed to find him. Fast.

Ingrid returned to the waiting room where a nurse crouched down in front of the girls, asking questions. She noticed Ingrid and smiled. "You're the one who brought them in?" An Irish accent, a face as broad as a warrior's shield.

"I guess."

"We've made contact with the council—"

Ingrid must have looked blank.

"—They arrange emergency housing. And Thames Valley Police will be here later. They just had a change of shift and they want to send the right team. You know, officers who have been specially trained." The nurse got to her feet. She was even taller than Ingrid. "I'm sure they'll want to talk to you too." She gestured to Ingrid's knees. "Do we need to take a look at that? I saw you're limping."

"I'm fine, thank you." Ingrid peered around the nurse. "I just need to speak to—"

"Yes, of course." She smiled again. "No problem."

Ingrid nodded at Katja who stood up. They walked a few paces down the hallway to get a little privacy.

"How are you feeling?" Ingrid asked, immediately realizing it was a stupid question. "Listen, I want you to have this."

Ingrid held out the burner phone Jen had bought.

"I'm going to call it, that way you've got my number." Ingrid dialed from Marshall's phone and the burner trilled. "Here. Take it. You can call your mom, too."

Katja pressed her lips together and a single tear rolled down her cheek. She took the phone. "Thank you."

"I'm really sorry that I have to go, but I want you to know you can contact me. For anything. I don't have the charger with me, but I can get it to you. Or, you know, you can pick one up."

Ingrid stopped talking because Katja had started to shake.

"What will happen? To me?"

Ingrid scratched her jaw. "You mean immigration?"

"No." Katja's eyes spilled over with tears that she did not wipe away. She lowered her eyes and said softly, "I killed him."

Ingrid placed a hand on Katja's shoulder and lifted her chin with the other. "Did anyone other than Chantana see?"

She shook her head.

"Then today, say nothing. I will speak to one of our lawyers for you." What she wanted to say, but didn't dare, was that Katja might be better off confessing to the crime. She would likely get longer on remand than the deportation process would take. A good attorney would claim self-defense and get her off. "I will call you. I promise."

Katja wiped her face with the back of her hand.

"Listen to me. The Al-Kareems are going to prison. You are safe now. They cannot hurt you."

Katja's nose streamed.

"Come on, let's find you a Kleenex."

They turned back toward the waiting room when Marshall's phone rang. "I need to take this. The restroom is just there, okay?"

Katja nodded.

"Jen, hi."

"How come you've got Marshall's phone?"

"Long story."

"Well, I don't have time for that. Whaddya need?"

Ingrid stepped to one side as two men rushed in, obviously in search of a loved one. Their anguished faces were drained of color. "I need to find Marcus Williams."

"Who's that?" Jen sounded distracted.

"The ambassador's son."

"Oh. Him. Hold on." A swishing sound scrunched over the phone. "Well, that's easy."

"It is?" Nothing was ever easy.

"You want me to give him a message?"

"Jeez, no, absolutely not. What are you doing, Jen?"

"Getting ready."

"What for?"

"It's the ambassador's ball tonight. At Winfield House. Remember?"

Somehow, it had slipped Ingrid's mind.

"I can check the guest list, but I'd be amazed if he wasn't on it." Jen paused. "Come to think of it, you're on it too. You had an invitation on your desk."

"True, but I'm meant to be dead."

"I doubt very much if they've, like, rescinded the invite or anything."

Jen was probably right, as usual. Ingrid ran her fingers through her hair, calculating her next move. The chance to confront Marcus Williams was too good to miss. There was just one problem. Where the hell was she supposed to get a ball gown from at such short notice?

34

The perimeter wall of Winfield House curved inwards, guiding traffic toward a double gate shrouded on both sides by trees and shrubbery. A discreet name plaque belied the scale of the house beyond. After Buckingham Palace, it was the biggest residence in London. Ingrid rolled down the window and a uniformed Marine approached.

"Invitation please."

"I was told it would be left here for me. By Jennifer Rocharde. My name is Ingrid Skyberg."

Rain droplets hemmed the peak of his white cap. "One moment, ma'am." He strode back toward the gatehouse and conferred with a colleague.

The black taxi was Ingrid's third mode of transport in a little over two hours. First, she'd driven the Range Rover back to Burnt Oak and dumped it where she'd hidden the Harley, then she'd ridden to Marshall's house. Needless to say, he hadn't had an evening dress in his closet, but Ingrid thought she was rocking a Kristen Stewart vibe in his tuxedo and Carolyn's Doc Marten's. She'd found enough makeup in Carolyn's bedroom to pull together what the fashion magazines might generously call 'a look'.

The Marine approached. He looked at the item in his hand closely, then scrutinized her. "Here you go." He handed her the invitation and her embassy ID badge still attached to its lanyard. That meant Jen had successfully retrieved the Prius from the Ilex forecourt. "You'll need to show your passport to the guys in the house."

"Thank you." Ingrid was about to buzz the window up, but he raised a hand.

"I'm afraid you can't go in this way. Your taxi is an unauthorized vehicle."

"Oh, okay. So?"

He opened the door. "It's just a short walk."

Ingrid paid the driver using Jen's credit card and stepped out into the night, stretching her left leg to stop her injured knee from seizing up. The hum of the city murmured from beyond the trees, and their wet scent sweetened the air. When the taxi had driven off, Ingrid spoke to the Marine.

"Am I very late?"

"Ma'am?" He stood to attention.

"Has everyone else arrived already?"

"Yes, ma'am. Most guests were here by twenty hundred hours."

"Am I the last?"

"No ma'am. There are still a few to arrive."

"And how many of us tonight?"

"Guest list of three hundred."

"That's a lot of hors d'oeuvres."

Ingrid realized they had met before. He had been the guy asleep in the mess room when Estevez had taken her to the Marines' frat house. He let her through the iron gate and directed her to a marquee with a sign that read 'security'. Parked beside it on the lawn was a USAF Sikorsky.

"Who came in the helicopter?" Ingrid asked.

"First Lady," he said with a smile. "And about seventeen Secret Service agents."

"Principal Brady is here? I didn't know she was coming." Excitement unexpectedly inflected Ingrid's speech.

"Get the impression it was all need-to-know."

Inside the marquee, a welcome blast of warmth wafted down

from overhead gas heaters. A young woman with a headset and clipboard stood in front of two airport-style security scanners. She looked at Ingrid and smiled. "May I see your invitation, please?"

The woman looked disappointed when she read Ingrid's name. "I thought you might have been…"

"No, no I'm not."

"Because you look a lot like her."

Ingrid smiled at her.

"And we've had a lot of other movie stars in here tonight."

Behind the woman, three tall men in dark suits observed Ingrid. They wore earpieces and the serious expressions of Secret Service agents.

"Your passport?" one of them asked.

Telling him she had surrendered it to Thames Valley Police wouldn't help.

"I wasn't told I needed a passport. Only ID." She offered them her embassy security pass. "It's clearly me."

"We are operating enhanced security tonight due the number of VIPs—"

"It's okay." A Marine stepped through the metal arch of the scanner. It was Carlos Estevez. "I know Agent Skyberg. You can let her through."

"Corporal. Nice to see you again." Ingrid gave him a smile.

"Looking good," he said, grinning broadly at the tux.

"Ha."

"I wasn't joking."

Ingrid felt herself blush.

He instructed her to place her jacket on the conveyor belt to be scanned, and then guided her through the body scanner.

"Please stand with your feet on the plate and face the camera," Estevez said.

Ingrid did as she was told, then collected her jacket.

"Have a great evening, Agent."

She turned back. "Say, did you get your laptop back?"

"Yes, ma'am."

"And your phone?"

He tapped his pocket.

Her invitation was inspected one more time before a Secret Service agent let her exit the marquee and walk up the driveway toward the residence. It cut through wide lawns on either side and ended at a large circular pond bordered with stone ramparts. Every parking space in the forecourt was taken. The expected mix of Lamborghinis and Maybachs formed a semicircle around the ornamental pond. A sign pointed toward the overspill parking lot where the lesser cars would be parked. At the end of the line of prestige cars was a stand of five motorcycles, including Marcus Williams' Suzuki Marauder with its 125cc engine, L-plate and polished panniers.

For the second time that day, Ingrid stared up at an enormous and impressive mansion. Winfield House was not nearly as old as Uppenham Hall—it had been built in the 1930s by Barbara Hutton, the Woolworth's heiress—but shared its grandeur. Made of red brick, it sat three stories high amid manicured lawns and was surrounded by the noble trees of Regent's Park.

Two Marines stood on the wide limestone steps leading up to the open front doors. They held carbines across their chests and had Beretta M9s holstered at their hips. Ingrid wasn't sure if, like the embassy, the grounds of Winfield House were technically American soil, or if the presence of so many dignitaries meant the use of firearms had been authorized by the Home Office. Both Marines looked straight ahead as she entered the house. The vestibule was reminiscent of a boutique hotel lobby. Another security officer checked her invitation, then compared her face against the photo that had been taken in the marquee and was now on his screen. Satisfied she was who she claimed to be, he nodded her through into the reception room, which was dominated by a giant Jeff Koons' balloon dog sculpture, its polished pink surfaces reflecting the twinkling Christmas lights. A waitress proffered a tray of champagne flutes and Ingrid took a glass.

"Thank you. Is that the way?"

"Yes, go straight through. You'll see everyone when you get past the stairs."

The oval lobby was bisected by a staircase that ran up to the second floor. A rope draped between the handrails bore a small 'Private' sign. Portraits of previous ambassadors lined the room and Art Deco light fittings hung from the ceiling like space rockets clinging to the underside of an improbable moon.

The gentle noise of the party—a piano, laughter, the tinkling of glasses—beckoned her forward. Ingrid stepped through a doorway into a grand hall and drank it all in.

The hall was understated, with white walls and smooth columns supporting a galleried balcony that ran down the entire length of the room. At either end, the balcony curled into a pair of spiral staircases that descended to the dance floor. Guests leaned over the balustrade and stared down at the dancers and networkers below. An enormous Christmas tree stood in the center of the room next to a table groaning with gifts for the ambassador. The far wall was lined with glass doors that, in summer, would open out onto a terrace over-looking the gardens. The attendees were mostly familiar but unplaceable. Her spruced up colleagues had obscured their everyday identities with close shaves, false eyelashes and the glassy expressions of people on their second drink of the evening.

"Ingrid?" The voice was uncertain, wavering.

Ingrid turned. It was Maisie Millane from the counterter-rorism unit. Maisie's hand covered her mouth.

"Maisie, hi. I almost didn't recognize you. You look so, well, so glamorous."

Millane's expression was unchanged. She was as still as a photograph. "I… Oh, my God." She let out the air from her lungs, bending forward slightly. "We thought you were…"

"Ah." Ingrid played with the stem of her champagne flute.

"And you're not."

"Um, no."

Millane blinked rapidly highlighting how expertly she had applied her smoky eyeshadow. "What happened? Does Jen know? She was… in bits."

Embarrassment made Ingrid look away. "Yes, yes she does. Seems it was a prank by someone who hacked into my email."

"Oh, Christ." Millane held a hand over her heart. "I can't believe it. We were all so... shocked."

Ingrid grimaced. "Guess people are in for an even bigger shock tonight when they see me."

"I'll say." Millane took a long sip of her drink. "Bold choice, by the way. The tux."

Ingrid didn't know what to say.

"Not many women can pull it off. But you've got the... height."

Someone tapped Ingrid on the arm and she pivoted.

"See, it is her!"

Ingrid smiled at the ridiculously well-groomed man in front of her. "Mr Kerrison, hello. How lovely to see you."

"Oh please, you know to call me Tom. Truman come say hello."

Maisie Millane looked on with bewilderment as Ingrid talked to one of the world's most famous couples. Tom Kerrison and his husband, the actor Truman Cooper, were old friends of the ambassador. Ingrid had got to know them on a case a few years back, and they had been so grateful for her help that Truman gifted her the Triumph Thunderbird.

"I saw some nice bikes parked outside. Any of them yours?" Ingrid asked Truman.

"Sadly not. How is the blue bird?"

Ingrid wasn't about to tell him. "Still being appreciated, every second I ride her."

"Have you seen the First Lady?" Tom asked, instantly bored with bike talk.

"No, not yet."

"She is wearing the most exquisite ice blue Vera Wang." Tom Kerrison was a fashion designer, famed for shoes that sold for four figures a pair. "She really doesn't deserve to be called Principal Brady. She looks surprisingly elegant," he lowered his voice, "for a woman of her age and build. She can't quite carry it off, but you, Agent Skyberg, would look amazing in it." He prodded at the shoulder pad of Ingrid's jacket. "Is this your boyfriend's?"

"Something like that."

"Don't be fucking stupid, Tom," Truman said, his propensity for expletives evidently undiminished. "Obviously any woman who wears a tux like that doesn't do boyfriends."

Ingrid pulled a face. "Actually, I have even less success with women than I do with men."

"Oh."

That threw him.

"I'm really sorry, but you'll have to excuse me," Ingrid said. "I'm actually on duty."

"Ooh. How exciting," Tom said. He had always been the friendlier of the pair. "Say no more. But please, darling, Dr Martens?"

Ingrid leaned in and whispered. "Nothing I'm wearing is mine."

"Glad to hear it."

She made her farewells and deposited her empty glass on the tray of a wandering waiter. She declined a replacement as she needed all her faculties operating at maximum capacity.

Ingrid picked her way through the hall, passing a central bar where cocktails were being blended with flare, and reached the piano just as the crooner started the opening bars of 'Jingle Bells'. She scoured the room and nodded and waved at colleagues, some of whom did double takes when they saw her. Out of three hundred guests, she was only interested in speaking to one of them.

Ingrid needed a better vantage point and edged her way between revelers toward the spiral staircases that led up the balcony. She was halfway up when she slammed right into a man running down toward the dance floor.

"Hello Marcus," she said. "Remember me?"

35

"Yes, hi. Of course." His tone—practiced, over-friendly—was a sure sign he didn't have a clue who she was. "How long has it been?"

Standing on the step above her, he appeared even bigger than when they'd crossed paths at the rowing club. He wore his collar open, and an undone black silk bowtie was draped around his neck. On his face was the easy smile of a man whose future was assured.

"Not long at all," she said, stepping to one side to allow two women in high heels to cling onto the handrail as they made their way down. Marcus watched them as they passed, his gaze focused on their buttocks. "Just two days ago."

"Oh, really?" He sneered slightly. If he couldn't remember her, that obviously meant she wasn't worth remembering. He ran a hand over his thick wavy hair. "You'll have to remind me." He was already looking over her shoulder for someone more useful to spend time with.

"At the rowing club."

He glanced down at her. "Really?"

"In the parking lot."

His expression hardened. His Adam's apple lowered as he swallowed.

She smiled. "Now you remember, right?"

He placed a hand on her forearm and leaned over her. "I heard you were dead. Drowned in a sewer."

"Yes, seems lots of people are seeing a ghost tonight." She removed his hand from her arm and pressed it into the handrail, her fingers gripping his wrist. "I know you were riding my bike, Marcus." She stared at him, but he refused to make eye contact, focusing on the partygoers below them instead. "And I know you killed a man."

She felt his forearm stiffen. Below them, Ingrid spotted Jen holding on to her fiancé as he talked business with a counterpart from the Far East.

"You might want to shut your mouth or I will arrange for it to be shut for you." He kept his voice low. He did not want a confrontation in this environment.

"Your friends at Red Box already tried to silence me. Worked out well, didn't it?"

His nostrils flared as he sniffed. He looked down, as if searching for someone in the crowd, anyone who would come and rescue him from her inquisition. "You're making some wild accusations…" He turned to her. "For somebody with no fucking evidence." He tried to shake her grip, but she kept his hand against the rail.

"Oh, your Red Box pals did a fine job of destroying the evidence. Just not fine enough. How do you think I found out it was you?"

He shrugged, feigning lack of interest. "You're pissing in the wind, Agent. You've got no CCTV, you got no DNA, you got no photographs. No phone records. Whatever you think you know, you're never going to be able to prove it." He really believed his life was Teflon-coated, and that daddy's money and mommy's contacts would protect him forever.

Ingrid's fingers dug deep into his wrist. "Let's pretend you're right about that for a minute—and you are so very, very wrong— even if I couldn't prove you killed Matthew Harding beyond all reasonable doubt, this is the internet age, Marcus. The allegation you killed someone and walked away, that you didn't even make an anonymous 999 call, will be online for the rest of your life.

Those rumors are going to hamper your chances when you apply for a job or, heaven help us, run for office. Teddy Kennedy might have been president if it wasn't for Chappaquiddick." She paused. "I thought I might start by editing your Wikipedia profile."

"You're a fucking fool."

"I'm a fucking FBI agent, Marcus." She leaned in. "I know how to make a prosecution stick. I know about the threshold of evidence and reasonable doubt, you dumb ass."

He smirked. "Not that dumb. Recognize them?"

Ingrid followed his gaze. Standing in front of the large Christmas tree were three men with physical builds and immaculate haircuts and their geeky sidekick: John, Paul, George and Ringo. Ingrid's skin prickled. She had always assumed Marcus's father had employed Red Box, but if they were at Frances Byrne-Williams's farewell drinks, then it must have been his mother. Ingrid had always thought the ambassador was one of the good ones, one of the honorable ones. She shook the thought away and parked her disappointment for another day.

"They did a good job," she said. "I'll give them that. They doctored the CCTV footage at the embassy. They put a block on accessing your phone records. They made sure the ANPR data got lost in the system, and they even fast-tracked the forensics, no doubt because they'd planted evidence on my bike gear."

The veins in his neck bulged, and the tendons in his forearm were rigid. Ingrid pushed her shoes firmly onto the stairs, anticipating he might try to push her. The fact he hadn't was a sign he wanted to avoid making a scene. And if that was his weakness, she was going to exploit it.

"But, seems they didn't know about busses."

He didn't respond.

"Don't suppose you've been on a bus in London, have you? So, let me fill you in. There are cameras on every bus in the city. They don't just record the passengers on the bus, they film the road in front of and behind the bus too." Ingrid hadn't heard back from Cath Murray at the Met, but so long as she could convince Marcus she had the footage, that was all that mattered.

"So, I requested the recordings from busses driving near the embassy the evening you stole my bike. Guess what the footage shows, Marcus? Or rather, *who* it shows."

Ingrid caught sight of Frances Byrne-Williams on the balcony above them. As she moved through the partygoers, they bunched and expanded like a murmuration of starlings.

"I'm confused, Marcus."

He looked at her.

"I thought you'd paid Red Box to buy you some time, so you could get out of the UK and return home away from the threat of extradition. So why are you still here?"

"I'm going to have to have a word with Director Leery," he said. "Do you know Director Leery? His son is a very good friend of mine."

"He's the head of the entire FBI," Ingrid said. "Of course, I know who he is."

"He really ought to know there's a hole in the training for Special Agents. It seems there are two very important words you missed out on at Quantico." He tried again to shake off her grasp but failed. "Diplomatic immunity."

Ingrid reeled slightly.

"The family of an ambassador can't be charged with a crime." His smiled stretched into a leer. "And besides, you're not going to be alive much longer to make an accusation, are you?"

"You going to arrange for my drink to be spiked?" Ingrid released her grip and stepped up so she was on his level. "Seems there was a gap in your education too. All your life you've been taught that the rule of law bends before wealth, but nobody told you about me." She was now blocking the path of anyone attempting to make it down the staircase. She took a step toward him. "See the thing is Marcus, you didn't just kill one person, did you?"

He rubbed his wrist where she had held him. "I don't know what you're talking about." His right eye twitched.

"And the problem you've got is you only confessed one crime to mommy. Told her it was an accident, and she agreed that you shouldn't have to pay for the error for the rest of your life, didn't she?"

A figure started to descend the staircase.

"I wonder if she'd have had the same reaction if she knew about the girl in your bed."

Williams glanced nervously upward to see his fuchsia-clad mother just a few steps away.

"The *underage* girl," Ingrid continued. "The girl whose body still has your DNA inside her." She smiled at the ambassador before whispering in his ear. "And because you didn't want to tell your dear mama about the girl, Red Box didn't investigate. Which is why they didn't kill the witness. The witness I now have in protective custody." She turned and forced a smile onto her face. "Ambassador, what a wonderful party."

"Thank you." Frances Byrne-Williams was wearing a tight-fitting satin dress with heels that had to be killing her. "What an inspired outfit."

"Your son here was just about to—"

"Give her the tour," Marcus Williams said, sweat beading in the crease in his forehead.

"Excellent idea, darling. Have fun kiddywinks." The ambassador waggled her fingers as she stepped gingerly downwards.

When his mother was out of earshot, Marcus grabbed Ingrid by the elbow. "It's this way."

Ingrid wondered where the hell he was taking her.

36

By the time Marcus Williams guided her into a bedroom on the second floor, he had regained his composure. Ingrid strode straight over to the bathroom door and checked they were alone. She opened the closet door and checked that too, then made her way to the window.

"Who showed you the footage?" he asked.

Ingrid had her back to Williams and didn't answer. She tried the window catch but the security bolts meant she could only open it a few inches. The only way out was the way they'd come in.

"I asked who showed you the footage?" His voice was deep and trembling.

Ingrid turned to face him. She leaned against the windowsill and folded her arms.

"Are we alone, Marcus?"

"Uh-huh."

"You want to step away from the door? Stop anyone from listening in?"

"Oh." He looked behind him as if he might see an eyeball at the keyhole, then stepped into the middle of the room. His stride was short, hesitant.

The bedroom, though small, was decorated lavishly. Striped

in rose and cream wallpaper was complimented by a carpet of dusky pink. Scalloped sconces concealed wall lights, and the quilted coverlet sported a tulip design. It looked like an old-fashioned five-star hotel right before the renovators moved in and sold the fixtures and fittings on eBay. The larger rooms would have hosted movie stars and Secretaries of State, but this would probably have been used by an aide or an intern.

"Shall I let you in on a secret," she said. "I haven't seen any footage, but I can guess what the Al-Kareems showed you. A dirty little sex tape of you forcing yourself on an underage girl?"

He blinked rapidly.

"And did they tell you not to worry about it, because they would take care of it? No one would ever know. Am I close, Marcus?"

His bottom lip protruded.

"Unless—I'm guessing at this point that the sheikh leaned in real close—you didn't help them out?"

He took a long time before answering. "You think you're so damn clever." The words shot out of his mouth like venom.

"It's what they do, Marcus. They find—or create—a weakness, then exploit it. If it makes you feel better, you're not the only one. They threaten the girls with the same tapes, promise to show their families."

Marcus Williams ran a hand over his chin, then cricked his neck. He stood a little taller, and his entire demeanor changed. "It's what we all do. You've really got no idea, have you?" He stepped toward her, but Ingrid remained leaning against the window, her body relaxed. "We've all got a little store of secrets to keep dry until they're needed. That's how the fucking world works you—" He stopped himself from launching an expletive in her face. "I know dirt about you and you know dirt about me and that way we all get along."

"And we all get rich?"

"Precisely."

Ingrid puffed out her cheeks and exhaled slowly. She pushed herself to standing and went toe to toe with Williams. "We're not talking about a trade, Marcus. This isn't two hundred points on the Dow. You're the son of a diplomat, one of the nation's most senior diplomats. Your mother is privy to state secrets."

His jaw twitched again.

"And for the child of a diplomat, for a man intent on pursuing power, I'm really rather surprised you don't know that right now the United States of America is supplying weapons to Saudi-backed forces who are killing soldiers from Jihar in Yemen. The United States is fighting a proxy war against the country your school chum Sammy will one day lead."

His mouth curled down at the corners. "What's that got to do with me?"

"Really?" Ingrid was just a few inches from his face. She could smell the wine and hors d'oeuvres on his breath. "You don't get it?"

His nostrils flared.

"We're arming their enemies, Marcus. We're killing their people, and you... your mother is one of our most senior ambassadors, and you are beholden to a hostile power. You're compromised. And that means our nation is compromised. Do you really not realize how serious this is?"

He turned on his heels and ran a hand through his hair. "You're a fucking child. You call it compromise because you're a... a prissy, holier-than-thou, do-good government employee... but in the real world we call it influence. It's soft power. Heard of that?"

Ingrid pressed her lips together to seal in her anger. "Actually, Marcus, I call it blackmail."

"Oh, grow up." Saliva flecked the corners of his mouth.

Ingrid closed her eyes and held them shut for an entire breath before opening them. "They put a lot of effort into recruiting you, Marcus. They really, really wanted something from you. What was it?"

He paced the room, constantly flexing and clenching his fingers.

"They probably had your compliance with the sex tape, but

they went further, didn't they? They made absolutely sure you would do their bidding."

He shot her a look. "You have no idea what you're talking about. They did me a favor, didn't they? They took care of the girl. Of course, I'm going to repay them, that's the way the world works. The real world."

He kept using that phrase, 'the real world', as if it was a justification for his actions, as if people like her couldn't possibly understand the gravity of the choices men like him had to make while they shouldered the future of the planet.

Ingrid fiddled with the buttons on the cuff of Marshall's jacket. "How did she die, Marcus?"

He didn't answer.

"Her name was Ayana, by the way."

He sucked in his cheeks and stopped pacing. He bowed his head and looked at the floor. "I don't know."

"Do you not remember?"

"I'd had a lot to drink."

"How much?"

"What is it with your stupid questions? Does it matter how she died?"

"What matters is you don't remember. What matters is that even though you have no memories of putting your hands around her throat, you never doubted that you had killed her."

His lips moved, but no words came out. His eyes narrowed. "What are you saying?"

Ingrid pushed her hands into her pockets. "You didn't kill her, Marcus."

He ran his fingers through his hair.

"They filmed you raping her, they spiked your drink, and when you had passed out, they killed her and left her in your bed."

He swallowed rapidly, his breathing quickened. "I... I..." He sat down on the edge of the bed.

"They wanted your compliance so badly they made you think you killed a girl. Taken a life. But I've got a witness that says you didn't do it."

"You mean I didn't?" Ingrid let him soak up the news. He pumped his fists into his thighs. When he started to shake his head, she knew she had him. "The greasy fuckers," he said.

"But," Ingrid softened her voice, "you did rape her. And you did kill Matthew Harding."

He whipped his head around to face her. "But I wouldn't have, would I, if they hadn't... hadn't done *that* to me. Obviously, I wasn't thinking straight." His shoulders slumped forward, like a doll that needed propping up. "It was their fault."

Ingrid held her tongue and sat down beside him. With great effort, she managed to keep her voice gentle. "Marcus, I know the Al-Kareems targeted you. But what I don't know is why. What did they want you to do?"

He chewed the inside of his mouth.

"Marcus, why did they go to so much effort? What have they asked from you?"

He sucked his teeth. "It doesn't make sense."

"What doesn't make sense, Marcus?"

"Like you say, to go to that much trouble."

"What did they ask for?"

He shrugged. "Hardly anything."

"What was it?"

He turned his head and examined her face, trying to decide if she was worthy of the truth.

"Marcus," she spoke firmly. "It is possible that whatever it is will have far more dire consequences than the deaths of Matthew Harding, Ayana Petrova and Steve Thompsett."

"Who the hell is he?"

"A friend of mine Red Box silenced to protect you."

A flash of fear ghosted over his face. "I didn't know." His eyes widened. "Shit. Really?"

"Marcus, I probably know a lot less about politics than you do, but I'm fairly sure I've heard the commentators on CNN and Fox say the real damage to reputation isn't caused by committing a crime, it's by covering it up. Your coverup has gone so spectacularly wrong it's gotten two more people killed."

He kneaded his fist into his leg.

"My concern—and I appreciate I'm just a sanctimonious, prissy, do-good government employee who doesn't have your experience of global politics—is that while those crimes are devastating for the victims and their families, whatever the Al-Kareems have asked you to do may be devastating for our nation. Now Marcus, what was it?"

He got to his feet in one muscular motion. The steel returned to his eyes. "You really think you're so goddamn clever, don't you? You think I'm some privileged frat boy who's got money instead of brains. You didn't even stop to consider I might be helping people here, did you?" He was pacing again. "You're right when you say I'm my mother's son, and one of the things I've learned from her is that diplomacy comes in many forms. And it takes *years*. It's friendships like mine and Sammy's that broker peace accords. They don't happen at Camp David or The Hague, they happen in clubs and drawing rooms."

Ingrid tilted her head. "I'm listening."

"Tonight is going to see the start of peace negotiations between the royal family of Jihar and the militia in Yemen."

"How so, Marcus?"

"Because the thing they asked me to do, this crime you're so sure I've committed, was to bring one of their negotiators with me. That's all they wanted. They wanted an introduction." He jutted out his jaw defiantly. "See? Real. World. Diplomacy."

Ingrid got to her feet. She formed fists inside her pockets to stop herself from grabbing him by the shoulders. "Who did you bring, Marcus? What was his name?"

"Her name." He was point scoring.

"What's her name?"

"Why does it matter?"

Ingrid pursed her lips and walked up to him. "In my world, Marcus, that's far too much effort to go to get an introduction. In your world she's here for a quiet word, in my world she's planning something."

He looked shocked.

"What is her name?"

"Hatoum. Arwa Hatoum. She's a scientist."

"And who did she want to meet?"

"A guy from the UN's office in Riyadh." He paused. "Where are you going?"

Ingrid had reached the door already. "I'm going to find out what Arwa Hatoum and the Al-Kareems really want."

37

Ingrid took the stairs three at a time. Her knee flamed with pain, and she was glad she wasn't in heels. She scurried through the ballroom, but pulled up suddenly. Lexi Traynor caught her eye. It wasn't that she looked like a Miss World contestant in the ball-gown around; it was who she was talking to: Ringo. Heat bloomed across Ingrid's face. Lexi was the embassy mole. She had been working with Red Box all along. Ingrid sniffed hard; now wasn't the time to get angry. She carried on running until she reached the lobby.

"Agent Skyberg?" Carlos Estevez stood to attention.

"Corporal." She caught her breath. "I need assistance."

"Yes, ma'am."

There were two other Marines and three security personnel in the lobby, waiting for the guests to start leaving. They all looked at her expectantly.

"I need to find a guest. You took photographs of everyone on arrival, right?"

"Correct."

"Can you show me what Arwa Hatoum looks like?"

"Yes, ma'am."

Estevez led Ingrid down a corridor into a small, darkened office. Another Marine sat at a bank of flickering monitors with live surveillance streams from various locations around Winfield House.

"Hi," Ingrid said.

The Marine looked at Ingrid's attire, nodded, then returned to his work. The glow from the screens reflected in his Buddy Holly glasses.

"What was that name again?" Estevez asked.

"Hatoum. Arwa Hatoum."

He rolled a chair over to a desk and logged into a computer. "Is she on a list? Do I need to escalate?"

Ingrid leaned over him. "It's a possibility," she said softly. "Let's just check her out first."

"Who is she?" he asked.

"I'm Googling her now." Ingrid said, pulling out Marshall's iPhone.

"Do you know what time she arrived?"

"Nope." Ingrid keyed in Hatoum's name and the word 'scientist' but her connection was poor and the results were taking ages to load.

"Why are you interested in her?"

Ingrid rested a hand on her hip. "I've received some intel. I'm worried she's not here for the appetizers."

"Everyone here wants something. Okay," Estevez said without taking his eyes off the screen. "Here she is."

Ingrid looked at the monitor. Arwa Hatoum was about fifty years old, five seven, slim and wearing a black pants suit with a black hijab. She wore wire-rimmed glasses and a warm smile. "Can you circulate her description?"

"Sure."

"Anyone sees her, have her quietly detained. Discretion, you understand?"

"Absolutely." He picked up a two-way radio and nodded at the screen. "Click the sidebar. That's her profile."

Ingrid read quickly. Arwa Hatoum was a physicist who had worked for a Californian engineering firm in the nineties. No current employer was shown. She had entered the UK in July on a six-month visa. She was married and had three children.

Ingrid turned to the Marine monitoring the surveillance cameras. "Have you seen her?"

He peered over and looked at Hatoum's photo. "Not especially."

"Can you look out for her?"

"No problem." His speech was slow, like he was stupid or stoned. He was probably just trying to act cool.

Estevez put down the radio.

"Anyone seen her?" Ingrid asked.

"No, not yet."

Ingrid gestured to the screen. "Can you search guests by employer as well as name?"

"I can try. Which employer?"

"The UN. I also want to find a man who works in their Riyadh office."

"Hold on."

Ingrid killed her dawdling Google search and called Jen. It rang and rang. Ingrid was used to her picking up instantly.

"Come on!"

Ingrid was about to hang up—leaving a message was a waste of time—when Jen answered.

"Ingrid?" The self-satisfied sounds of the party filled the background. "Are you here?"

"Can I borrow you for half an hour?"

"Totes. Whaddya need?"

Ingrid gave her instructions to find the security room and ended the call.

Estevez looked up at her. "These are the people here from the UN." He jabbed a finger at the screen. "None work in Riyadh."

Ingrid's vision swum momentarily, making her dizzy. Either Marcus Williams had lied about what the Jiharis wanted, or they had lied to him.

"What should we do, Agent?" Estevez asked. "The First Lady is on the premises. If there is a security breach, I have to escalate. Who is she?"

He was right. "I am concerned she obtained her invitation by deception."

Estevez picked up his radio, ready to call. "What kind of deception, Agent?"

Ingrid scrunched up her mouth. Had she over reacted? Plenty of guests would have employed a little blackmail to secure an invitation to the ball. She reminded herself that other people's use of blackmail probably hadn't included murder. "I think someone was blackmailed to put her on the list."

Estevez pressed the call button on his radio. "Red One, this is Red Six. We have a situation, over."

Somebody yanked the door open, filling the room with light. Jen stood in the doorway, breathless, her shoes in her hand. Estevez leaped to his feet, the radio still clamped to his ear.

"It's okay," Ingrid said. "She's with me. Jen, Corporal Estevez; Estevez, Jennifer Rocharde."

They nodded their greetings.

"Red One, this is Red Six." He wasn't getting an answer.

"What do you need?" Jen asked, balancing on one leg to slip her shoes back on. "Nice outfit, by the way."

"Not my first choice." Ingrid turned to the other Marine. "Sorry, I don't know your name."

"Sergeant McWhorter, ma'am."

"Can Jen take this computer, sergeant?" She gestured to one on the other side of the booth.

"Don't see why not."

With four bodies and an excessive amount of electronic equipment, the temperature in the tiny room was shooting up. A bead of sweat ran between Ingrid's shoulder blades, making her shiver.

"Jen, I need you to find out everything you can about a woman called Arwa Hatoum. McWhorter?"

"Yes?"

"Can you track someone from the moment they came in? Can we see where she went? You got facial recognition on that?"

He sat a little straighter. "No ma'am, we don't. Not yet, but Estevez should be able to take you through her movements. I gotta stay on the live feed."

"Understood." She turned to Estevez, who nodded his

compliance even though he was still trying to get through to his superior.

"Red One, are you there? Red Two, this is Red Six, please respond." He wasn't getting anywhere. He lay down the radio and switched his attention to his monitor.

"Is it possible to open a window in here?" Ingrid asked. She took off her jacket and hung it over Jen's seat. "You able to get online?" she asked.

"Yup. Reckon I can remotely access the embassy's servers, see if she's on one of our lists." Jen turned and looked up at Ingrid. "Who is this woman?"

"I'd never heard of her until five minutes ago. Get me everything you can."

"Aye, aye captain."

"Agent?" Estevez turned his head. "You want to take a look with me?"

Ingrid leaned on the back of his seat.

"This is Hatoum entering the lobby—"

"Can we rewind? Can we see her arrive? At the gate, I mean."

"Um, sure."

After a bit of trial and error, Estevez pulled up the gate camera and scrolled back in time.

"Is that her?" Ingrid asked. Her throat was dry.

Estevez pressed play, and they watched Hatoum getting out of a black taxi—alone—and approach the gate. She was clutching a small leather purse under her arm.

"Can you zoom in? Get the plate?"

He clicked a few times, but the image was too fuzzy.

"Jen?"

"Yep?"

"You're not busy, are you?"

"Nope, not at all. Twiddling my thumbs here."

"That's what I thought. Can you find out which black cab dropped off a passenger outside here at..." She peered at the time stamp on the recording. "Seven thirty-two."

"No problemo."

"I want to speak to the driver." Ingrid placed a hand on Estevez's shoulder. "Okay, let's go."

Estevez followed Hatoum from one camera to another. They saw her passing through the security equipment in the marquee, which at least meant she had not brought a weapon with her, then walking past the fountain to the front door. The next camera picked her up chatting to the woman and a man as they entered the lobby. The cameras tracked through the hallway and into the oval room where she stopped to look at the photos of previous ambassadors, before disappearing behind the private staircase.

Estevez switched to footage from the main hall and scrolled to where she stepped into the reception. The hall was already busy with guests standing in small clusters. On fast forward, it was easy to spot a pattern among guests who universally moved counter clockwise around the large Christmas tree when they entered, before lingering at the display of gifts on the table, before moving on toward the bar and from there to the French windows overlooking the garden. Hatoum declined a flute of champagne on arrival, then moved more slowly, making her easy to follow.

"Ingrid?" Jen said.

"Yes?"

"Um, I don't know why you're, like, interested in Arwa Hatoum but I thought you might like to know there is an Arwa Hatoum whose husband was killed in Yemen last year."

Ingrid's stomach lurched so violently she had to grip the back of the chair for support. "Dear God." If Hatoum's husband had been killed by an American-made weapon, the threat level just skyrocketed.

"How did someone with her background get on the guest list?" Jen asked rhetorically.

Ingrid wasn't really listening. She was too focused on the action on screen. "Go back, will you?"

Estevez clicked rewind.

"There. Play."

They watched Hatoum approach the table of gifts. She stopped, examined them, then lifted one up.

"What is she doing?" Estevez said.

Hatoum took a small white box off the table, turned away for twenty seconds, then put the box back down.

"Did she take something?" Estevez asked.

"Let's assume she did." Ingrid ran her fingers through her hair. If someone had left something in the box for Hatoum, it meant she wasn't working alone. The air pressed in around her. "Corporal, you need to get back on the radio. This woman needs to be detained. Immediately."

"Yes ma'am." He picked up the radio. "Red One, this is Red Six, do you copy?"

"Jen?"

"Yep?" She swiveled around.

"I need Corporal Estevez here to tell you how to work this thing. We need to see who brought this white box into the party and left it on the table."

" Okeydokey."

Estevez put the radio down. "Lieutenant Preston is not responding."

"Who's he?"

"He's the one who can raise the threat level."

Estevez and Ingrid looked at each other. "Is he the type of guy who would ignore your call?"

"Absolutely not."

Something hardened inside her. She pointed to his radio. "You got another one of those?"

"Yes, ma'am."

Ingrid grabbed the handset and turned for the door. "Corporal Estevez, Sergeant McWhorter, you need to alert all security teams on site to the threat, and then you need to get the First Lady to safety."

"What are you going to do?" Estevez asked.

Ingrid swallowed hard. "I am going to find Arwa Hatoum."

38

In the main hall, the pianist was jazzing up 'Little Donkey' and the waitstaff circulated with cloth-wrapped bottles of champagne. A civilian security agent stood to one side of the entrance. He wore a black suit, black shirt and an earpiece.

"Have you seen her?" Ingrid asked.

"Seen who?" He didn't make eye contact and kept his gaze on the partygoers. He had an English accent and was built like a quarterback. With any luck, he was ex-military.

"Arwa Hatoum. There was a radio request to locate her."

He shrugged.

"Corporal Estevez told you all to look out for her."

"I didn't hear anything. The radio's not been working for the past ten minutes."

Not a good sign. "She's five seven, about a hundred and thirty pounds, glasses, hijab."

"What's that?" He kept scanning the hall and evading her gaze.

"Headscarf."

"Oh, that." He rolled his shoulders and stuck out his neck like a chicken. "Definitely not seen her."

He was not grasping the severity of the situation. "What's your name?"

He finally looked at Ingrid, granting her a sideways glance. "Rob."

"Rob, I am Special Agent Skyberg with the FBI. We have a security incident and we need to locate Arwa Hatoum and detain her. Repeat the description I just gave you back to me."

He turned. His lip curled. "You serious?"

She raised an eyebrow.

"Headscarf. Glasses."

That'd do. "You trained in detention techniques?"

"Nah, but if I see her, I'll sit on her." He thought he was being funny. Not ex-military, then.

Ingrid figured the civilian security was on a different radio network to the Marines. She pushed through the crowd toward to the table of gifts. It groaned with neatly wrapped boxes topped with expertly tied ribbons and bows. One even had twinkling lights.

A woman saw Ingrid scouring the display.

"It's beautiful, ain't it?" A southern belle in a red dress trimmed with white fur. "Real cutesy."

Ingrid smiled at her, reached right into the center of the table and picked up the small white box.

"I don't think you can do that," the woman said.

It was an origami box that came apart with a squeeze. It was empty. Ingrid threw it back on the table and raced up one of the spiral staircases to the balcony. Endorphins flooded her system, quickening her pulse and sharpening her vision.

"Excuse me." She pushed a flirting couple out of the way to get a better view of the room.

"And a Merry Christmas to you too," the man said.

Out of three hundred people, only a handful would have their heads covered. Surely it would be easy to spot a woman in a hijab? Ingrid's breaths deepened as she surveyed the room. Ingrid pressed the transmit button on the radio. "This is Skyberg. Is the First Lady safe?"

The receiver hissed with interference. "Still trying to locate her," Estevez said.

Ingrid scanned the dance floor. She zeroed in on a woman

near the French windows. Black jacket, black… hair, not a hijab. Ingrid drummed her fingers on the balcony rail. She pressed transmit again. "Jen, can you hear me?"

"Hold on." McWhorter's voice. "Handing you over."

"Ingrid?"

"Any luck with who delivered the gift?"

"Not yet," Jen said

"Stay on it."

Ingrid stood upright and turned her attention to the guests on the balcony. Maybe Hatoum would also want to make use of the vantage point? Ingrid checked the people leaning over the balustrade, then looked behind them where three coffee tables were surrounded by couches and upholstered stools. None of the people having intense conversations was Hatoum.

Ingrid didn't have time to waste. If Hatoum wasn't in the main room, that meant she needed to go find her. Within seconds she was back down on the dance floor and running straight for Rob the security guard.

"Where's the restroom?" She asked.

"The what?"

"The goddamn ladies."

"Oh, right. Down the corridor. You'll see the signs."

Ingrid powered down a white marble hallway lined with dark paintings in round frames like presidential seals. The radio bleeped.

"Skyberg."

"Thought you'd like to know," Jen said. "The First Lady has been located. The Secret Service are escorting her to safety."

"Excellent work."

"Still working on the gift giver."

Two women, arms linked, heads inclined, tottered toward her. Ingrid powered past them. "She must be bursting," one of them said.

There was a line of women outside the restroom.

"Hey!" one shouted as Ingrid ran in front them and barreled into the bathroom. Several women washed their hands and reapplied lipstick. Others waited for a cubicle. None of them were

Hatoum. There were five cubicles. Ingrid knocked on the far door.

"Hey, just a minute."

"Ma'am. I'm FBI. I need you to identify yourself."

"Fuck off."

"Ma'am, I'm serious."

The middle cubicle door opened. An older woman with skin as white as her hair gave Ingrid a look of chastisement.

"Ma'am," Ingrid said again to the closed door. "I need your name."

"For heaven's sakes."

It didn't matter, it clearly wasn't Hatoum. Ingrid rapped on the next door. "Ma'am."

"Oh, that one's out of order, honey."

Ingrid turned to a woman in the line. "Really?"

"I've been here ten minutes and no one's come out of there."

"You sure?"

Ingrid's heart boomed. She examined the doors. They were set into the wall so each cubicle formed its own little room. There was no climbing under or over them. Ingrid shouldered the locked door, and it rattled against its bolt.

"Anyone got a dime?" she asked. "Ten pence?"

Seven women looked at her like she was an idiot. Her radio babbled with static and muffled instructions.

"I need to open this lock." There was a groove in the mechanism she could twist if she could just get a coin or a knife.

Some of the women pulled apologetic smiles. "My husband carries the money."

"I got a fifty," one of the lipstick appliers said, "if you can make change."

"Never mind." Ingrid took a step back then aimed a Dr Marten sole at the lock, sending the door flying open to an intake of breath from everyone in the room.

Inside the cubicle, something was on top of the closed toilet seat. Ingrid felt her pulse in her fingers as she picked up a piece of black material. Below it was a folded black jacket. Ingrid was holding Hatoum's hijab. The edges of her vision narrowed. The sounds of the restroom pulsed in and out like a badly tuned radio. This was not good. This was really not good. She dropped the hijab and turned to the women. "You." She picked one at random. "You are in charge of making sure no one touches this, you understand?"

Ingrid didn't wait for an answer before dashing out into the corridor. She talked into the radio. "This is Skyberg."

"Go ahead." McWhorter's voice.

"I just found a hijab and a black jacket in the ladies' room off the marble hallway."

There was a pause. "Shit."

"You need to check the CCTV from outside the restroom. We need to know what Hatoum looks like now and you have to circulate her current description."

"Yes, ma'am."

"Ingrid? Can you hear me?" Jen's voice.

"Loud and clear, Jen. What have you got?"

"The gift? The white box?"

Ingrid slowed a little. "Yep."

"It was brought in by Marcus Williams."

It took a second for the impact to hit her. She stopped running. Fuck. Was Marcus Williams even subject to security checks? This was his London home, after all. That meant anything could have been in the box. "Do you know where Williams is?"

"Not currently," McWhorter said.

"Send out the order to apprehend him on sight."

"Roger that."

Williams might still be in the room where she'd left him. Ingrid found a staircase at the far end of the corridor and took the steps three at a time, her knee complaining with each footfall. She sprinted down the hallway as fast as her injury would let her and flung the door open. The room was empty.

"Damn."

It was time to evacuate. They had no idea what the threat was, and that meant they had no option but to get everyone to safety. Ingrid lifted the radio just as Jen's voice crackled through.

"Ingrid? You there?"

"What is it?"

"I have a description of Hatoum." She sounded serious. Scared, even.

"Go ahead."

"White shirt, open at the collar, black slacks, hair tied back in a ponytail." She paused. "Ingrid?"

"Yes?"

"She's wearing an earpiece and what looks like a fake Secret Service ID."

The floor beneath Ingrid seemed to wobble. The walls appeared to move. She knew what was coming.

"Ingrid, I think she's the Secret Service agent we saw escorting the First Lady."

39

"Where was she taking her?" Ingrid headed for the stairs.

"They were stepping into an elevator."

"Which one?"

"Like… I don't know."

"What does it look like?"

"Um, it's in a long marble corridor. There are circular paintings on the wall."

"I know it. Can you see on the footage which floor she took her to?"

"How would I tell that?"

"Is there a display above the door? Can you watch and see where it stops?"

"I'll get back to you."

Ingrid hit the stairs and started heading up. She lifted the radio to instruct McWhorter to get on with the evacuation. She was about to press transmit and take another flight of stairs when she looked again. That wasn't a pile of laundry, was it?

Ingrid sprinted down the corridor. The pain meant she limped a little. The laundry was a body in a white uniform. It was a Marine.

Her jaw swung low and her breaths became shallow. There was a bullet hole in the back of his head and a patch of carpet glistened darkly beneath him. Ingrid crouched down. By his feet was a discarded white plastic rectangular object. She knew immediately what it was. A 3-D printed gun. She pressed the transmit button.

"Man down, second-floor corridor."

The static on the radio seemed endless. It felt like it was coming from inside her ears.

"Skyberg. McWhorter here. You need medical assistance?"

She reached down and turned him over.

"Too late, you need to start an evacuation." She swallowed, attempting to lubricate her dry throat. "McWhorter. I'm real sorry, but it's one of yours. He's been shot."

Ingrid looked down at his still-pristine uniform and read his name badge. Lieutenant Preston.

"I'm sorry," she repeated. "It's Preston."

"Oh man." His voice was suddenly weak. "Shit. This is what we train for, right?"

"You have to start the evacuation."

"Yes, ma'am." He inhaled deeply. "Is his weapon still on him?"

His holster was empty. "Negative. We must assume we have an armed hostile."

Ingrid got to her feet and ran back toward the stairs. Up ahead, a man bowled out of the stairwell and into the corridor. He ran toward her, his navy blue jacket flapping like a cape. He wasn't slowing down.

"You need to turn back," she said, her pace slowing. She put out her arms to create a barrier. "Sir, you need to—"

In his hand was a compact semi-automatic. He took another step before raising his arm. Ingrid ran at him hard and reached up to grab his wrist before he could make the shot. She smashed his hand into the wall, forcing the gun from his grasp. He grabbed her throat, rotated her, and pushed her against the wall. His meaty fingers pressed down against her trachea. She couldn't breathe.

He didn't fit the Red Box mold. He was fatter, scruffier, darker skinned. He was Jihari. Ingrid brought up her knee and felt his flesh compress as she made contact with his groin.

"You prissy bitch."

Prissy? Again?

His grip relaxed fractionally and Ingrid twisted free. She bent down for the weapon, a Beretta M9. His knee cracked into her forehead, blinding her before sending her reeling backwards to the floor. She blinked at the paneled ceiling as the pain radiated across her skull. She heard the gunshot but did not feel it.

Then another gunshot.

She looked up at him. His eyes were wide, his mouth was twisted. The two holes in his white shirt were ringed with red. She rolled onto all fours and saw Estevez at the end of the corridor, his Beretta steady in both hands. Her attacker sank to his knees, landing hard before slumping sideways, streaking blood down the gold embossed wallpaper. He stretched out a hand for the M9, but Ingrid kicked it away.

"Who sent you?" Ingrid demanded.

Estevez kept his aim on her assailant and approached.

"Why are you after me?"

The man's eyes were blank, but his chest still heaved.

"Why?" Her jaw trembled with anger. "Tell me!"

He moved his lips, but no words came. He tried to spit at Ingrid, but his saliva dribbled down his chin. His breathing stopped.

"He's with Hatoum," Estevez said, holstering his Beretta. "There are at least three more of them."

Ingrid stood up. Bright lights spiraled across her vision from the kick in the head. She gestured at the broken 3-D printed gun.

"They're only ever good enough for one bullet," Estevez said.

"They only needed one bullet," she said, looking at Preston's body. "Then they took his weapon."

Ingrid crouched down and swiped up the Beretta.

"Preston's not the only casualty," Estevez said. "That M9 belongs to Private Sorensen. I found him on the terrace. One bullet in the back of his skull. There was a 3-D printed gun next to his body too."

She swallowed.

"Not sure how they got the bullets past us."

"My guess would be the little white box on the gift table," Ingrid said while checking to see if the Beretta was loaded. "Any other casualties?"

"Four operatives not responding," Estevez said. "Preston and Sorensen are accounted for. The other two are Secret Service."

Ingrid stared down at the dead man. Something he had said was bugging her. What was it? It didn't matter. She couldn't let it distract her right now. "The civilian security radios aren't working. Are the Secret Service on their own wave band?"

"Don't know. But it might explain why the evacuation hasn't started."

They ran toward the staircase.

"But McWhorter's on it?" Ingrid asked.

"Affirmative."

"Then let's get Hatoum."

They reached the top floor and Estevez held out a hand. He signaled she would go right and he would go left. She nodded that she understood and inhaled hard. This was really happening. Estevez counted them down on his fingers. Middle. Index. Thumb. They stepped up and turned into the hallway.

"Clear," Estevez said.

"Clear."

They were in a door-lined corridor that stretched right and left. It was less grand than the one below, and at either end, the passageway turned away from the front of the residence. They stopped and listened. The sound of the party and the piano wafted up from below. Keeping the M9 steady, Ingrid reached for the radio with her left hand. "Jen? You hear me?" She ran her tongue over her lips to moisten them. "Where has Hatoum taken the First Lady?"

"Skyberg. This is McWhorter."

"Yes?"

They stood still.

"We have a visual on the First Lady. Mrs Brady is on the roof.

Repeat, the First Lady is on the roof. Hatoum is with her. We do not know where her Secret Service detail is."

Estevez and Ingrid both looked at the ceiling. The First Lady was above their head somewhere.

"You thinking what I'm thinking?" Ingrid said.

"One of these doors has got to lead to a hatch, right?"

They walked slowly, Estevez aiming ahead, Ingrid covering the rear.

"You have snipers out there?" Ingrid asked. "In the grounds?"

"Two. If they're still standing, that is."

"But none on the roof?"

"Negative."

Ingrid and Estevez exchanged looks.

"Don't worry. We got this," Estevez said. His smile almost convinced her.

"Is that the US Marines' new motto?"

"In Latin, yep."

Ingrid slipped the radio back into her jacket pocket. "Why take her to the roof? It doesn't make sense."

Estevez kept both hands on his Beretta. "Dunno."

Ingrid tried a door handle. Locked. "If they want her dead, Hatoum could have killed her already."

They took another step.

"If they don't want to kill her, what do they want?" She tried the next door. Also locked.

Estevez did not answer. His arms moved in a narrow arc as he swept his weapon from left to right. Ingrid tried another door. It opened onto a small room that was empty apart from a bare bed. They carried on down the hallway. When they reached the end, they turned the corner together, weapons front and center.

"Shit," Ingrid said.

The wall ahead was sprayed with blood. On the carpet in the middle of the corridor was a body wearing black. They approached the downed Secret Service agent slowly. Her body lay at the end of a long streak of blood. She had crawled for over thirty feet before she died. A Glock 19 was still in her hand. Estevez picked up the weapon and tossed it to Ingrid. "Back up."

She checked it was loaded and tucked it into her waistband.

Further along the corridor was an open door. In front of it was what looked like a dark shadow. As they got closer, they saw the shadow was tinged with red. In the doorway was a body. He wore a black suit, fake ID, and earpiece. He had also crawled several yards. Both legs had entry wounds and the amount of blood indicated his femoral artery had been hit.

"What do you reckon?" Ingrid asked.

"Shoot out? Both got hit?" He glanced down the corridor at the Secret Service agent's body. "He probably died first, then her radio wasn't working, so she tried to get help."

"Has he got a weapon?" Ingrid asked.

Estevez crouched down to retrieve it as their radios crackled with Jen's voice. "Ingrid?"

Ingrid reached into her pocket for the handset. "Go ahead."

"Does the name Abdul Miah ring any bells?"

Really not the time for a quiz, Jen. "No."

"He's the ISIL guy behind the attacks in Bombay, Tripoli, and Denpasar."

"Wasn't he killed?" Ingrid was more breathless than she'd realized.

"Apparently not. He's been in Iraq." She inhaled deeply. "The thing about those attacks Ingrid, is they were sequenced. Guns first, then a bomb, or the other way around, then another attack when the emergency services got there."

Ingrid did not like the sound of this. "Oh God, is he here?"

Estevez shoved the dead man's weapon into his waistband and got to his feet. He indicated they should move back into the corridor.

"No," Jen said. "But he's Arwa Hatoum's mentor. Her social media is full of him."

"Jesus, what are they planning?" Estevez said.

"What about the evacuation, Jen?"

"McWhorter's working on it."

Ingrid ended the call and looked at Estevez.

"What now?" he asked.

"We leave the evac to McWhorter and we damn well find a way of getting up on the roof."

They tried every door knob until they came to a set of double doors. They stood on either side. Estevez reached over to turn the handle. "One, two…" On the count of three he pushed and Ingrid swung in, both hands gripping the M9. Lights flickered on automatically.

They had found the servants' quarters. The carpet was threadbare, and the doors were smaller and closer together. They took a side each and tried every door in turn to reveal small bedrooms and storage areas.

"Here!" Estevez shouted. "It's here!"

Ingrid spun around. An open door revealed a narrow wooden staircase that led up to the roof. Estevez's feet crunched on glass. "I can't find a light."

"Your eyes will adjust."

Estevez's footsteps made the old stairs creak as he climbed up into the darkness. A flash of the face of the man he had shot surfaced. That look of bewilderment before he fell. And then it came to her. The thing that had bugged her about him.

He had called her 'prissy', the exact same word Marcus Williams had used. *Prissy*. It wasn't the first time she'd been called it, but the way her attacker had used it sounded like he was repeating it phonetically, without understanding it. He'd used it like a swear word.

"Christ, no."

"What was that?" Estevez asked from inside the darkened stairwell.

"Sorry," Ingrid said. "Nothing."

It couldn't be a coincidence. The Jiharis must have listened in. Either Marcus Williams had taken her to a room under surveillance or the Jiharis had had installed malware on Williams's phone. They had been using it as a listening device. It would have been easy enough to do when they'd drugged him. She felt weak. They would have harvested his passwords, his emails, his contacts. If he'd used the WiFi in the embassy, there was no telling how deep the data breach might go.

Ingrid needed to get the entire system shut down. Immediately. She needed to find Williams and destroy his phone. Every second she delayed, the State Department's cyber infrastructure was compromised.

But before she could do that, Ingrid needed to save the First Lady.

40

"Skyberg?" Estevez called down from the darkness above her head.

"You see anything up there?"

"I think I hear voices."

Ingrid stood still and listened. All she could make out was the wind and the hum of her radio. She stepped further inside the stairwell. Her shoes crunched on the broken glass. A light bulb. Hatoum hadn't wanted to make it easy for anyone to follow her. Estevez' white uniform was just about visible in the gloom above. Ingrid climbed onto the first step knowing her eyes would adapt.

"Anything?"

"Not sure. Not anymore." Estevez was breathing hard.

Ingrid took another step. Her eyes were starting to make things out. The walls and treads were made of rough-hewn timber. It was an access point for contractors.

"What now?" Ingrid whispered.

"I tried the door. I think it opens, but the moment we make a noise—"

"Will be the moment Hatoum kills the First Lady."

"It might also be booby-trapped."

"So, what, we wait for the snipers?"

Estevez took a beat before answering. "If they could take the shot, they would have by now."

"Either they're dead, or they can't get a clean shot?" Ingrid said.

"No one wants to be the guy who shot the First Lady."

"So, it's down to us?" Ingrid said.

Estevez didn't respond.

"Okay," Ingrid said. "I'll create the diversion. As soon as you hear a commotion, ram that door open and take Hatoum out."

"What are you going to do?"

Ingrid inhaled sharply. "I'll think of something."

She dashed back into the hallway and tried all the door handles. The only open door she'd seen on the top floor had a body lying across the threshold. She ran back to it, the carpet oozing as her DM trod in the congealing blood. She stepped over the corpse and reached the window. Ingrid looked down to the forecourt below. The circular driveway, bounded by parked cars and motorbikes in front of the residence, enclosed a round pond with a fountain at its center. Beyond that, the gravel driveway retreated into the trees and the front gates beyond. Spotlights illuminated abstract sculptures on the lawn. She couldn't see anything that might explain why Hatoum had taken the First Lady to the roof. Three black-clad Secret Service agents burst out of the front door and ran across the driveway, onto the wet grass and moved into positions behind the fountain and sculptures. McWhorter had finally organized the response. The evacuation was imminent.

Ingrid tried the window. No lock. She lifted the sash and listened through the open window. A voice. An American voice. The First Lady's.

She would have had hostage training. Mrs Brady knew to keep her captor talking. Ingrid stepped back over the downed Jihari's body and raced down the corridor. If the First Lady was audible at the front of the house, Ingrid needed to get to the rear. She sprinted down the hallway and traced a route that took her to the back of the building. She winced with the pain. Breathless, she tried a door. Locked. She tried the next one. Then the next.

On the ninth attempt, a door opened. A small storage room stacked floor-to-ceiling with cardboard boxes.

Ingrid squeezed between the boxes to get to the window. She tugged on the sash and it opened easily, letting in a fierce blast of December. The wind turned her sweat-soaked shirt to ice. Ingrid stuck her upper body through the opening and looked around. The window was in a dormer, an arch-shaped box protruding from a sloping roof tiled with slate. Below her, a few hardy guests were bathed in rectangles of light from the French windows in the ballroom. They dragged hard on cigarettes She leaned out further and the radio bashed into the window frame, dislodging it from her jacket pocket. It skittered down and came to rest in the guttering.

Ingrid shimmied back inside then, leaning out, reached down for it. Even at a full stretch, it was several feet beyond her grasp. From now on, she was on her own. She checked the Beretta had its safety on and pocketed it. She would need both hands to get onto the roof.

Ingrid slid her top half back out the window and hauled herself through it until she was sitting on the sill. The Beretta dug into her thigh. The Glock in her waistband pressed into her back. She reached up, gripped the wet dormer arch and pulled herself to standing. Her knee buckled, but she held on. She glanced down at the ground. The smokers were oblivious.

The window frame was slick with rain and Ingrid's foot slipped. A burst of adrenaline fired through her veins. Her heart ricocheted inside her chest.

Easy, she said to herself. *Easy*. She took a deep breath.

Ingrid assessed her options. The sloping roof extended about another yard above the height of the window. The only way to get eyes on the First Lady was to climb on top of the dormer.

Ingrid moved her left foot out from the window sill and stepped sideways onto the slanted slate tiles. She pressed her shoes in hard and grasped the top of the window frame. Her fingers were so cold she couldn't grip properly, but tile by tile, she climbed upwards until she could hook a leg over the dormer. Her breath steamed with the exertion.

Ingrid hauled herself up and straddled the dormer. She took a moment to let her lungs recover. The rain pressed through her pants, driving the cold into her thighs, but it wasn't enough to numb the searing pain in her left knee. She pulled the Beretta out of her pocket and took off the safety. She reached up and placed it delicately on the flat roof a few inches above her head.

Here goes.

She squeezed her thighs against the dormer. Ingrid contracted her abdominals and sat up straight. She could now see over the lip of the roof. The figures of Arwa Hatoum and the First Lady were silhouetted against the lights at the front of the residence. Also black against the haze was the roof access hatch where Estevez was waiting. It protruded from the flat surface like a small garden shed. Hatoum held her hostage in front of her, jabbing Lieutenant Preston's Beretta into her side. The First Lady's Vera Wang dress billowed in the fierce breeze.

Ingrid wasn't trained to use an M9. She had never fired the weapon in her hand before. Her fingers were seizing up with the cold. Her target was eighty yards away. There were trained firearm colleagues taking up position. She was not the best operative for the job, but she was the only one with eyes on. She needed a way to separate Hatoum and her hostage to make sure she didn't shoot the wrong woman.

A loud piercing sound ripped through Ingrid's eardrums. She flinched so hard she almost lost her balance. The pulsating wail drove deep into her skull. She turned her head. An alarm sounder was attached to the neighboring dormer. Down below, the French doors opened and a stream of party goers joined the smokers. The evacuation was finally underway.

Hatoum was shouting. Ingrid couldn't hear what she was saying, but she did not seem panicked by the alarm. Ingrid peered down and saw security guards directing partygoers to the front of the building. She smelled smoke.

Oh, God. No.

This was all part of the plan, wasn't it? What had Jen said? Something about sequenced attacks. McWhorter hadn't set off the alarm. A fire had. The only people who would light a fire with three hundred guests in the building would be Hatoum's accomplices.

Shit.

Kidnapping the First Lady was just a small part of what they wanted to achieve, wasn't it? They had deliberately set a fire and when everyone was at the evacuation point, they were going to do something horrific, weren't they? A bomb? A mass shooting?

Still flinching from the alarm, Ingrid looked across the wet roof. Did she save the First Lady? Or did she warn everyone else?

41

The alarm drilled into her ear. She couldn't think straight. Ingrid picked up the Beretta. Her hands trembled. Her heart beat in double time. It was three stories down, and there was no pulley to grab hold of. She breathed deeply, releasing a funnel of steam into the night.

Ingrid rested the Beretta's muzzle on the lip of the roof to steady her aim and lined up the sights. Hatoum was too close to the First Lady to risk a shot. She had to separate them. There had to be something she could use.

She took her left hand off the pistol and dipped it into her jacket pocket. Her cold hands found the solid rectangle of Marshall's iPhone. It would have to do. Her fingers were so numb it was difficult to curl them around its hard edge. She couldn't drop it. She lifted it out and placed it jerkily on the flat roof. The muscles in her thighs, squeezing hard against the dormer, started to twitch. She had to control the shakes. She couldn't hit the wrong target.

Ingrid kept her right hand on top of the M9 and picked up the phone with her left. She pulled her arm back and hurled it across the roof. It skimmed over the asphalt and landed to the left of Hatoum who turned to see what it was. As she peeled apart from the First Lady, Ingrid aimed low and pulled the trigger. The recoil made her lose her balance.

Hatoum twisted around, her leg collapsing beneath her, as the roof access door burst open. A flash of light ripped through the dark. Hatoum fell and Estevez rushed toward the First Lady.

Ingrid dropped the pistol and felt for the radio, then remembered it was in the gutter. Marshall's phone was out of reach. She shouted to Estevez as he hurried Mrs Brady inside, but he couldn't hear her over the alarm. Ingrid had to warn everyone about a sequenced attack. She had to get to ground level.

Ingrid's legs were so stiff from the cold, she had to lift her injured leg with her hands. She levered herself off the dormer and rested for a few moments on the sloping roof. She fought to ignore the pain as she crawled back through the open window and into the store room. It was only then she realized she'd left the Beretta on the roof. She pulled the Secret Service agent's Glock out of her waistband and hobbled out into the corridor and straight into a spray of water. The sprinkler system had been activated. The alarm pulsed through her brain and her skin burned with the cold and the wet. Her lungs struggled to draw down air as she hurried toward the staircase. She planted a hand on the banister and vaulted down into the stairwell. She took the stairs four, five, six at a time ignoring the pain in her knee. When she reached the next level, she stumbled and fell out into the corridor where Preston and the Emirati agent still lay on the floor.

A dark figure ran toward her. He reached inside his jacket.

Fuck.

Ingrid tumbled and rolled across the carpet beneath the bullet as it ripped down the hallway. Ingrid straightened her arms and pulled off a shot. She righted herself in time to see Ringo fall against the wall. She fired again, catching his neck. Blood slashed across the wall. She didn't hang around to watch him thud down onto the carpet.

She practically fell over as she reached the bottom of the stairs and raced along the marble corridor on the ground floor. She skidded on the wet floor as she powered toward the front entrance. The alarm bounced off the white stone, penetrating her skull from every angle. Guests covered their ears as they jostled to get outside.

"Stop!" She pushed the wet hair off her face as she ran toward them. "Stop!"

She couldn't make herself heard over the alarm. She forced her way through and entered the lobby. Several men had given women their jackets to put over their heads, and their drenched shirts clung to belly rolls and previously hidden tattoos.

"Stop! It's a trap."

One woman turned to her but didn't understand.

"Stop," Ingrid shouted. "You have to go back inside."

She was met with a look of bemusement. She grabbed the woman's arm. "You've got to turn back."

"There's a fire," the woman said. "They want us out."

Ingrid turned to the man behind her. "Sir, please listen. You all need to go back."

Everyone wanted to escape the sprinklers. They wanted to get away from the wailing alarms. They were desperate to get out and Ingrid was unable to stop them. She didn't have a badge. She didn't have ID. But she couldn't give up. She barged through the throng to reach the front door.

"Hey, we all want to get out!" A woman tugged at her, but Ingrid struggled free. She needed to get to the door, she had to prevent them reaching the assembly point.

"Let me through! Please, just let me through."

Either they couldn't hear her or they didn't believe her. An elbow to her stomach told her to know her place. Ingrid waved to a security guard to get his attention. "Stop them. Please, stop them!"

She forged a path through the horde to reach him. He was also soaking wet. He scanned everyone's face, looking for hostiles.

"You've got to help me," Ingrid said to him. He was tall and angular, like a long-distance runner. "You have to stop them."

He didn't look at her. He had his orders to apprehend Hatoum. "This is an emergency. We need everyone at the evacuation point," he shouted.

EVA HUDSON

"Where is that?"

He nodded at the doorway. "By the fountain."

The forecourt was the worst possible assembly point. There were cars parked all along the front of the house. They were perfect cover positions for gunmen. What if the cars weren't hiding assassins, but bombs?

Ingrid pushed her way outside and shouted at the guests to get away. They stared at her but didn't move. They were taking their instructions from the men with uniforms and ID badges. She was going to have to try something else. The gun in her pocket bumped against her thigh as she ran. She pulled up.

The Glock might do it. It would certainly get people to run if she started firing. She reached in and fingered the hard metal. There were armed Marines. There were Secret Service agents. Pulling the gun here was suicide. She needed another plan.

Ingrid ran back to the door and drove through the swarm of drenched people surging out into the cold night.

"No one's allowed in," the guard said.

Ingrid shrugged off his grip and barged her way against the tide.

"Whatever it is, it's not worth dying for," a woman said.

A foot landed deliberately on top of Ingrid's, but she kept pushing. "Let me through."

She tugged at people's shoulders and forced her arms between them to make space for herself. She weaved to the edge of the throng, then broke free and ran down the marble corridor and powered up the stairs. With the Glock in both hands, she kicked open the door of the bedroom Marcus Williams had taken her to earlier. She knew there was no point in opening the window.

Are you really going to do this?

Think.

It was potentially a suicidal move.

Ingrid turned back and locked the door. She dragged over a nightstand and wedged it under the handle. It would buy her a few seconds when they came for her.

266

A shiver ran over her skin, starting at her left shoulder, spreading across her back, up her neck, then down into her waist. She faced the window and examined her reflection.

This is the right thing to do.

Ingrid took aim and shot into the glass, shattering her reflection. Between the pulses of the alarm, she heard screaming from outside. None of the snipers immediately returned fire.

She hurried over to stand beside the window, out of the line of fire. She aimed the Glock down at the huddled guests. From her vantage point she could see them spreading out from the front door, then drifting across the forecourt, not sure where to go. Directly below her was the cluster of motorcycles, followed by a row of polished, dark vehicles reaching toward the entrance. She needed to get them away from the cars.

A bullet whipped into the top sash, sending a dagger-like shard of glass onto the carpet. Marksmen would be at the bedroom door within seconds. This was her only chance.

Making sure she was well hidden, Ingrid aimed at a patch of gravel close enough to the guests to scare them, but not so close to risk injury. She squeezed the trigger. She fired again, and again, and again. With each bullet, more people started running. Some tripped over as they ran, pushing past each other to reach the bushes, some hid behind cars but most ran across the lawn. She kept firing. She had no idea how many rounds were in the mag, but she kept pulling the trigger as the snipers' bullets flew through the window and tore into the wall opposite.

Ingrid felt the blast before she saw it.

The force threw her from the window, across the room and slammed her into the bed. The room filled with white light. Glass shards filled the air like a shoal of whitebait. The explosion deafened her. She couldn't hear anything. She could barely see. Liquid ran down her face. Was she even breathing?

Ingrid staggered to her feet, then fell against the wall. She looked out of the window. Two people lay on the gravel; everyone else had gotten far enough away. She slumped down onto the floor. Vomit squeezed up from her stomach as she hit the carpet. She thought she might pass out. The only thing she could be sure of was the bomb had gone off directly below her. It had been packed into one of the motorcycles.

She didn't need to be told whose bike it was.

42

The paramedic picked the shards of glass out of Ingrid's cheek as a young constable from the Metropolitan Police looked on through the open doors of the ambulance.

"Really, it's okay," Ingrid said. "I'll be fine."

The EMT wore a headlamp and scrutinized Ingrid's cheeks for tiny reflective pieces. "There's another one," she said before her tweezers moved to the delicate skin under Ingrid's eye. "You're lucky. A centimeter the other way and you'd be in hospital."

"At least that'd delay my interview with the police."

The uniformed police officer rubbed his hands together to warm them. His nose was a seasonal shade of Rudolf red. "It's procedure," he said. "I think you can be sure of an easy ride."

After the explosion, Ingrid had waited in the bedroom for the Secret Service to arrive, figuring it was the best way to stay alive. She'd shouted through the bullet-riddled door that she was an FBI agent, that she had tried everything to get everyone to safety.

"There's a nightstand in front of the door. I'm going to move it, okay?"

She scraped it to one side.

"I'm now going to unlock the door. You hear me?"

"Step away from the door, Agent."

"I am unarmed. Repeat. I am unarmed."

Ingrid raised her hands, and the door opened. A Secret Service agent stepped in, his gun leveled and aimed at her head. A second agent scanned the room, his weapon moving through an arc in search of an accomplice.

"ID?" the second agent said. He was compact and lean, like a martial arts specialist.

"I don't have any. But I've worked with most of the people out there on the lawn for four years. Did everyone get to safety?"

He looked at the discarded Glock on the bed. "That yours?"

"No, sir."

"Whose is it?"

"It belongs to one of your colleagues." She paused. "I found her body on the top floor."

The two men prowled the room and checked the closet and the bathroom. The first agent turned to her. "You're bleeding."

Ingrid raised a hand to her face.

"You will likely need treatment," he said. "Unfortunately, I still need to detain you. And the Metropolitan Police will almost certainly need to arrest you."

"It's a formality," added his colleague. "We are aware you did not aim at targets. It's probable you saved a lot of lives tonight."

Outside the ambulance, the lawn of Winfield House strobed with blue flashing lights. Six fire engines, eighteen ambulances, and enough police cars to fill a multistory parking lot had responded. At least two helicopters hovered overhead. Three Jihari operatives had been detained, three more had been killed. In total, the authorities had counted ten bodies: three Marines, three Secret Service agents, the Jiharis and Ringo. Two guests had been airlifted to the hospital with life-threatening injuries.

Ingrid had requested legal counsel from the Bureau's pool of UK lawyers before talking to the police. The forensics would clearly show Ringo had been killed by the gun she had used and there would have to be an investigation. Then there was also the minor matter of the pre-existing warrant for her arrest issued by Thames Valley Police. She knew the risk of prosecution was low, but there would be a lot of explaining before she was released.

The constable stood a little straighter. "Oh," he said. "Oh." He straightened his uniform.

A Secret Service agent appeared at the open doors and without talking to the police officer looked inside the ambulance. His jacket was not wet, but his white collar was sprayed with blood. "Are you Skyberg?" he asked.

"Yes I am."

"Excuse me," he said to the EMT, "I'm going to have to ask you to step outside."

She tilted her head to one side. "This is my ambulance, mate."

"Ma'am, it will just be a for a few minutes."

Ingrid and the EMT shuffled forward.

"Not you, Skyberg."

"Oh."

Behind him, the police officer was smiling. When the paramedic jumped out, her mouth widened into a capital O.

"One moment," the agent said before stepping back. "Ma'am."

Ingrid stared out at the flashing lights, unsure what was happening. A stretcher bearing a body bag was carried across the lawn by two London Ambulance Service crew. She wondered if it was Hatoum.

"Agent Skyberg?"

Ingrid recognized her face immediately and stood up, hitting her head on a storage cabinet. "Ma'am?"

"Sit down, please."

The First Lady grabbed the hand rail and climbed onboard, shooing away the offer of help from her security detail. Ingrid rubbed the back of her head. It wasn't too hard a hit.

Wrapped in a blanket with her wet gray hair scraped off her face, the First Lady still managed a smile. She was much less austere in person than she appeared in photos. More of a favorite grade school teacher than a forbidding Principal. "May I?" she asked, sitting down on the cot. Beneath the blanket, the hem of her sapphire satin dress was slashed with blood. She held out a quivering hand and Ingrid shook it.

"It's an honor, ma'am," Ingrid said, her voice desperately in need of a mouthful of water.

"The honor is entirely mine." Mrs Brady pressed her lips together, contorting her familiar features, before leaning forward. "Corporal Estevez tells me I owe you my life. That you were the one who fired the first shot?"

Ingrid nodded.

"I also hear mine is not the only life you saved." Her deep brown eyes glistened with tears. "Tonight would have been a far greater tragedy had it not been for you. This will not be forgotten. Now," she said, composing herself. "Have you got everything you need? Can I get you some supplies?" As she pushed a strand of wet hair behind her ears, Ingrid noticed her earrings.

"Ma'am, thank you. I am being taken care of. How are you?"

She seemed genuinely surprised at the question. Her shoulders moved in the tiniest of shrugs. "Shaken, I guess." Mrs Brady looked down at her hands. "We've all seen some awful things tonight." Her bottom lip quivered as she relived the horrors of the preceding hours. Ingrid sensed that Ringo's death, the way his neck had been ripped open by her bullet, would never leave her.

"Ma'am?"

"Yes?"

"Why did Hatoum take you to the roof? I've been trying to work it out."

The First Lady widened her eyes, then nodded. She swallowed. "She said she wanted me to know what it was like." She blinked back tears. "Hatoum said she had seen too many people torn apart by bombs. She wanted me to bear witness. Then, having witnessed the destruction, she wanted me to phone my husband and tell him to stop our country selling arms to their enemy."

Ingrid shook her head. "Really?"

"If he refused, which he would have done, of course, she would have put a gun to my temple and tried to bargain me for a deal." Her voice trailed off and she inhaled sharply to sniff back more tears. "It would never have worked."

They fell silent as they both recalled the images they knew they would never unsee.

"Ma'am?"

"Yes?"

"Are you visiting other people? Here? Tonight?"

"I'm pretty sure the Secret Service want to get me out of here."

"If you can, can you please try to find a woman called Jennifer Rocharde."

The First Lady inclined her head. "Go on."

"She deserves so much credit. People like me, we're trained for this, but Jen is my assistant and—by the way, she is a huge fan of yours—she was so cool under pressure tonight. If it wasn't for her on the other end of the radio, I would never have known there might be a bomb." Ingrid realized she was crying. Tears fell like acid into the cuts on her cheek and it was hard to get the words past the lump in her throat. "She's… she's amazing. If you can…"

"I will, I promise." Her Secret Service detail was making noises. "Thank you again, Agent. You must let me know if there is something I can do for you." She shuffled toward the edge of the cot and stood to go.

"Actually," Ingrid managed, wiping her face with her sodden sleeve. "There is."

The First Lady turned back, more than a little surprised. "Yes?"

"This is going to sound dumb."

"Okay."

"And totally inappropriate."

"Probably not okay." Her smile twisted into awkwardness.

"It's for Jen, you understand. Christ," Ingrid was burning with embarrassment. "I can't believe I'm going to ask you, but Jen is getting married, and I know she wants to wear a pair of earrings like yours." Ingrid sat a little straighter. "Could you tell me where you got them?"

The First Lady's features pinched together, then cracked into a wide-open smile that never appeared in photoshoots for magazines. "Oh honey," she said. "I don't think either of us can believe you just asked me that." She reached up and unfastened the earrings. "You had me really worried there for a second. Here," she offered them to Ingrid. "You give them to her."

"Really?"

The First Lady took a step toward her and opened Ingrid's palm.

"Thank you, ma'am." Ingrid gripped them in her fist as the First Lady climbed out of the ambulance, reluctantly accepting assistance from her Secret Service agent. Suddenly overcome, Ingrid bent forward and buried her head between her knees. The sobs made her entire body heave and when she opened her eyes again, the constable was once again standing in front of the doors. He had an apologetic look on his face.

"Is it time?" Ingrid asked.

"'Fraid so."

"Shall we get it over with then?"

"Like I say, it's a formality. It'll all get sorted, I'm sure. You've got nothing to worry about."

Ingrid nodded. "Go on then."

He sniffed in hard. "Ingrid Skyberg, I am arresting you on suspicion of unlawful use of a firearm. You do not have to say anything, but it may harm your defense if you do not mention when questioned something you later rely on in court. Anything you do say may be given in evidence."

43

"Ladies and gentlemen, I thought I'd give you a little update from the cockpit." The pilot's British accent was authoritative and reassuring. "We've made good time across the pond and we should be on the ground in about thirty-five minutes. The weather in Washington is a bracing minus five with light snowfall, so I hope your thermals aren't in the hold. Cabin crew, prepare for landing."

The other passengers started shifting in their seats, looking out the windows to see if they could spot the familiar shape of Long Island or Chesapeake Bay. Others got to their feet for a stretch before the seatbelt was turned on. Ingrid checked her new watch. The timing had to be precise.

When the digits clicked over to 23:00, GMT, Ingrid unclicked her seatbelt, stood up and stretched out her knee. The cortisone injection had done an amazing job. She walked toward the curtain separating economy from business class. Immediately, a member of the cabin crew approached.

"Can I help you?"

Ingrid raised her finger to her mouth and showed the woman her ID.

"Oh, gosh, it's you. You were in the paper, weren't you?"

Ingrid managed a smile.

"God, if we'd realized… Well…"

Ingrid had deliberately asked to be booked into economy. She would have been forced to decline an upgrade if they'd offered.

"It's an honor to have you onboard."

Ingrid didn't know what to say. She was going to have to get used to the hero treatment. There was already talk of a medal from the director of the FBI and a reception at the White House. The prospect of resigning had become a little more… distant.

"I just need to…" Ingrid pointed toward the business class passengers. "Five minutes."

"Of course."

Three rows down, Ingrid slipped into an empty seat. The man next to the window was watching the latest Tom Cruise movie. Annoyed his space had been invaded, he turned. A scowl was already etched onto his mouth.

"Hello, Marcus."

His face hardened. He removed the headphones.

"Enjoying the movie?"

Marcus Williams looked like he wanted to spit at her. Ingrid clipped herself in and made a show of getting comfortable.

"Because I've got something else you should watch. Much more compelling than Mission Unbelievable. Wanna see it?" She fetched her brand-new iPhone out of her back pocket.

"What the fuck do you think you're doing?" he said, keeping his voice low.

She found the footage and held the phone for him to look at. "Recognize her?"

He peered briefly at the screen. "I asked you a question," he said.

"I also asked you one." She jabbed the phone in his direction. "Take a look."

He barely glanced at the video. "Don't care." He rolled his tongue over his teeth, making his cheeks bulge.

"Oh, you should," she smiled. "You really should. If I turn the sound up, you'd hear your name being spoken a lot. An awful lot."

Anxious, he took a slug of his whisky and peered at the screen.

"Her name is Katja. You probably don't remember her, either because you only met her once, very briefly, and you were a bit distracted. Or because she was a servant."

He withdrew, pressing his back into the armrest.

"She was the girl you found in the hallway at Uppenham Hall. Remember now? You probably do because it was the day you woke up to find a dead girl in your bed."

Marcus glanced around nervously, but no one was paying them any attention. No one was coming to his rescue.

"Can you see where Katja is, Marcus?"

His expression was one of utter disdain.

"That's a police interview room. She's giving her testimony to Thames Valley Police." She pressed pause on the video. "She can put you at Uppenham Hall just minutes before you killed Matthew Harding on the bike you stole from me." Ingrid put the phone away. "Oh. Nearly forgot. Now that your coverup is an international incident, guess what?"

Fury furrowed his brow. His skin glistened with sweat.

"Not going to guess? Don't want to play?"

He rubbed his nose.

"Okay, I'll tell you." Ingrid was enjoying this a little too much. "Your phone records have—miraculously—been found. It took MI5 to get them. The ANPR images from outside the embassy have materialized too. One piece of evidence puts you in the vicinity of the accident, and the other shows you riding a bike you don't have a permit for. So—"

"So nothing." He jutted out his jaw as his nostrils flared. "Diplomatic immunity, remember?"

Ingrid had to stop herself from smiling. "Ah, yes. About that. When was the last time you spoke to your mother?"

His eyes popped. Fear narrowed his mouth.

"Because it would have been the last time for a while. At twenty-three hundred hours GMT, so," she looked her watch for emphasis, "about two minutes ago, she was taken into custody—"

"You fucking—" He reached for her throat, but Ingrid grabbed his wrist and forced his hand back onto his own knee.

She plastered an insincere smile on her face. "Your lovely mom has just been charged as an accessory to conspiracy and collusion. She thought she could end her career with an unblemished record, but I don't think any jury is going to look kindly on a senior diplomat who knowingly hired a private security company to hide her son's crimes."

His face was reddening. "You're lying." His spittle flecked her face.

She reached over and tapped his knee. "You'll be able to turn your phone on when we land. See the headlines for yourself."

The seatbelt sign illuminated, and a steward made an announcement asking all passengers to take their seats.

"Also," Ingrid drew out the syllables. "You know what you were saying about diplomatic immunity?"

His breathing quickened. A vein pulsed in his forehead.

"It's bullshit. Did you know that? Your friend Sammy, for example, he's been charged with human trafficking. It really doesn't matter that his dad's a prince. His dad will be charged too."

"You're lying," he spat. "If you're dumb enough to try, you'll never make it stick. The State Department, the Foreign Office, they're going to make you sweep it under the carpet." He sounded so sure of himself yet, Ingrid noticed, his eye had started to twitch. "Welcome to the real world, Agent."

That phrase again. "Talking of the real world, Marcus, you should prepare yourself to come down to earth with a bit of a bump. You might be right about parking tickets and lewd behavior cautions evaporating for those with diplomatic immunity." She edged over and placed her hand on his forearm. "But you colluded with a foreign power, Marcus. You never asked whose crimes your mom was being charged as an accessory to, did you? But then you didn't need to, did you? Because they're yours. You've committed an act of aggression against the United States, Marcus. You can take it from me, diplomatic immunity does not apply." She unclicked the belt and got to her feet, then leaned over the seat. "It's true you were probably never going to be extradited for the killing of Matthew Harding, but when we land, me and few of my buddies from the Bureau will take real good care you."

He wiped his nose.

"Enjoy your drink, Marcus, because the moment you land on American soil, it will be my pleasure to arrest you for the crime of giving aid and comfort to an enemy of the United States of America."

His lip started to quiver.

"You can look it up if you like. It's also known as treason."

GET AN EXCLUSIVE SKYBERG NOVELLA

Want to read more about Ingrid Skyberg? For FREE? Join Eva's mailing list at evahudson.com and receive RUN GIRL, a novella featuring Ingrid Skyberg's first assignment in London for free. You'll also be kept up-to-date when new books in the series are released.

Visit evahudson.com

THE INGRID SKYBERG THRILLERS

Run Girl - Prequel (A novella)

Secretary of State Jayne Whitticker is in the middle of delicate negotiations when her favorite grandchild disappears from Paris.

Special Agent Ingrid Skyberg is hauled out of her FBI training session at Scotland Yard to head the hunt for the eighteen-year-old girl, who the FBI believe is now in London. Will she succeed in her unexpected mission? Or will her failure lead to the collapse of the crucial peace talks?

FREE to download when you join Eva's mailing list.

Fresh Doubt - Book One

A story of lies, secrets and deadly mind games.

Two hours ago, brilliant American psychology student Madison Faber found her roommate lying in a pool of blood. Now she is in police custody and suspected of murder. Madison persuades Special Agent Ingrid Skyberg to find the real killer, but the investigation soon puts Ingrid in danger. Can she unmask the murderer before she becomes a victim herself?

Kill Plan - Book Two

An American trader is poisoned in his office in the City of London. Two days later, a Latvian immigrant is discovered floating face down in the River Thames. These seemingly unrelated crimes are the work of an audacious serial killer working on both sides of the Atlantic.

When Special Agent Ingrid Skyberg starts putting the pieces together, she also puts herself in the firing line.

Deep Hurt - Book Three

In a seedy hotel in central London, the baby daughter of a US Air Force pilot lies lifeless in his wife's arms. Accused of killing the fourteen-month-old in an uncontrolled rage, Kyle Foster flees, taking his eight-year-old son with him.

Will Ingrid find Foster before he hurts anyone else? Or will she succumb to the old demons she's been trying to escape for the last eighteen years?

Shoot First - Book Four

A teenage girl disappears after witnessing a gangland murder in Chicago. Nine months later, and heavily pregnant, she arrives in London only to disappear again.

Special Agent Ingrid Skyberg has just two days to find the girl and get her to testify or else a brutal killer walks free. But Ingrid isn't the only person looking for the girl, and a war that started on the streets of Chicago is about to explode in the peaceful English countryside.

Below Zero - Book Five

Stockholm is under siege. A bomb has gone off, a series of high profile people have been kidnapped, and the city is in lockdown. Unfortunately for Special Agent Ingrid Skyberg, everything is kicking off on the same day she is in town to complete a dangerous assignment that is so secret, and so illegal, that neither the FBI or the US government can ever know about it. Her instructions are simple: no ID, no credit cards, no trace. If she ends up in jail, or floating face down in the harbor, there can be no way of identifying her.

No badge, no gun, no backup: this time Ingrid is on her own.

Final Offer - Book Six

A shadowy UK-based group has been trying to hack the US elections. When Special Agent Ingrid Skyberg is assigned to find out who's funding the hackers, she finds herself up against an invisible enemy who is extremely powerful and utterly ruthless.

To bring them to justice, Ingrid must go undercover and infiltrate the world of super-rich Russian oligarchs. But money buys all kinds of protection and Ingrid soon realizes that by taking on this battle she's putting everything on the line – her career, her future, her life.

In a nail-biting race against time, Ingrid sets out to solve the mystery and unmask the conspirators before they can silence her. Forever.

Flight Risk - Book Seven

Ingrid is ready to walk away from her life. She wants out of London. She even wants out of the FBI. But when she attempts to board a flight at Heathrow and sneak away without telling anyone, she's arrested on suspicion of causing the death of a man she's never heard of.

Now Ingrid must stay in the country, and the Bureau, to prove her innocence. There's just one problem: she can't remember if she killed him or not

---

EVA'S OTHER BOOKS

The Loyal Servant

Winner of the Lucy Cavendish Prize for Fiction, *The Loyal Servant* is a whistleblower thriller that topped the Amazon political fiction chart. Investigative reporter Angela Tate investigates scandal and corruption in the corridors of Westminster.

The Senior Moment

Sixty-five-year-old Jean Henderson arrives in New York to find her son and his pregnant wife missing from their apartment. When she reaches out to the cops for help, Jean discovers how invisible older people really are and concocts a plan to get noticed: by robbing a series of banks.

The Deadly Silence (formerly The Third Estate)

Thirty-three years ago two little girls disappeared. Today, the man convicted of murder three decades ago is back on the streets as another girl vanishes. Angela Tate covered the first disappearances and is dragged into discovering the terrible truth behind the latest.

ABOUT THE AUTHOR

Eva was born and raised in London. She worked as a local government worker, web editor, dot com entrepreneur, portrait artist and singer. In 2011, Eva won the inaugural Lucy Cavendish Prize for Fiction for her first novel, *The Loyal Servant*. The book was also shortlisted for ITV's People's Novelist Award.

In 2013, Eva published the first Ingrid Skyberg Thriller and never looked back.

To find out more about Eva or Ingrid, please visit evahudson.com. You can get the latest on all things Skyberg at twitter.com/eva_hudson and facebook.com/evahudsoncrimewriter.

Made in the USA
Las Vegas, NV
30 June 2021